EVERY
BITTER THING

EVERY
BITTER THING

Leighton Gage

This one is dedicated to Eide:
For thirty-two years, and counting
You Are My Sunshine.

Copyright © 2010 by Leighton Gage
All rights reserved.

First published in the United States by
Soho Press, Inc.
853 Broadway
New York, NY 10003

Library of Congress Cataloging-in-Publication Data

Gage, Leighton.
Every bitter thing / Leighton Gage.
p. cm.
ISBN 978-1-56947-845-5
eISBN 978-1-56947-846-2
1. Silva, Mario (Fictitious character—Fiction.
2. Police—Brazil—Fiction. 3. Murder—Investigation—Fiction.
4. Brazil—Fiction. 5. Mystery fiction. gsafd I. Title.
PS3607.A3575E94 2010
813'.6—dc22
2010029141

Paperback ISBN 978-1-56947-998-8

Printed in the United States of America

10 9 8 7 6 5 4 3 2 1

To the hungry soul every bitter thing is sweet.

PROVERBS 27:7

IT WAS NORMA PALHARES who first steered her new husband toward the offshore oil platforms. At the time, it seemed like a judicious course to follow. In the end, it set their marital ship on the rocks.

Jonas would spend only two days a week at home; but the money was good, and he'd only do it for a year or so, just until they had enough saved up to buy a bigger house. But the kids they'd planned on never came, so they'd never needed that bigger house. And, in the meantime, their expenses just kept going up and up. New cars every year, flat-screen televisions all over the house, imported wines, designer clothing, the most expensive restaurants, the finest club in the city, the best hairdressers. Jonas kept bringing the money in, and Norma kept shoveling it out. A year became two, then three. And by the time the divorce became final, they'd been together for more than seven.

Jonas moved in with a colleague and began to do what he'd wanted to do for quite some time—embrace the good life.

The colleague was another petroleum engineer who had taken a small flat on a busy shopping street in the Leme neighborhood, six blocks from the beach. He, too, had recently separated from his wife and, burdened by child support, would have been happy to have Jonas stay on and help with the rent. But Jonas, who'd managed to conceal a bundle of money from Norma and her lawyer, had no kids and no financial problems. He wanted a place of his own.

He settled first in Santa Teresa, taking a small house with

a high wall and a big garden. The house, situated in the highest part of Rio's highest neighborhood, was conveniently located, less than fifty meters from the nearest streetcar stop. The single-story structure was of just the right size: big enough for Jonas's needs, but small enough to be maintained without a full-time maid. A cleaning lady, who came in three times a week, kept it tidy.

From his backyard, Jonas could look down on the mouth of the bay. The headlands, seven hundred meters below, were so close to one another that a Portuguese navigator had once, on a long-ago January day, mistaken them for the entrance to a river. It was he who'd given the place a name it would bear forever after: Rio de Janeiro, River of January.

The spectacular view was further enhanced by the Christ Statue up on the Corcovado. The monument, almost forty meters in height, was actually four kilometers away, at almost the same altitude as the house. To Jonas's visitors, it looked like a copy in miniature set into the recesses of his garden among the banana trees.

It was all very lovely, but the neighborhood's newest resident soon came to a rude awakening: the charm of Santa Teresa was offset by a lack of security. It had become a dangerous place to visit, and an even more dangerous place to live.

After being held up at the point of a gun three times in nine months, Jonas, frightened and fed up, paid the penalty for canceling his lease and took an apartment in Ipanema.

There, smack-dab in the middle of Avenida Vieira Souto, his terrace faced the brilliant yellow sand of the beach. The South Atlantic was only a hundred meters from his front door. Beyond the curling waves, islands floated on a sea of blue. Farther out, the superstructures of ships dotted the horizon. And on weekends, Jonas was treated to the sight of tiny forms, climbers, scaling the gray walls of the Sugarloaf.

But unlike the house in Santa Teresa, he hadn't chosen the apartment in Ipanema for the view; he'd chosen it because the neighborhood attracted many visitors and many of them were tourists. The city fathers didn't like it when tourists were assaulted, so Ipanema was heavily patrolled, not only by the civil police but also by a special battalion dedicated to the protection of tourists. Jonas Palhares was confident that he'd moved to a place of absolute safety.

His confidence was misplaced.

On the fatal day, a little before noon, he was surprised to hear the doorbell ring. It was thirteen days before Christmas, a holiday he'd planned on spending with his widowed mother in Minas Gerais.

Back in November, on his most recent trip to the States, he'd bought presents for her and his sisters. They were wrapped and stacked in a neat pile on his bed, the final items he'd pack. But before leaving for Belo Horizonte, he had work to do. A leak had been reported, an oil slick was staining the sea around platform P-23, and a helicopter was on its way to fetch him.

The pickup point was Santos Dumont, the little airport not twenty minutes away. There'd be no long cab ride to Galeão, and that, at least, was a blessing.

Jonas's apartment was in a luxury building. Doormen were downstairs to screen visitors. No one should have been allowed to simply board the elevator, show up in front of his door, and ring the bell. But this was Rio, and in Rio one comes to expect such things. Service personnel tend to be lax. The guy charged with announcing his visitors might have dropped down to the bar on the corner for a quick coffee, or more likely a *cachaça* and a beer. On the other hand, the doorman *might* be at his post. And, if he was, the person standing outside in the corridor *might* be his girlfriend,

Chantal. *The doorman wouldn't stop Chantal. He's used to see-ing her come in at all hours.*

He went to the door and, without looking through the peephole, jerked it open.

It wasn't Chantal.

And less than four minutes later, Jonas Palhares's hopes for an enjoyable future were dashed forever. He was just another statistic, one of Rio de Janeiro's unsolved homicides.

Chapter Two

IN THE EARLY YEARS of the twentieth century, the small town of Brodowski, in the heart of São Paulo State's coffee-growing district, was populated almost exclusively by Italian immigrants. They labored on the plantations, maintained their language and customs, married one another, and largely kept to themselves. In the winter months, Ribeirão Prêto, the closest city of any size, could be reached by a single-lane dirt road. But in the springtime, when the rainy season began, the dirt turned to mud, and the mud isolated Brodowski from the world.

A hundred years later, the coffee was gone, replaced by the new century's more lucrative cash crop: sugarcane. The grandchildren and great-grandchildren of the original residents had been assimilated, the road had long since been paved, and Ribeirão had swollen to more than a million residents.

But one thing hadn't changed: Brodowski was still a sleepy little town. And yet Brodowski was famous. Famous because it was here, in 1903, that Cândido Portinari had been born. Portinari grew up to be Brazil's most famous painter. By the beginning of the twenty-first century, his work was selling for hundreds of thousands of reais and gracing the walls of some of the most prestigious art museums in the world.

Then, in late 2005, something else happened to put Brodowski on the map: the famous social psychologist Paulo Cruz bought a house there.

Doctor Cruz's first book, *Trabalhando nos Campos do Senhor* (*Toiling in the Fields of the Lord*), was a weighty tome on Evangelical sects in Brazil. It earned high praise in the world of academe, but the first—and only—printing numbered a mere thousand copies. And more than half of them were pulped.

His second work, released in 1998, under the title *Namoro e Noivado* (*Courtship and Engagement*), was a different case altogether. Cruz's colleagues lamented the lack of scholarship. The critics turned up their noses. The scientific journals panned it. And it went through seven printings in four months, each one bigger than the last. His publishers, attempting to explain the phenomenon to the astonished author, compared Cruz's work to that of the American Alfred Kinsey in the 1950s.

They were right.

The author's detractors, almost exclusively professors of sociology and social psychology, ascribed his success to prurient interest. They accused Cruz of titillating his readers under the guise of educating them.

And they, too, were right.

But, after seven printings in four months, there was no stopping Doctor Paulo Cruz. He wrote two more books in quick succession.

O Casamento (*Marriage*) appeared in 1999, and was re-released in 2000 with a lurid new cover and a new title: *Sexualidade no Casamento* (*Sex within Marriage*). Cruz followed it up in 2003 with *Sexo e a Familia* (*Sex and the Family*). And that became the biggest hit of all, ultimately translated into thirty-two languages. Cruz's reputation was made, and he was offered a lucrative sinecure in the psychology department at the University of Ribeirão Prêto, which he accepted.

By 2005, he was traveling the world, delivering—over and over again—variations of the same speech. It was a talk he constantly updated by introducing new and different slides. The slides were of attractive and well-endowed men and women photographed in "scientific" poses.

The professor, required to show his face in a classroom no more than once a week, and not even that if he was away on a speaking engagement, could permit himself to live quite far from the campus. He hit upon Brodowski, selected the house and grounds of a former coffee planter, and settled in as the town's newest resident. Living in the great house, and playing the lord of the manor, suited Cruz well. So, too, did his domestic arrangements.

He met a young psychology student named Florinda Gomes, who soon became his mistress. Florinda assumed Cruz was going to marry her. In that hope, as with many other things in their life together, she was disappointed. Cruz's research on male/female relationships in general had convinced him that a fixed union was not for him. He liked feminine companionship, he even liked children, but he didn't want to have a wife or offspring living with him in the same house, and he certainly didn't intend to entangle himself in a marriage.

He forbade Florinda to move in. If she had, within a few short years the law would have considered her his common-law wife. But by setting her up in an apartment of her own in downtown Ribeirão Prêto, all she could hope for, should he tire of her, was child support. Officially, and before the law, Professor Paulo Cruz remained a bachelor.

Florinda's mother, a widow named Eustacia Gomes, lived almost fourteen hundred kilometers to the north, on the island of Itaparica. She visited her daughter infrequently, offering as an excuse that the arthritis in her knees made it difficult to travel. All of them knew this to be a lie. The truth of the matter was that Eustacia Gomes didn't like Paulo Cruz.

The island's sandy beaches and lukewarm seas made it an ideal place for a family vacation. During the summer months, January through March, it seldom rained on Itaparica, and Paulo and Florinda's three kids, released from the imprisonment of their school back home, were in their element.

That year, taking advantage of the drop in airfares after the Christmas season, Florinda scheduled a visit that was to last a month. Cruz remained behind. He always did. In the absence of his mistress and their brood, he coveted his solitude. The lack of distraction also had a concrete advantage: it would enable him to make significant progress with his next book, a work he'd provisionally titled *Sexualidade Entre Doze e Vinte* (*Sexuality between Twelve and Twenty*).

Cruz's insistence on being left alone while in the throes of creation was well known. Friends and family were aware that they'd meet with a cold reception if they attempted to visit, or even to telephone, at such times.

So his murder remained undiscovered for quite some time. The medical examiner's estimate was that Professor Paulo Cruz had already been dead eight to ten days before Florinda returned and found him. The local police had no clue as to the motive for the crime, and had no suspects. The rarity of murder in the vicinity of Ribeirão made undertaking a murder investigation difficult for them. It was already being chalked up as the work of a random killer, an unsolvable crime.

Chapter Three

CHIEF INSPECTOR MARIO SILVA of the Federal Police suppressed a yawn.

He'd been up late the night before, struggling through yet another crisis with his wife, Irene. They were coming up to the anniversary of little Mario's death, always a bad time of the year.

Then, too, his boss's urgent summons had come between him and his second jolt of morning caffeine.

Add to those two facts another: an urgent summons from Sampaio was commonplace. Sampaio was an alarmist, a chronic worrier. Most of what he considered urgent turned out not to be urgent at all.

But Silva still had had no choice but to hurry to the office.

It wasn't until the director of the Brazilian Federal Police dropped his bombshell—"Somebody killed Juan Rivas"—that Silva came instantly and completely awake.

But he was an optimistic man, and he remained hopeful. "Please tell me Juan Rivas is no relation to Jorge Rivas," Silva said.

"His son."

Silva's hope evaporated.

Jorge Rivas was the Venezuelan foreign minister. In the days when he'd been ambassador to Brazil, Rivas had forged links with everyone who mattered in the Brazilian government. The president liked him, and the minister of justice liked him, so it was a sure bet that Nelson Sampaio, ever eager to emulate his superiors, would declare a liking for him as well.

"I like him," Sampaio said, as if in response to the thought. "He's a fine man, and a great representative of his country."

"I see," Silva said.

What he saw was trouble ahead. The murder of Rivas's son would be a killing with political implications, the kind of case he hated above all others.

"Tell me the kid wasn't killed on federal property," he said.

"The *kid*, as you choose to call him, was thirty-two years old. And he wasn't."

"Kidnapped, then?"

Sampaio shook his head. "The murder took place in his apartment."

Silva sat back in relief. "Then it's a concern of the civil police. We're out of it."

"Don't kid yourself. You think we can hide behind our mandate? Mandates don't mean squat if I get a direct order from Pontes."

"You got a direct order?" Silva felt a headache coming on.

"Any time now. A call is coming. You can bet your ass on it."

When Sampaio predicted a call from the minister of justice, Silva didn't doubt him. The director was never wrong about the machinations of Brazil's federal bureaucracy.

"Now, in case the seriousness of this situation isn't clear to you," Sampaio said, "let me spell it out: no one gets to be foreign minister of Venezuela without being a buddy of the clown who runs the country. And nobody in this government wants to get on the wrong side of The Clown. This isn't just a murder, Mario; it's a major political incident."

"Because of the oil," Silva said.

"Of course it's because of the oil. What else? You think the president shows up in all those pictures hugging The Clown because he *likes* The Clown?"

A green light started flashing on Sampaio's telephone. He punched a button and picked up the receiver.

"It's him?" he asked.

Ana, in the outer office, said something Silva couldn't quite hear. Sampaio grunted and punched another button.

"Good morning, Minister," he said, morphing, in a flash, from querulous superior into solicitous subordinate. But then his smile turned to a scowl. "Yes, yes," he said rudely, "put him on."

A second passed. The smile returned.

Silva couldn't hear what was being said, but the gravelly voice and the imperious tone were unmistakable. It was Pontes, all right. The director, sycophant that he was, sat listening to the minister as if he was hearing the Voice of God.

After almost a full minute's harangue, Pontes stopped to draw breath.

Sampaio leaped into the breach. "I have to tell you, Minister," he said, "that I'm truly shocked." His voice, if not his expression, carried complete conviction. "I've just arrived at the office. This is the first I've heard of this." Sampaio was a consummate liar, a fact he didn't bother to conceal from his subordinates. "His apartment, you say?"

The minister droned on. Like Sampaio, he'd rather talk than listen.

"I'll give it first priority," Sampaio said when the droning stopped, "and put my best man on the case." Sampaio didn't mention Silva by name. He never did. "And I'll go there personally to give impetus to the investigation. Give me an hour or two, and I'll call you with a firsthand report."

Sampaio seldom missed an opportunity to rub shoulders

with the Great and Powerful, even if the shoulder rubbing was only via telephone.

The minister dealt out more advice, this time about ten seconds' worth.

"Yes, Minister. Of course, Minister. Goodbye, Minister."

Sampaio's scowl was back before the telephone hit the cradle.

"You'll do the grunt work, of course," he said to Silva without missing a beat, "but I'll be giving you my full support. You have my cell number. If you need advice, feel free to call, twenty-four seven."

Silva let his eyes drift to the window. A cloud, harbinger of an oncoming storm, was just emerging from behind the Ministry of Culture.

"Ana has the address," Sampaio concluded. "We'll go separately."

He stood and went into his private bathroom. The audience was over.

In the outer office, Ana Tavares, Sampaio's long-suffering personal assistant, was extending a sheet of paper.

"Crime-scene address," she said. "I called Arnaldo. He's on his way to your office."

"Thanks, Ana. Efficient as always."

She ignored the compliment.

"Mind if I ask you a question?"

"You can ask," she said. "I may not answer."

"Do you always make Sampaio jump through hoops, make him talk to the minister's secretary first? I can't recall a single occasion—"

"I have no idea what you're talking about," Ana Tavares said.

Chapter Four

LUCIO COSTA HAD PROJECTED Brasília as a city of two hundred thousand people and not a single traffic light. Brazil's brand-new federal capital was to be a city designed around the automobile, a place where roads fed into roads, and where the flow of vehicles would never stop.

Six decades later, the population was pushing three million, there were traffic lights galore, and the city's traffic problem was a national scandal.

"Goddamn it," Silva said, as his car bumped over a pothole.

Arnaldo, accustomed to both the condition of Brasília's streets and the asperity of Silva's complaints about them, ignored the outburst. "How come Sampaio didn't offer us a ride?" he wanted to know.

"Steals his thunder," Silva said, signaling a left turn and glancing in the rearview mirror.

They were in Silva's twelve-year-old Fiat. *Agente* Arnaldo Nunes was Silva's longtime sidekick. Silva had just finished telling him the little he knew about the case.

"You figure Sampaio tipped the media?" Arnaldo asked.

"Tipped them, or knew they'd been tipped," Silva said. "No reason for him to put in an appearance otherwise." They rounded the corner. "Look."

"Jesus," Arnaldo said. "So that's why you took your time getting here."

Two television vans were pulled up in front of the murdered man's building. Their masts were extended, their dishes pointed at some faraway satellite.

A barrier of yellow crime-scene tape, supported by stanchions, ran in a wide arc around the front door. A crowd of reporters flocked like pigeons fighting for crumbs. Nelson Sampaio, bathed in the light of sun guns and camera strobes, stood in their midst. If Silva had arrived ten minutes earlier, those reporters would have been surrounding *him*.

Silva parked between the director's BMW and a Ford sedan with a staff of Asclepius affixed to the license plate. A young cop came over to shoo them away, but Arnaldo flashed his badge, and the youngster backed off.

On their way to the front door, the two federal cops passed within a few meters of Sampaio's impromptu press conference. They were close enough to see the expression on the director's face, one of indignation mixed with sympathy, which even Silva had to admit was a neat trick. Sampaio was calling the reporters by name as he fielded their questions.

Arnaldo held up the tape, Silva ducked under it, and they headed for the duo stationed in front of the entrance. One was sporting a red-and-gold uniform, a high-brimmed hat, and white gloves. It reminded Silva of costumes he'd seen at a performance of *The Merry Widow*.

The other guy, in sharp contrast, wore a rumpled suit with a badge pinned to his lapel. For some reason, both of his shoes were untied. Silva and Arnaldo offered their warrant cards, but the guy in the suit waved them aside.

"Good morning, *Senhores*," he said. "Third floor front."

Silva nodded his thanks. The guy in the uniform did what he was there to do: he opened the door. The two cops stepped into a marble-lined foyer. As they made for the elevator, the detective behind them murmured something into his radio.

"Calling ahead," Silva said.

"Sartorially challenged," Arnaldo said, "but well trained. What's with the shoes?"

"Looked new," Silva said. "Probably hurt his feet."

The elevator was descending, but he pushed the button anyway. The doors opened and Lucio Cavalcante, Brasília's chief medical examiner, stepped out. The ME was carrying an aluminum case.

"All done up there, Lucio?" Silva asked.

"What are you guys doing here?"

"Political implications," Silva said.

"Son of a friend of The Clown, right?"

"Right. What can you tell us?"

"I just briefed Pereira. I'm busy. Get it from him."

"When's the autopsy?"

"Tomorrow. Or maybe the day after."

"I don't think so," Silva said.

One of the ME's eyebrows moved toward his hairline. "What's that supposed to mean?"

"You're going to get a call from someone. He'll want you to finish this one before dinnertime."

"The hell I will. Rivas waits his turn, just like everyone else."

"Not if the guy who's calling is the minister of justice, he doesn't."

"You think that's likely?"

"I think it's more than likely. He spent ten minutes on the telephone talking to my boss about this."

"Fuck Pontes." The ME bristled. "And fuck your boss."

"What a lovely thought," Arnaldo said.

"Your buddy, the ME in São Paulo," Cavalcante said, addressing Silva. "What's his name again?"

"Couto. Paulo Couto."

"Him. I'll bet he doesn't have to put up with all this political shit."

"Perhaps not," Silva said. "You considering a move?"

"To São Paulo? Ha! Besides, that's where Pontes is from."

"True, but now he's here."

"*He's* here, all right, but there are thousands more like him back where he comes from. São Paulo is a fucking nest of vipers."

"Hey," Arnaldo said. He also stemmed from São Paulo.

But Cavalcante wasn't listening. He hurried out the front door, ducked under the tape, and headed for his car. Some of the reporters broke off from the group surrounding Sampaio and followed, shouting questions as they went. Cavalcante waved them off. The last they saw of him, he was disappearing behind the pack of newshounds.

Silva and Arnaldo boarded the elevator. The doors slid shut with scarcely a whisper.

"Nice," Silva said, looking around at the burnished wood, beveled mirrors, and polished brass.

"This elevator? Or the fact that Sampaio just lost half his audience?"

"That too," Silva said.

The doors slid open to reveal a slight man with a big moustache. *Delegado* Walter Pereira headed up the homicide division of Brasília's civil police.

"Morning, *meninos*," he said. "Caught the hot potato, did we?"

"I'm afraid so, Walter," Silva said.

Independent of the mayhem surrounding him, Pereira customarily wore a ready smile along with his loud sports jackets. This morning, he was wearing a frown.

"What's with you?" Arnaldo asked.

"Your goddamned boss is what's with me," Pereira said. "He's doing his dog and pony show as we speak. There's a television in one of the bedrooms. Want to have a look?"

"Not on your life," Arnaldo said.

Silva bent over to look at the damage to the apartment's front door.

"Perp did this?" he asked.

Pereira shook his head. "We did."

Silva studied the floor. A trail of blood stained the carpet.

"Let's not get off the subject," Pereira said. "Your god-damned boss—"

Silva waved a dismissive hand. "You don't have to tell me, Walter. I work with the man."

"The way I heard it, the *filho da puta* doesn't work at all. The way I heard it, you guys do all the work, and he takes the credit. He is, by the way, currently positioning himself to do just that. He's live on Channel Five."

"Of course he is," Arnaldo said. "His public demands it."

"His public doesn't know shit. They think the blowhard is a twenty-first-century Eliot Ness. What kind of a background does Sampaio have in law enforcement, anyway?"

"None whatever," Silva said. "He was a corporate lawyer. He made a substantial contribution to the president's election campaign. The rest, as they say, is history."

"Watcha got?" Arnaldo asked.

"Just answer me this: is he, or is he not, a filho da puta?"

"He's a filho da puta of monumental proportions," Arnaldo said. "Watcha got?"

Pereira finally broke into a grin. The teeth under his moustache were movie-star white.

"I got it solved, is what I got," he said.

Silva sensed a weight being lifted from his shoulders. "Solved?" he said.

"Ninety-nine percent."

"You make an arrest?"

"Not yet."

"Who did it and why?"

"Allow me my little moment," Pereira said. "First, come and have a gander at my body."

"Can't wait," Arnaldo said, looking him up and down.

"The corpse, Nunes. The corpse."

"Very proprietary," Silva said. "My body, indeed."

"We still have jurisdiction, Mario. Until somebody tells me otherwise, the civil police still have jurisdiction."

"I don't doubt it," Silva said. "And you're welcome, I'm sure."

Pereira pointed. "In there."

Following the trail of blood, they advanced into the living room.

The place was a slap in the face to minimalism. Every square meter of wall space was occupied. Where there wasn't a window, there was a tapestry, or a case of books, or a painting, or a shelf. Many of the shelves contained images of saints—antique ones, by the look of them. And there were bigger images too, freestanding and scattered about the floor, some of them almost as tall as a man. The décor reminded Silva of stately homes he'd visited in Europe; it was totally incongruous in the heart of a city only six decades old. He wrinkled his nose. The room was warm. Juan Rivas was beginning to get ripe.

"What did this guy do for a living?" Arnaldo said. "Run a pawnshop?"

"He was a student," Pereira said.

"A student? And he owned all this stuff?"

"'Student' is a polite euphemism for 'playboy.' The guy never did a lick of work in his life. And there's an explanation for the stuff."

"Which is?"

"His old man is a friend of the clown who runs Venezuela."

"We know that. So what?"

"Being a friend of The Clown is akin to owning your own oil well. Old man Rivas, if he wanted to, could buy half the politicians in this town. Can you imagine the pressure we'd get on this one if I wasn't about to ride in on my white horse and finger the perpetrator of this dastardly deed?"

"Your histrionics are ruining my morning, Pereira," Arnaldo said.

"I'm glad, Nunes. Ruining your mornings is one of my few joys."

"Who found the body?" Silva said.

"His cleaning lady."

"Still here?"

"Nah. I let her go home. She's a little thing, maybe a meter thirty, maybe fifty kilograms. Name of Carmen Fonseca. There are twelve-year-olds bigger and stronger than she is."

"What's big and strong got to do with it?"

"You'll know when you see my body. Anyway, she didn't have much to tell, said she was surprised the front door was only on the latch, not dead bolted as usual. She locked it behind her, walked around the couch, spotted the body, and fainted. A little while later, she came to, crawled to the phone, and called it in."

"Why did you break down the door?"

"Her legs gave out. She couldn't get up to open it. When the first guy came in, she crawled over to him, grabbed his ankles like he was a rock and she was being carried out by the tide. Hysterical, he said, would be an understatement."

"Young woman?"

"A hag. Fifty-four, according to her identity card."

"Not old at all," Arnaldo bristled.

"Not for one of the few remaining dinosaurs in law

20   *Leighton Gage*

enforcement," Pereira said, "but if it makes you feel any better, she looks even older than you do. In her case, I put it down to a hard life. You? Well, I don't know. All that sitting around on your ass and those long lunches, maybe?"

"It comes from nailing bad guys, Pereira. What's *your* conviction rate? Two percent?"

They were walking as they spoke. The trail of blood ended behind one of the couches, and there they stopped. The victim wore pajamas and a bathrobe. The bathrobe was up to his waist, the pajamas down to his ankles.

"Found like this?" Silva asked.

Pereira shook his head. "Cavalcante stuck a thermometer up his ass."

"Okay to approach the body?"

"Go ahead. We're done with him."

Rivas's feet were bare, the toenails enameled red. Both legs were bent at unnatural angles. His cheekbones were caved in, his forehead indented, the top of his skull crushed. Silva's overall impression was that of a broken doll. In almost thirty years of law enforcement, he'd never seen a more brutal beating.

"Ouch," he said.

The corpse was still wearing a wristwatch, or rather the shattered remnants of one: a Cartier, with a gold case and wristband.

"You find his wallet?" Silva asked.

Pereira nodded. "In his bedroom, out in plain view, full of money. We left a few small bills."

Silva wasn't entirely sure he was kidding.

Arnaldo walked around the body. "It computes," he said. "A guy beats anyone that bad, it's not robbery. It's personal."

"Sometimes, Nunes," Pereira said, "your deductive powers amaze me."

"I gotta admit," Arnaldo said, "that such a reaction is not uncommon, even among highly experienced operatives."

"What's Cavalcante's estimate on the time of death?" Silva said.

"Between 10:00 P.M. and 2:00 A.M."

"Murder weapon?"

"Good question. Look here."

Pereira bent over and pointed. Only then, amid all the gore, did Silva see the bullet hole. It was a palm's breadth above Rivas's groin.

"Cavalcante thinks the shot came first," Pereira said, "and it probably would have killed him. But the murderer decided not to hang around and wait. The other wounds were inflicted by some kind of blunt instrument. There's nothing in the apartment that fills the bill. No gun either."

"You notice those red toenails?" Silva asked.

"Hard to miss. How often do you see a guy with painted toenails? Was Rivas gay?" Arnaldo asked.

"He was," Pereira responded, "and I'll get to that in a minute. So, what's your take on the shot? If it wasn't meant to kill him, why shoot him at all?"

"You put a bullet into a man's abdomen," Silva said, "it's like giving him a punch in the gut. He's going to bend over forward." Silva extended his left hand as if he was shooting a pistol, and raised his right as if he was holding a club. "Then the perp hits him on the back of the head to bring him down." He brought down his right arm, matching action to words. "Once he's on the floor, there's no escape. And the killer can see him suffer while he finishes him off at leisure."

Pereira rubbed his chin. "Makes sense," he said. "But how come Rivas just let him stroll in with a club in one hand and a gun in the other?"

"Maybe the little he was able to see through the peephole didn't seem like a threat."

"Anyone in the building hear a shot?"

Pereira shook his head. "No one we talked to, and that's all the adjoining neighbors except for the guy downstairs. He isn't home."

"According to you," Arnaldo said, "you have the case ninety-nine percent solved. How about sharing? It would be really nice to get out of here before lunch."

"Let's start with a motive," Silva said.

"I have one," Pereira said. "Sexual jealousy."

"Evidence?"

"Plenty. I have . . ."—he paused for effect—"letters."

"Did I hear a fanfare of trumpets just before you said 'letters'?" Arnaldo said.

"What kind of letters?" Silva said.

"Let's move on to the next exhibit, shall we? Right this way, gentlemen."

Pereira ushered them through an arch, across a dining room, and through an open door.

Half of the space was occupied by a breakfast nook, the rest by a modern kitchen. Seated at a table, wearing a pair of latex gloves, was a young man in shirtsleeves. His suit jacket hung neatly over the back of a chair.

"Chief Inspector Silva, Agent Nunes," Pereira said, "meet Detective Vargas."

Vargas blushed and got to his feet.

"Heard of you, Senhor. Heard of you both."

Silva offered a hand. The young man snapped off his right glove before he took it. Then he shook hands with Arnaldo.

"Tell them about the letters," Pereira said.

"They're all in order," Vargas said. "From the thirteenth of August up until . . . well, I don't know exactly. The last seven were never opened. I thought we'd let the forensics people do that. I just finished putting the others into plastic envelopes." He picked one up and held it between Silva and Arnaldo, not sure who should get it. "The series starts with this one."

"*Tell* them," Pereira said. "They can read later."

Vargas turned an even brighter shade of pink. "They're love letters, and in the beginning they're pretty much like any other love letters, but then they turn abusive. The writer, who was older than Juan, knew Juan was ditching him for someone younger."

"Knew, or thought?"

"Knew, Senhor. He mentioned the other party by name."

"And that name was?"

"Gustavo."

"Were the letters signed?"

"With a single letter, a 'T.' Look here. See?"

"Any return address?"

"No. No stamps, either. They're dated, though, on the outsides of the envelopes."

Silva turned to Pereira. "Hand-delivered?"

Pereira shrugged. "Or stuffed in his mailbox, or slipped under his door."

"Did you question that guy out front? The one dressed like the Student Prince."

Pereira shook his head. "I was just about to when you guys showed up."

"Let's do it together," Silva said.

While they were waiting for the doorman to come up, Pereira took the federal cops on a tour of the apartment. There were two bedrooms, but only one bed showed signs of having been slept in. Pereira tapped his fingers on the drawer of a bedside table.

"Here's where we found the letters," he said.

"If the guy who killed him wrote the letters," Arnaldo said, "why didn't he take them with him?"

"He probably wasn't thinking about anything except beating the shit out of Juan," Pereira said.

Arnaldo shook his head. "Doesn't fit," he said. "He took his weapons, didn't he? So why not the letters?"

"Stop constructing alibis for my perp," Pereira said.

"What if Senhor T already *has* an alibi?" Arnaldo said.

Pereira glared at him.

"What is it with you, Nunes? How come you always try to rain on my parades?"

"What else did the ME have to say about that blunt instrument?" Silva asked.

"Some kind of a bludgeon; thicker than a cop's baton, round, no sharp edges."

"Take us through the business of the dead bolt one more time."

"According to Carmen, Juan was a security freak. One time, she came in and forgot to engage the bolt. He had a fit, damned near fired her."

"But when she arrived this morning?"

"The dead bolt wasn't engaged. That much we managed to get out of her."

"So Rivas almost certainly let the murderer in," Silva said, "and the murderer almost certainly let himself out. Begs a question, doesn't it?"

"What question?"

"Juan wasn't suspicious of his caller. Wouldn't you be suspicious of someone who was sending you abusive letters?"

Pereira gave an exasperated snort.

"Look, you guys want to do the devil's advocate thing,

that's okay. Me? I'm a man who looks for the most obvious solution."

A voice intruded. "José de Araujo, Senhores."

The detective from downstairs, his shoes now tied, was in the doorway. Behind him, standing on tiptoe to look over the detective's shoulder, was the guy in the operetta costume. Under the polished leather brim of his hat, his eyes were big with curiosity.

"Is he here?" he said.

"Who?" Pereira said.

"Senhor Juan. I heard he was . . . killed." Araujo gave a delicious shiver.

"You heard right," Pereira said. "The body's in the living room, behind the couch."

The doorman looked disappointed. "Behind the couch, huh?" For a moment, Silva thought he was going to ask if he could see it.

Pereira fished a notebook out of his pocket. "What's that name again?"

"José de Araujo, Senhor."

Pereira made a note of it and pointed his pen at an upholstered chair. "Sit down, José." The doorman did, and Pereira took a seat facing him. The detective waited until Pereira waved him off, and then left without a word.

"How long you worked here, José?" Pereira said.

"Six years, Senhor."

"How well did you know Juan Rivas?"

"Very well, Senhor. I greeted him every day. I opened the door for him. I delivered his packages. When he had a visitor, I called him on the interphone. When he needed someone—"

"Okay, okay, I got it," Pereira said.

"Can I smoke, Senhor?"

"No, you can't. Did Juan have any special friends?"

A sly look came over the doorman's face. "So you know," he said.

"Know what?"

"Know he was a *viado*, Senhor. I guess I can say that. Now that he's dead. And you being the police."

"He didn't make any secret of it, then?"

"Only sometimes."

"Such as when?"

"When he got a visit from his father, Senhor. His father is a very important man. A Colombian, I think. Or maybe a Uruguayan. Not an Argentinean."

"You think his father was unaware of Juan's homosexuality?"

"What?"

"You figure Juan's old man didn't know his son was a viado?"

"*Sim*, Senhor. That's what I think."

"Why?"

"Senhor Juan always acted differently around his father, Senhor Jorge."

"Acted differently? How?"

The doorman took off his cap, revealing a bald patch, and scratched the top of his head. "He just . . . did. Most of the time, you could see that Senhor Juan was a viado, see it before he opened his mouth. You didn't have to see him hugging and kissing that friend of his. You just knew."

"Friend? You saw him with a friend?"

"All the time, Senhor."

Pereira glanced at Silva. A smile curled one corner of his mouth.

"An older man, was he? This friend?"

"Sim, Senhor."

"How much older?"

The doorman considered the question. "Thirty years older. Maybe more," he said after a short pause.

"Brazilian?"

"No, Senhor. They always spoke *Castelhano* together. And also with Juan's father."

"Juan's father knows this man?"

"Sim, Senhor. They are friends."

"You know the friend's name?"

"His name is Garcia, Senhor. Tomás Garcia."

"Tomás with a T, right?" Pereira asked, making a show of writing it down.

"Sim, Senhor. Is there any other way to spell it?"

Pereira snapped his eyes from notebook to doorman. "You trying to be a wiseass, José?"

"No, Senhor. I honestly don't—"

"You have any idea how to get in touch with this Tomás Garcia?"

"But of course, Senhor." José de Araujo pointed a white-gloved finger at the carpet under his feet. "Senhor Tomás, he lives downstairs on the second floor."

Chapter Five

"MOTIVE, MEANS, AND OPPORTUNITY," Pereira said when the doorman was gone. "I am *so* going to nail this guy Garcia."

"What's that proverb?" Arnaldo asked. "Something about not counting your eggs until the hen lays them?"

"Nunes," Pereira said, rubbing his hands in satisfaction, "even you, your pithy proverbs, and your half-assed suppositions are but minor irritations on this fine day. Share my joy. Think of the comedown for that boss of yours. He's down there shooting his mouth off, and I'm up here solving the case."

"Pithy?" Arnaldo said. "Did you say pithy?"

"I did," Pereira said. "And I even know what it means."

"I'd approach this one with caution," Silva said. "Believe me, Walter, you don't want to be proven wrong."

"I'm *not* wrong. Senhor T-for-Tomás is our man. You guys want to be in on the collar?"

"The wise thing to do," Silva said, "would be to get rid of Sampaio first."

"True," Pereira said. "We don't want him horning in on the interrogation. That alone would give him grounds for another goddamned news conference. Hey, how come it's taking him so long to get up here?"

"Body's still here," Arnaldo said.

"So what?"

"Sampaio gets weak in the knees if he sees a corpse. Corpses give him nightmares."

"That's your twisted sense of humor again, is it, Nunes?"

"No, Walter," Silva said. "It isn't."

"Wait a minute. Wait a minute. You're serious? Corpses give him nightmares? And a wimp like that heads up the Federal Police?"

"And a wimp like that does," Arnaldo said.

***

ARNALDO AND Pereira watched as the body, now zipped into a black bag, was lifted onto a gurney and rolled out the door. Silva came out of the kitchen, putting his cell phone in his pocket.

"I told Sampaio," he said. "He's on his way."

"And all this time he's been talking to those reporters?" Pereira asked. "How does he do it?"

"It's a talent," Silva admitted.

"Filho da puta. How much are you going to tell him?"

"Mushroom treatment," Silva said.

"Meaning?"

"We're going to keep him in the dark and feed him shit."

The words were no sooner out of Silva's mouth when the door opened and The Mushroom bustled in. "Senhores," he nodded curtly, taking in the group. Then he extended a hand to Pereira. "I don't think we've met."

Pereira took the hand. "Pereira. Civil police. I've heard of you, Senhor, seen you on television."

"Have you indeed?" Sampaio preened. "Heard good things, I hope."

Pereira looked at Arnaldo, then back at Sampaio. "Absolutely, Senhor. Nothing but good."

Sampaio gave a perfunctory smile, as if he'd expected nothing less. Then the smile vanished.

"How long has the victim been dead?"

It seemed like a strange choice for a first question. Silva looked at Pereira.

"The medical examiner's preliminary conclusion," Pereira said, "puts the murder between 10:00 P.M. last night and 2:00 A.M. this morning."

"And your people were called shortly before 7:00, correct?"

"That's correct, Senhor."

Sampaio scratched the nonexistent whiskers on his immaculately shaved chin and let them wait for his next comment. His body language said he was privy to important information. When he spoke, it seemed like an anticlimax.

"The father of the victim, as these gentlemen know, is a Very Important Person, Jorge Rivas, foreign minister of Venezuela."

"Yes, Senhor, I'm aware of that."

Sampaio stopped scratching and looked at each of them in turn.

"The president instructed our foreign minister to call Rivas personally, communicate the death of his son, and express the sympathy of the Brazilian government."

"Thoughtful of the president," Arnaldo said.

Sampaio paused for a moment, apparently concluded—erroneously—that Arnaldo was being sincere, and continued. "The phone call," he said, "was placed about an hour ago."

Pereira couldn't contain his curiosity. "How'd you find that out?" he said. "You got a contact in the Foreign Office?"

Sampaio fixed him with a fish-eyed stare. The director had many sources of information, none of which he shared. Knowledge was power. The silence went on for so long that Pereira started to fidget. When Sampaio deigned to resume, his tone was cold enough to freeze water.

"Kindly show me the courtesy," he said, "of not interrupting again." Pereira's eyes narrowed, but the director stared him down. "Our foreign minister was unable to complete the call. It seems that Senhor Rivas *had already been informed of his son's death. He is, even as we speak, approaching Brasília.* So my questions to you, gentlemen, are these: Who the hell told Rivas about the death of his son? Which one of you, or which person reporting to one of you, felt he had the right to do that? And if the informant proves to be someone unassociated with you people, how did that person find out about it?"

Arnaldo and Silva exchanged a look. "We will endeavor to discover the answer to those questions, Director," Silva said.

"You're goddamned right you will. And when you do, you'll tell me first, is that understood?"

"Understood, Director."

"What else have you got?"

"Nothing else at the moment," Silva said.

Sampaio looked deeply into his chief inspector's eyes. They stared at each other for a long moment, the exemplary communicator versus the master at concealment.

Sampaio blinked first. "All right," he said, "keep me posted. I've got to get out to the airport. I want to be there when Jorge Rivas's flight arrives."

Without even a nod in Pereira's direction, he bustled off in the direction of the elevator.

"Prick," Pereira said when Sampaio was safely out of earshot.

"You have no idea," Arnaldo said.

Silva glanced at his watch. "Unless he's a gentleman of leisure, the odds on Garcia being home at this time on a weekday morning aren't good."

"No, but we can still toss the place, question the maid, get handwriting samples, maybe even find the murder weapon. I have Judge Carmo's number right here."

Pereira pulled out his cell phone.

Caio Carmo was what the cops termed a "friendly judge,"

willing to issue a search warrant on the thinnest of evidence. The two federal policemen stood waiting while Pereira tried first Carmo's home, then his chambers. Carmo, as it turned out, was in court.

Pereira left an urgent message and the cops adjourned to a nearby *padaria* to drink coffee and wait.

***

TOMÁS GARCIA's front door was opened by Garcia's maid, a young woman with bad teeth and a Bahian accent. From the glazed look she gave Pereira's ID, Silva concluded she couldn't read. She said her name was Safira Nogueira and, when prompted, produced a dog-eared identity card.

Her employer wasn't there, she said, hadn't been home when she showed up for work that morning. She normally arrived at nine, left at six. Normally, too, he'd be there to greet her and to see her out.

Vargas read the warrant and explained, in layman's language, what it gave them the right to do. She asked them to wait while she tried to reach her employer. But, as it turned out, Tomás Garcia wasn't picking up his cell phone. Reluctantly, she admitted them.

The interior of the apartment was in sharp contrast to the one upstairs, as if the younger man was striving to appear older, while the older was clinging to vestiges of youth. The palette in Juan's apartment had been a mélange of dark reds and browns; Garcia's place was a riot of color, the decoration contemporary and minimalist.

Pereira and Silva sat on a yellow leather couch, Safira on an upright chair, upholstered in cerulean blue, designed for aesthetics more than for comfort. The other two cops began to search the premises.

"Were you aware of the fact," Pereira asked, kicking off

the questioning, "that Tomás Garcia and Juan Rivas were lovers?"

Safira showed no surprise. "Yes," she said. "Sometimes Senhor Juan would come down here to spend the night. Sometimes Senhor Tomás would go up there. They used to call each other, too. Sometimes five or six times a day."

"But not recently?"

"No, Senhor. Not recently."

Vargas came into the living room with a sheaf of papers in his gloved hand. He hadn't been away for more than three minutes.

"From his desk," he said. "The same handwriting as the letters."

Pereira smiled, as if the young cop had given him a present.

"How about the club?" he said. "Or the gun?"

Vargas shook his head. "Not yet, Senhor."

"Keep looking," Pereira said.

Just then, there was a rattle of keys at the front door. Vargas, without being told, crept over and stationed himself behind it. Pereira rose to his feet, looked at Safira, and put a finger to his lips.

Silva, too, stood.

Keys in hand, a figure in his late fifties, or perhaps in his early sixties, entered the apartment. He froze when he saw the men standing in front of the couch.

"Senhor Garcia?" Silva asked.

"Who are you people? What are you doing in my apartment?"

"I'll take that for a yes," Silva said.

Garcia sensed a movement behind him and turned to find Detective Vargas gently shutting the door. He took a nervous swallow, and his prominent Adam's apple bobbed up and down.

"No need to be alarmed," Silva said. "We're police officers. Here's my identification."

As Garcia read, the stiffness drained out of his neck and shoulders. He slouched, looked very tired; defeated, even.

"A police ID doesn't give you the right to invade my apartment," he said.

"No," Pereira said. "But this does." He produced Judge Carmo's warrant and held it out. "Read it, if you like."

"I certainly will," Garcia said. His Portuguese was fluent, but heavily accented. He snatched the paper out of Pereira's hand and started to examine it.

"That will be all for now, Safira," Silva said.

The maid looked to her employer, but he kept his eyes glued to the paper. Safira nodded at Silva and left the room.

Garcia was wearing a tailored suit and a Versace tie, but he'd done a bad job shaving. Narrow swatches of whiskers clung to his chin. He smelled of Scotch whiskey and mint-flavored mouthwash. Folding the warrant, he licked his lips and looked at Pereira.

"Were you aware, before you read that"—Pereira pointed at the papers—"that Juan Rivas was dead?"

"I was aware," Garcia said, cautiously.

He could hardly have said otherwise what with the circus going on downstairs. If he hadn't known before he got home, someone in front of the building would have told him.

"We found your letters," Pereira said, "the ones you wrote to Juan about Gustavo."

Tomás Garcia turned a shade paler. His eyes moved from side to side as if seeking an avenue of escape.

"You want to tell us about it?" Pereira asked. "Get it off your chest?"

"I loved him," Garcia said. "We had a spat. We were

estranged, I admit that. I was angry, but I would never have. . . ." His voice trailed off.

"Have what?" Pereira said.

"Killed him."

"And yet your letters. . . ."

Garcia put a hand over his eyes and sank down onto the sofa. "Oh, God," he said. "You don't believe me, do you?"

Pereira didn't reply.

"All we want," Silva said, "is the truth. If you're innocent, you have nothing to fear."

Garcia, apparently surprised by Silva's gentle tone, lifted his head. "This is one of those good cop/bad cop routines, isn't it?"

"It's not a routine. I'm not trying to trick you. I honestly want you to tell me what happened."

Garcia began speaking in a rush. "You say you want the truth? All right, here's the truth: I wanted to patch it up between us. I'd tried everything else, so I threatened to kill myself, and—"

"Wait. You threatened to kill yourself?"

Garcia frowned. "You said you read the letters."

"Not all. There were a few unopened."

"A few? How many is a few?"

"Seven."

"Seven. The last seven?"

Silva nodded.

Garcia stared past him. A tear pearled out of his left eye and ran down his cheek. He made no attempt to wipe it away.

"Yesterday," he said, "I spent the day with a bottle. I got shitfaced. I passed out for a while, woke up, and started drinking again. Sometime around midnight, or maybe it was later, I heard banging around upstairs. His living room is . . .

was . . . just above this one. I thought to myself, *He's with that bitch Gustavo Fernandez.*"

"One moment, Senhor Garcia," Silva said. "You said you heard 'banging around.' Did you hear a shot?"

"A shot? No."

"You're sure?"

"Of course I'm sure. I know what a shot sounds like. There was no shot. Why do you want to know if there was a shot? What does a shot have to do with anything?"

"Who's Gustavo Fernandez?"

"Gustavo Fernandez is a whore. Gustavo Fernandez is a filthy, money-grubbing whore Juan met in a sauna."

"A sauna?"

"In Miami. Gustavo is Cuban, one of those so-called exiles. Always complaining about how Che Guevara and the Castro brothers took their island away, but they wouldn't go back to it if you paid them."

"And this Gustavo? He's here now? In Brasília?"

"I thought he was. He's been here twice before. Juan paid for his tickets both times. Business class, no less. The little bitch said he wouldn't fly tourist."

"And now you think he's here again?"

"I assumed he was when I heard the noise."

"You think Gustavo killed Juan?"

"How should I know?"

"I'm not asking you what you know, Senhor Garcia. I'm asking you what you *think*."

"Then I think . . . not. Gustavo had a good thing going. He was in it for the money. Why should he kill a goose that was laying golden eggs for him?"

"Could Juan have done something to make Gustavo jealous?"

Garcia shook his head.

"Impossible. Gustavo didn't care about Juan. I couldn't get Juan to see that, but it's true."

"All right, so you heard this banging around. . . ."

"And it sounded like they were having a rough fuck on the carpet. I couldn't stand it. I was drunk. I went up there on an impulse."

"Drunk," Pereira repeated. "And angry too, I'll bet."

"Angry too, I admit it. Being angry isn't a crime."

"Murder is," Pereira said.

"Goddamn it! I've already told you. I didn't kill him!"

"Senhor Garcia," Silva said, "please."

Garcia took a deep breath.

"I took the elevator. When it stopped on three—"

"Wait a minute. You took the elevator? For one floor?"

"Normally I'd walk up the stairs, but I was so drunk, I decided to take the elevator. As I got off, I heard the metal fire door to the stairwell slam shut. All the banging had stopped. I walked into the apartment—"

"You walked into the apartment? Are you telling me the door was open?"

"I used my key."

"So the door was locked, as usual?"

"Not as usual. Juan likes to keep it on the dead bolt. He has a lot of art in there."

"But this time it was only on the latch?"

"Yes."

"As it would have been," Silva suggested, "if an intruder had walked into the corridor and pulled it shut behind him."

"Yes. Yes, that's right."

"Please go on. You entered the apartment, and. . . ."

"And at first, I didn't see anything. I called Juan's name. He didn't answer. I was on the way to his bedroom when I passed the couch and saw him . . . lying there. It . . . it was

awful. Can you imagine my shock? My horror? Seeing someone you loved, seeing them like *that*?" Garcia raised a hand
to his face. "His left eye was almost—"

"I saw it. What did you do then?"

"I panicked. I was afraid the criminal might still be there.
I ran down here and locked myself in."

"And then?"

"And then I made myself another drink to settle my
nerves. And I got to thinking. That stairwell, it goes down
to an exit at the back of the building. It's normally locked,
but if it isn't, you can get out without being seen by the doorman. I got my courage up, went downstairs, and checked the
door. Someone had broken the lock."

Pereira told Vargas to go downstairs and examine the
door.

"The night doorman works from midnight to eight,"
Garcia continued. "He must have a day job, because he
sleeps half the time. He sacks out on a couch in the lobby.
You have to pound on the glass if you want to get in. I
thought about waking him up, telling him about Juan, about
the door."

"But you didn't?"

Garcia hung his head. "No."

"Why not?"

"I knew he'd call the police. Then I'd have to explain the
whole thing, my relationship with Juan, all of it. I knew the
press would tear into me like a shoal of piranhas. I didn't
want that."

The penny dropped for Silva. He suddenly realized he had
an answer to Sampaio's questions.

"So instead of calling the police, you called Jorge Rivas,
Juan's father?"

Garcia nodded. "I called his mobile phone, his private

number. He leaves it on, day and night. It's one of those satellite things, so he can be reached anywhere, anytime. He's an important man, a minister in the government."

"We know."

"I didn't think Jorge would forgive me if I called anyone else first. Jorge and I have been friends for a long time."

"Good friends?"

Garcia paused before he answered. "What the hell. I might as well tell you. Jorge and I were . . . intimate. It started years ago. We went to boarding school together. We remained friends, even after he was married. He used to swing both ways, you see. Not me. I only like men. Anyway, he got me my job here at the embassy, back when he was the ambassador."

"You work at the Venezuelan embassy?"

Garcia nodded. "I organize cultural events, parties, that sort of thing."

"So you're the cultural attaché?"

"No. Not the cultural attaché. I just . . . organize parties and things."

"And you stayed on after Jorge Rivas went back to Caracas?"

"Yes."

"How did the current ambassador feel about that?"

Garcia shrugged. "He didn't like it very much, but what could he say? Jorge is his boss, and Jorge instructed him to keep me on."

"And you wanted to stay because. . . ."

"Because Juan wanted to stay. It's as simple as that."

"Does Jorge Rivas know you've been intimate with his son?"

Garcia looked at his lap.

"No," he said. "He doesn't even know Juan is . . . was gay."

"All right," Silva said. "So you spoke with Juan's father. What, exactly, did you tell him?"

"I told him I'd let myself into Juan's apartment."

"He didn't find it unusual? You having a key?"

"He knows we take care of each other's plants whenever one of us is traveling. Juan goes to Miami a lot. He likes the nightlife there, the clubs on South Beach. And the saunas, too, although I didn't know *that* until . . . until Gustavo Fernandez came into our lives."

"So you told the elder Rivas you let yourself in, and then. . . ."

"I told him the same thing I told you, except I didn't say I was drunk, didn't say I thought I'd heard Fernandez and Juan fucking. I said I heard suspicious noises, thought it might be burglars, said I went up there, saw Juan's body, panicked, and came back here."

"Did you tell him about the emergency exit, about the lock being broken?"

"Yes."

"How did he take it?"

"What do you mean?"

"Within a very short time, Senhor Garcia, we're going to deal with a bereaved father who is also the foreign minister of your country. The case has political overtones. We, the police, are going to be under a great deal of pressure, and I want to be as prepared as I possibly can. Tell me, please, how Senhor Rivas reacted to the death of his son. Was he devastated? Angry? Hysterical? What?"

"He . . . he was none of those things."

"What, then?"

"He was . . . offended."

"*Offended?*"

"He took it as a personal affront," Garcia said.

"Don't you think that's a strange way for a father to react?"

"Jorge isn't your average father. He has . . . how can I put this . . . a tendency to interpret everything in terms of himself."

"Megalomania? Egotism?"

"I didn't use either of those words."

"Tell me what he said."

"I don't remember exactly, but it was something like didn't the killer realize who he was dealing with? And then, *How dare anyone do something like this to me?*"

Silva raised an eyebrow. "To *me?*"

Garcia gave the faintest of nods. "Jorge wasn't always as hard as that, but when he got to be an ambassador. . . ."

"He got carried away by his own importance?"

Garcia bit his lip, looked out of the window, looked back at Silva. "In all fairness, neither man was fond of the other. Jorge used to call Juan *that little prick* and Juan referred to his father as *the old bastard.*"

"Nice family," Pereira said.

"When you spoke to him," Silva said, "did he give you any instructions?"

"He told me to call the police and report it."

"Anything else?"

"He said he'd get here as soon as he could, said it wouldn't look good if he didn't come."

"Let me get this straight," Silva said. "He as much as told you he was coming for the sake of appearances?"

"I told you what he said. You can read into it what you like."

"All right. You ignored his instructions to call the police. Why?"

"I wasn't ignoring them. I took a drink to fortify myself.

Then I took another one. And I . . . fell asleep. I woke up this morning, looked out the window, and saw the police cars and the ambulance."

"What time was this?"

"About half past nine."

"What did you do then?"

"I drove to the airport to meet Jorge's flight. The Foreign Office already knew he was coming, gave him the VIP treatment, and drove him off to have coffee with the foreign minister. He knew I'd be waiting, so he sent someone with a message. I was to go home; he'd be here as soon as he could."

"Here?"

"He owns this apartment. He owns the one upstairs as well. You don't have to tell him, do you? About Juan and me? It has nothing to do with the murder."

"Doesn't it?" Pereira said.

"No, goddamn it! It doesn't. And he wouldn't want to hear it. These days, Jorge is what he chooses to call *reformed*. But he only uses that expression to me. For the rest of the world, he's never had a homosexual relationship in his life."

"What kind of an attitude is that?" Pereira said. "I mean, like, who gives a shit these days?"

"Our president does. He'd never permit the presence of a gay man in his government. He'd consider it a national embarrassment."

Vargas came back with his report. The lock on the exit door had been intentionally smashed. The news didn't impress Pereira. He was reaching for his handcuffs when Silva hustled him into the hallway.

Chapter Six

"I want to discuss this," Silva said.

"What's to discuss?" Pereira said. "Who cares about some broken lock? I sure as hell don't. Garcia might have done that himself." He started to turn back toward the living room. "I'm going to bust him."

Silva gripped him by the arm. "Wait," he said.

"Why?"

"What if you're wrong? What if he doesn't confess?"

"He'll confess. I'm gonna lean on him. When I'm done, he'll own up to it even if he didn't do it."

"Walter, listen to me. As soon as you finger Garcia Sampaio will steal the ball and run with it. He'll take credit for solving the case."

"Surprise, surprise. What else is new?"

"If Garcia is innocent, Sampaio will have to eat his words. It'll make him look like an idiot."

"Garcia *isn't* innocent. And Sampaio *is* an idiot."

"Yes, he is. But you don't want to give him cause to take offense."

"I might give a shit if I reported to him. But I don't. Let go of my arm."

Silva did, but he kept talking. "Sampaio has this thing he calls a favor bank. He does something for somebody, and they wind up owing him one. He can call in chips anytime he wants to and, believe me, Walter, if you incur his enmity, he'll find a way to call in the chips on *you*."

"Filho da puta!" Pereira said, but now he was paying close attention.

"And how about your own boss, Meireles?" Silva said. "I hear he's angling to become secretary of public safety."

"True. But Meireles is different."

"Is he?"

"He's a real cop, for one thing."

"Tolerant of honest mistakes, is he?" Silva said.

"I'm not making a mistake!" Pereira said.

"Keep your voice down, Walter. Let me give you an alternative scenario: What if this guy Gustavo and his friend Juan had a falling-out? What if Gustavo doesn't have an alibi? What if someone saw him and the victim together a short time before the murder?"

"That's all circumstantial bullshit."

"And what do *you* have?"

"I got—"

"You've got letters and an established association. What you *haven't* got are the murder weapons. Rivas and Garcia were lovers. Latent prints and hair samples are going to be all over that apartment. They'll be useless as proof. And, anyway, Garcia has already told us he was there last night. Without solid forensic evidence, or an admission of guilt, your case won't hold water."

"I'm gonna get an admission of guilt. I'm gonna get a full confession."

"Garcia isn't some punk you can sweat until he says what you want him to say. He's connected."

Pereira bit his lip. "You think he's got diplomatic immunity?"

"I don't know. But I *do* know he's a friend of the foreign minister of Venezuela. An *intimate* friend, as you just heard."

"How long do you think that's going to last? When Juan's old man hears about Garcia's little game of hide-the-banana with his son, he'll—"

"You heard what Garcia said. No gays in The Clown's government. It's not much of a stretch from there to no *fathers* of gays in The Clown's government. You think Jorge Rivas is going to thank you for making his son's affair public?"

Pereira rubbed the stubble on his chin. "What's my alternative?" he said.

"Give me time," Silva said, "to check our database."

"What database?"

"The one we've got on violent crimes countrywide, the one your people are supposed to be contributing to."

"Oh, that one. Right. We *do* contribute to it."

"I'm glad to hear it. Not everybody does. Think about it, Walter. This murder is unusual in three ways: one, the bullet to the abdomen prior to the beating; two, the extreme violence of the beating; three, the absence of the murder weapons. Suppose we don't find the weapons, or suppose we find them and can't link them to Garcia. If there's one more murder, *just one*, that fulfils the other two conditions, and if Garcia can prove he was elsewhere when it happened, a case against him won't hold water. How many victims are gutshot and then beaten? How many corpses have you seen that suffered as much physical abuse as Juan's did?"

There was a soft knock on the door. Silva opened it.

"What is it, Safira?"

"Excuse me," she said. "Senhor Jorge Rivas is here."

Silva grimaced. "Already?"

"Sim, Senhor."

"Let's go, Walter," Silva said. "Think about what I said."

"I'm thinking," Pereira said. "Goddamn it, I'm thinking."

***

IN THE living room, Rivas had his hand on the shoulder of a weeping Tomás Garcia and was studiously ignoring Detective Vargas. The young cop's cheap suit had classified him as a man of no importance. No importance, at least, to the Foreign Minister of the Bolivarian Republic of Venezuela.

The minister was a diminutive man, a fact about which he must have been sensitive, because he was wearing shoes that added about four centimeters to his height. His eyes were dry and clear, those of a man who'd learned to sleep comfortably on a first-class airline recliner, those of a man who'd done just that.

His striped dress shirt was starched and unwrinkled, certainly changed since his arrival. An Hermès tie, firmly knotted, was pulled up to the limits of his collar and held in place by a gold pin. Otherwise clad in a splendid example of the Italian suitmaker's art, he exuded an air that reminded Silva of someone else he knew: Nelson Sampaio. Rivas's first words added weight to that impression.

"Who's in charge here?"

"This is Delegado Walter Pereira," Silva said, "head of Homicide here in Brasília."

"Who the hell are you?"

"Mario Silva, Chief Inspector for Criminal Matters, Federal Police."

"Your boss went to the airport to meet my flight."

"Did he, Senhor?"

"If he's an ass-licking shit called Sampaio, he did."

"That's him," Arnaldo said.

"I'll be sure to tell him you said that. Who the fuck are you?"

"Agent Haraldo Gonçalves, Senhor," Arnaldo Nunes said without missing a beat. "Federal Police."

"Two of you, huh? Two federals and"—he glanced back and forth between Vargas and Pereira—"two civils. Well, you're not stinting on the manpower, at least. What do the Federal Police have to do with this?"

Silva formulated his answer with care: "Consideration for your position, Senhor."

"You know what it looks like to me? It looks to me like your ass-licking boss stuck his nose into my son's case so people would pay attention to *him*. He may have thought I didn't notice him at the arrival gate, but I did. When he wasn't fawning on one of his betters, he kept trying to stick his head into the shots so he could get on camera. When we got to the VIP lounge, away from the reporters, he button-holed me. Told me you people were going to crack this case in short order. Have you? Have you cracked the case?"

Silva looked at Pereira.

"What?" the Venezuelan said, shifting suspicious eyes from one to the other.

"No, Senhor," Pereira said at last. "We haven't yet cracked the case."

"Well, what are you doing hanging around here? Get out and solve it. Leave me and my friend alone. We have grieving to do. Christ, I wish I was in Caracas where the cops know their jobs."

Pereira flushed and opened his mouth for a sharp retort, but Silva surreptitiously stepped on his foot. "We're finished here, Senhor," he said. "But before we move along . . ." Tomás Garcia, with the mien of a dog fearing a blow, took a step away from Rivas and lowered his head between his shoulders. ". . . I'd like to offer you my heartfelt sympathy on the death of your son."

"Thank you," Rivas said stiffly, then turned his back on the four cops and led Garcia off toward the bedrooms.

***

"How the fuck do you do it?" Pereira whispered, when the door closed behind them.

"Do what?" Silva asked.

"Keep your patience with a blowhard like that."

"We get a lot of practice," Arnaldo said.

"Reminds me of that filho da puta, your boss."

"Like I said. Practice."

"All right, Mario," Pereira said, "I still think you're wrong, but I'm gonna go along for the ride. What do you expect me to do while you're checking that database of yours?"

"Talk to the other doormen. Find out when Rivas came home for the last time. Find out if he was alone. Find out if he had any visitors. Continue looking for the murder weapon. Believe me, Walter, you have nothing to lose by playing it this way. You might even uncover something that will strengthen your case against Garcia."

"Or absolve him completely," Arnaldo said.

Pereira stuck out his jaw. "Somebody teach a course in ballbusting at that federal police academy of yours, Nunes?"

"You're looking at him," Arnaldo said, exuding false modesty.

"Gustavo Fernandez," Silva said, thinking aloud, "is a Cuban exile, probably an American citizen now. Either way, he would have needed a visa, which means we'll have a record of his address in Miami. I can get a friend, an American cop, to do a background check."

"For all the good that's going to do," Pereira said.

"Stop being so damned negative, Walter. We may just come up with something."

"When pigs fly," Pereira said.

Chapter Seven

ANOTHER DAY, ANOTHER MURDER. It was very early in the morning. The sun was just coming up. Pereira was standing near the body, making notes, when a young patrolman touched him on the shoulder.

"A telephone call, Senhor, patched through on the radio."

"Who is it?"

"Chief Inspector Silva, Federal Police."

Pereira went to his car and grabbed the microphone. "It's not a good time, Mario. I'm busy."

There was a crash of static, then Silva's voice. "This will only take a minute. Can you hear me okay?"

"I can. So can half the cops in Brasília."

"I'm aware of that. You recall your remark about airborne pigs?"

Pereira thought for a moment, and then said, "Yeah. What about it?"

"I've found others in the database."

"Others? As in more than one?"

"Four. All with the same characteristics."

"Four? Jesus Christ! Where are you?"

"In my office."

"I'll come to you. Give me half an hour."

"Ask for Arnaldo."

Pereira groaned. "Not Nunes again! What a crummy day this is turning out to be."

***

ARNALDO MET Pereira in the reception area at Federal Police headquarters and led him to a windowless conference room. The furnishings consisted of a round wooden table, four chairs, and nothing else. There was a hole in the ceiling where some kind of repair had taken place to the pipes or conduits. A notebook computer was plugged into a socket halfway up one of the walls. The only other objects on the table were an overloaded ashtray and a pad of paper with a few notes. The stench of ten thousand dead cigarettes hung in the air.

"Christ," Pereira said, "what a dump."

"This is the VIP room," Arnaldo said. "You should see the new one."

"Worse than this?"

"It will be. The coffee staining of the carpet and the filling of the ashtrays are scheduled for tomorrow."

"Why aren't we meeting in your office, Mario?"

"Security reasons."

"Hiding from your boss?"

"Exactly."

"So you're still keeping him in the dark?"

"If Sampaio was a portobello," Arnaldo said, "he'd be the size of this table."

"Have a look at this," Silva said. He moved the mouse, and the computer's screen came to life. It showed the image of a horribly mutilated corpse.

"Jonas Palhares," Silva said, "petroleum engineer, thirty-four years old, divorced, no children, lived alone."

"Lived where?"

"Rio de Janeiro."

Silva clicked the mouse. The next photo was also of Palhares, taken from a slightly different angle.

"When did it happen?" Pereira said.

"About two weeks before Christmas."

"Suspects?"

"One. His girlfriend, Chantal Pires."

"You sound like you doubt it."

"I do."

"Why?"

Silva pointed at the screen. "Look at him. Women are into poison and pistols; they don't do things like that."

"Depends on the woman."

"For once," Arnaldo said, "I agree with Pereira. Take my mother-in-law."

Pereira ignored him. "No chance it could have been a robbery?"

"No," Silva said. "Palhares's wallet was still in his pocket, his watch was still on his wrist. There was no sign of a break-in."

"Just like Rivas."

"Just like Rivas."

"That girlfriend you mentioned. She live-in?"

"No. And she's one of the few people he knew in Rio. He's from Belo Horizonte originally, only been in Rio for about a year."

"She a local?"

Silva nodded. "They met on the beach."

"She have a key to his place?"

"Yes."

"And this guy . . . what's his name again?"

"Palhares."

"Palhares was also shot in the gut?"

"He was."

"Who called it in?"

"The girlfriend. And long after the murder."

"Another reason to believe she didn't do it."

"Exactly."

"You guys going to talk to her?"

"We are. I sent a man from São Paulo." Silva glanced at his watch. "He should be arriving there as we speak."

"Why? You've got a field office in Rio, haven't you?"

"Yeah," Arnaldo said. "But we haven't got Babyface."

"Babyface?"

"Haraldo Gonçalves," Silva said. "We call him Babyface."

"I'll bet he loves that."

"Hates it," Silva said. "But that's beside the point. When it comes to females, he's our secret weapon. Women open up to him."

"In every way you can imagine," Arnaldo said.

"You got a dirty mind, Nunes."

"It comes," Arnaldo said, "from excessive association with homicide detectives."

Silva chose another file on the computer's desktop and opened it. The image on the screen showed the body of a young man. His blond ponytail looked like a mop used to soak up blood. The blood was his; it had dried and was more brown than red.

"Victor Neves," Silva said, "twenty-six years old, exporter of leather goods, lived in Campinas, engaged to the same woman for over three years. Murder was"—he checked his notes—"almost a month ago. The vic's mother found the body. He was her only child. She's been under sedation ever since."

"Suspects?"

"The cops in Campinas like Neves's partner for it. He has no alibi, and they say there's something shifty about him."

"You sending someone?"

"I am."

"Okay. Number three?"

Silva clicked the mouse. "Paulo Cruz."

"*That* Paulo Cruz?" Pereira said. "The guy who wrote the sex books?"

"That Paulo Cruz. He lived in Brodowski. It's a little town near Ribeirão Prêto."

"I know where Brodowski is. Everybody does. Portinari came from there. You ever read any of Cruz's stuff?"

"No. You?"

"Every single one."

"There were only three," Arnaldo said.

"So I read three."

Again, Silva clicked the mouse. The upper part of Cruz's body now filled the screen.

"Are those little white things what I think they are?"

"That, Walter, would depend upon which little white things you're referring to."

The next photo was even tighter. It framed the victim from the middle of his chest to the crown of his head. Some of Cruz's teeth were lying on the rug. There were smaller objects as well, not quite as white.

"Maggots," Silva said.

Pereira pinched his nose, as if the smell was there in the meeting room with them. "Yuck," he said. "Took a while before they found him, huh?"

"Over a week. He was working on a book. His girlfriend was away in Bahia."

"No maid?"

"He had one, but she was on vacation."

"Live-in girlfriend?"

"She wasn't live-in. But they did have three kids."

"And he never married her? Betcha *she* did it. Hell hath no fury and all that."

"She didn't do it," Silva said. "I told you. She was in Bahia."

"She got any proof of that?"

"Plenty."

"If it was me, I'd take a closer look at that proof. She's a natural for it."

"The cops in Brodowski thought so too. But her alibi is rock-solid."

"No other suspects?"

Silva shook his head. "And Brodowski isn't exactly an epicenter of violent crime. The locals are well out of their depth. They'd already filed a request for help."

"You said four. Who's the fourth?"

Silva frowned. "That one confuses me."

He clicked the mouse. A black man in knee-length shorts was staring at the camera with one eye. The other was mashed to a pulp. His bloodstained polo shirt bore the Lacoste crocodile emblem.

"Nice shirt," Pereira said. "Who's he?"

"He's The Man Who Doesn't Fit. João Girotti, a thug with three convictions, one for armed robbery, one for burglary, one for auto theft."

"A man still in search of his vocation," Arnaldo said.

"Good riddance," Pereira said. "Where did this punk end his days?"

"In an alley, in back of a bar, in Brasilândia."

"Brasilândia?"

"A suburb of São Paulo," Silva said. "A slum. Girotti lived there whenever he wasn't a guest of the state."

"Was he gay?"

"Not as far as we know."

"And the other three you just showed me all had girl-friends. How do we tie four straights to a gay like Rivas?"

"I don't think we can. I think we're going to have to

discard your original hypothesis of homosexual jealousy as a motive for Rivas's murder."

"I'm still gonna find out if Tomás Garcia was here in Brasília when these people were killed."

"And you should. But I'm now convinced he's not our man."

"Okay, okay, I have to admit, it's looking pretty thin. But tell me this: what's a lowlife like Girotti have in common with four respectable citizens?"

"Maybe they were only *apparently* respectable citizens," Arnaldo said.

"Okay, so how do we connect Girotti to four *apparently* respectable citizens?"

"That's the question, isn't it?" Silva said. "I don't have an answer."

"Any ballistics results on the bullets?"

"Not yet. But. . . ."

"I know, I know, don't even bother to say it. The MO is just too similar. It's the same killer. But it doesn't necessarily follow that the *victims* are connected. We could be dealing with some sick bastard who picks them at random."

"That's possible."

"But you don't think it's likely?"

"No, I don't."

"Why?"

"São Paulo, Campinas, Ribeirão Prêto, Rio, and Brasília; one killing in each city. That's almost *too* random to *be* random. I think the killer had a reason to go to those places, and I think that reason was that he wanted to kill those specific people."

"Who was the first?"

"Girotti, the thug."

"And when was that?"

"Back at the end of November."

"So it's been going on for over two months?"

"It has."

"All right, Mario, I admit it. You were right, and I was wrong. You saved my ass, and I owe you one. Thanks."

"*De nada.*"

"What about that guy in Miami?"

"Gustavo Fernandez."

"We rule him out?"

"Not just yet. I've got a friend, a cop in Miami. He'll talk to Fernandez."

"When?" Pereira said.

"Today, when he gets up. It's three hours earlier in Miami."

Chapter Eight

THE BUILDING WAS THREE stories tall, ugly, and painted flamingo pink. A concrete sign to the left of the door identified it as the Ocean View.

Detective Sergeant Harvey Willis glanced at the opposite side of the street. "Bullshit," he said. The building over there was considerably taller and effectively blocked any possible view of the North Atlantic.

But view or no view, the three-story monstrosity he was standing in front of would command healthy rents. The Miami Beach of picture postcards, Bermuda shorts, and tourist-pale knees was only four blocks to the north.

Pierre "Pete" André, Willis's partner, looked at his watch.

"If he's a night owl," he said in his soft Creole accent, "he's not gonna be happy."

It was a quarter to ten, still very early by Miami Beach standards.

***

THE MAN who answered their ring was wearing a light blue T-shirt, darker blue pajama shorts, and an attitude.

"Gustavo Fernandez?" Willis asked.

"What's it to you?" the man said.

"Detective Sergeant Willis, Miami Beach PD. This"—Willis jerked a thumb toward the black man standing next to him—"is Detective André."

The man ran a hand through his unkempt hair and stared at them out of bleary, brown eyes. He didn't seem in the least intimidated.

58 *Leighton Gage*

"Cops?"

"Cops."

"Got any ID?"

"Sure."

Willis had his badge ready.

The man fish-eyed it. "Something with a picture," he said.

Willis turned the badge case over and let Fernandez scrutinize his warrant card.

"What do you want with me?" Fernandez said, finally admitting to Willis's identity. "I didn't do anything."

"I didn't say you did," Willis said. "May we come in?"

"*Carajo*, do you know what time it is?"

"It's about ten."

"Middle of the fucking night."

"Can we come in?"

"Wait," Fernandez said and shut the door in their faces.

They heard voices from within, Fernandez and another man.

"Ah," André said. "Like that."

A minute later, the door opened again. The apartment had been pitch-black. Now the overhead lamp was on.

"I hope you're going to make it quick," Fernandez said and stepped aside.

The place was a studio, a single room with a kitchenette in one corner and a king-sized bed in the other. Beyond a door on their right, someone flushed a toilet.

Fernandez pointed at a table encircled by four chairs. "Sit there," he said.

He walked to the window and pulled aside a heavy blackout curtain, revealing the wall of an adjoining building.

"Ocean view, my ass," Willis whispered to his partner.

On his way back to the table, Fernandez switched off the overhead lamp. "What's this all about?"

Willis took the lead. "You were an acquaintance of Juan Rivas, right?"

"What's with the *were* shit? We're still acquaintances."

"You don't know?"

"Know what?"

"It was in the *Herald*, him being the son of the Venezuelan foreign minister and all."

"I don't read the fucking *Herald*. Where are you going with all this?"

"Juan Rivas is dead."

"No shit?" Fernandez didn't look devastated or even concerned, just curious. "What happened to him?"

"He was murdered."

"Huh."

"The way we hear it," André said, "you and he—"

Fernandez looked at the door to the bathroom, held up a hand, and lowered his voice.

"He was a friend. That's all, just a friend."

"Uh-huh," Willis said. He reached into his pocket, took out his notebook, and glanced at a page. "According to our information, you also know a guy by the name of . . ."—he found what he was looking for—"Tomás Garcia?"

"That old fart? Yeah, I know him. So?"

The shower in the bathroom went on; it made a lot of noise. Fernandez looked relieved.

"According to Garcia," André said, "you and Rivas were an item."

"That's a load of crap," Fernandez said.

"Is it? The Brazilian cops have Rivas's telephone records. They told us the two of you spent a lot of time chatting with each other."

Fernandez cast another glance at the bathroom door.

"Okay, okay: at one time. But no more. That's history."

"So the two of you haven't spoken for a while?"

"What did I just say? History."

"What happened?"

Fernandez shrugged.

"I moved on," he said.

"You broke up?"

"There was nothing to break. Casual sex, that's all it was. What have you guys got to do with any of this? Juan was murdered down in Brazil, right?"

"What makes you think that?"

"You mean he was here?"

"No. It happened in Brazil, all right." Again, Willis consulted his notebook. "There were three occasions when you didn't exchange telephone calls for over a week. The first was from the tenth to the eighteenth of August."

"I was in Brazil."

"And from the third to the thirteenth of October?"

"Again, Brazil."

"That the last time you were there?"

"Yeah. Last time."

"Can you prove it?"

"Hell, yes, I can prove it. I've got the stamps in my passport."

Willis turned the page. "The third time period in which the two of you weren't calling each other," he said, "was from the fourteenth to the twenty-second of November."

In the bathroom, the sound of the shower stopped. Fernandez lowered his voice. "He was here."

"He stayed with you?"

"No, I mean here in Miami. He took a hotel suite. He was after a good time. I showed him around."

"Did you stay with him? There in the suite?"

"What if I did?"

"When did you first meet him?"

Fernandez thought for a moment. "July. It musta been the first or the second. I remember taking him to the fireworks on the Fourth. You done?"

"Just a few more questions. What did he tell you about his relationship with Garcia?"

"That the old fart wouldn't let go, couldn't get it through his head that Juan was finished with him. He kept slipping letters under Juan's door."

"Did Juan show any of those letters to you?"

"He read a few when we talked by phone. We laughed about them. Hey, you think the old fart killed him?"

"Do you?"

Fernandez shrugged. "How would I know?"

"Did Juan talk to you about any of his other relationships?"

"No."

"Did Juan ever tell you about anyone he was afraid of?"

"No."

"Anything you can think of that might lead to finding his killer?"

"No," Fernandez glanced at the bathroom door. "How much longer is this gonna take?"

Willis stood up and André followed suit.

"We'll be out of here," Willis said, "just as soon as you show us those stamps in your passport."

* * *

"HELLO, BABYFACE."

"You know I don't like that nickname, Chief Inspector."

It was 4:30 P.M. in Brasília. Haraldo Gonçalves was calling in from Rio de Janeiro.

"Sorry," Silva said, smoothly. "It just slipped out. What have you got?"

"*Nada*. Chantal Pires is a dead end. She's no killer."

"Chantal Pires? That would be Jonas Palhares's girlfriend."

"The very same."

"All right, let's hear it."

"They met on the beach."

"So?"

"The girls you meet on the beaches in Rio, they're all dressed alike, which means in bathing suits about the size of postage stamps. And nobody is stupid enough to wear jewelry or a watch, so you don't know whether you're dealing with an heiress or a whore until she opens her mouth."

"And often not even then."

"And often not even then. You must be younger than you look, Chief Inspector."

"What's that supposed to mean?"

"Nothing, Senhor. It just slipped out. Chantal told me Palhares had her in bed two hours into their first date."

"How forthcoming. Go on."

"Palhares lived in a rental apartment, a duplex penthouse on Vieira Souto in Ipanema. The guy went through a divorce, for Christ's sake! You gotta ask yourself how he could have afforded it."

"So you went there and had a look?"

"I did. There's a stain where he bled out on the rug. The air-conditioning had crapped out, and Palhares's corpse was there for a while before they found him. The whole place still stinks. The owners have got some work ahead of them before they can rent it out to someone else."

"Find anything of interest?"

"Nothing."

"The Rio cops have any other suspects?"

"Not one. And they're backing off on Chantal. As well they should."

"What makes you so sure they can rule her out?"

"The way she talked. When he brought her home the first time, she took one look at that apartment and thought she'd found the duck that lays golden eggs."

"In the fairy tale, it was a goose."

"Whatever. She told him she was a model."

"But she isn't?"

"No, Senhor. But she sure as hell looks like one."

"So he bought it."

"He bought it. She let him tell her long, boring stories about oil rigs, fed his ego, waited on him hand and foot, fucked him until he was cross-eyed. And, apparently, things were going just fine, and she was already thinking of herself as Senhora Palhares."

"And then someone came along and killed him."

"And then someone did. And if Chantal knew who it was, she'd kill him with her bare hands."

Chapter Nine

HECTOR COSTA WAS BOTH the head of the federal police's São Paulo field office and Mario Silva's nephew. Late the following morning, he drove from São Paulo to Campinas. It was a pleasant drive through verdant hills studded with small farms, and he made good progress until he reached the outskirts of the city. But then things started to go wrong.

Campinas, now numbering over three million inhabitants, had recently introduced a number of one-way streets. He was in town for more than an hour before he located the precinct housing the homicide squad.

But he'd called ahead, and when he gave his name to the desk sergeant, he was immediately directed to the office of Delegado Artur Seixas.

Seixas was a man pushing sixty. On the wall behind his desk was a small blackboard with a label. *Days Until Retirement*, it said. The number 27 was scrawled in white chalk.

"From today?" Hector asked.

"Including weekends," Seixas said. "First thing I do every morning is pick up the chalk and change the number." He stuck out a hand and Hector shook it. "It was my wife's idea. She keeps telling me how great it's going to be, and I go along with the game. But the truth is I hate the idea. You'd think thirty-five years would be enough, wouldn't you?"

"Yes."

"Well, it isn't. Not for me. I don't fish, I don't hunt, I got no hobbies at all. I'm afraid I'm gonna go nuts. You want to go get some lunch?"

***

THEY SAT at a counter and ate sandwiches.

"I understand you have a suspect," Hector said when the conversation turned to the Neves case.

"You talking about Eduardo Coruja, his business partner?"

"Him."

"Nah! That turned out to be a dead end."

"No other suspects?"

"Nope."

"Any forensics that might help?"

"We got the bullet and sent it to Brasília. My understanding is you're going to compare it to the one you took out of that Venezuelan."

"We are. Anything else?"

"Nothing else. And our forensics people are first-class."

"Unicamp, huh?"

Seixas opened his hands, as if the answer was obvious. And indeed it was. Unicamp, the Campinas branch of the University of São Paulo, trained the best criminal forensics people in the country. The professors who worked there were often called upon, nationwide, to consult on difficult cases.

"No offense," Hector said, "but I'd still like to have a look at that apartment."

"None taken," Seixas said. "We can go over there right now. I brought the key."

***

NEVES HAD lived in a high-rise bordering the university's campus. The neighborhood was packed with bars, boutiques, and trendy restaurants. The building's security guard recognized the grizzled cop from previous visits and buzzed them through at once.

An elevator was waiting. The indicator panel skipped

every other number. "Lofts," Seixas said. "Every apartment takes up two floors."

Victor Neves's place was on seventeen. His front door opened onto a living area backed by windows rising two stories to the ceiling. A counter divided the living/dining area from the kitchen. An open door led to a guest bathroom. A stairway curved upward.

"Watch your feet," Seixas said, indicating some dried bloodstains just inside the front door.

"Must have shot him right here," Hector said.

"Uh-huh," Seixas agreed. He pointed to a much larger bloodstain near the sofa. "And beat him to death over there." One side of the blood pool had a straight edge. "There was a carpet," Seixas said. "They took it for analysis."

"And?"

"Lots of fibers and stuff. Some interesting blond hairs, so they tell me, but we've got nothing to compare them with, so they're all pretty useless at this stage."

"I take it Neves's girlfriend is not blond."

"You take it right. She's a brunette."

The downstairs area was small, the furnishings sparse. The kitchen had all of the modern conveniences, including a dishwasher, but everything in miniature. The apartment was spacious enough for a couple, but not for a couple with kids. Telltale smudges of black fingerprint powder showed on many of the surfaces.

"What's upstairs?" Hector asked.

"A bed and a bathroom. Go ahead. Have a look. I'll stay here. I've seen it already, and I have bad knees."

Hector climbed the stairs, stood at a metal rail, and took in the view of the city. Beyond the urban sprawl, a mountain range showed bluish in the haze.

Seixas looked up at him from below. "The shades were

down when Neves was found," he said. "He'd probably closed them for the night."

Closets with sliding doors lined the far side of the sleeping area. Next to the bed was a small table with a clock radio, a reading lamp, and a copy of a novel written by Paulo Coelho. Hector picked up the book and absently flipped through the pages. A bookmark slipped out and fell to the floor. He picked it up, looked at it, and went downstairs to show it to Seixas.

* * *

"NEVES WAS reading *Guerreiro da Luz*. He left it on the nightstand next to his bed. Guess what he was using for a bookmark?"

"Tell me," Silva said.

"A boarding pass for a flight from Miami International to São Paulo Guarulhos. Neves's name was on it. He was in Miami last November."

"And so was Rivas. Is that what you're getting at?"

"A long shot, I know—"

"A very long shot." Silva grabbed a ballpoint from the porcelain mug on his desk. "Date?"

"The twenty-second of November."

"Airline?"

"TAB."

"Flight number?"

"8101."

"Got it. Did you get a chance to speak to Janus?"

"I did."

Janus Prado was the head of São Paulo's homicide squad.

"Did he have anything more on that thug João Girotti?"

"He was busted on a burglary charge, but in the end they couldn't hold him. The witness, the *only* witness, recanted."

"Bought off?"

"Or scared off. Girotti was released on the afternoon of the day he was killed. If he'd stayed in jail, he might still be alive. The term 'protective custody' comes to mind."

"Don't be a wiseass. You're starting to sound like Arnaldo."

"Heaven forbid."

"What else?"

"Prado's guys are doing no more than go through the motions. Their feeling is that whoever killed Girotti did the city a favor."

"Did they question the people in the bar?"

"Only briefly. Girotti was there celebrating his release. He drank nonstop from about five in the afternoon until nine or nine thirty at night. Then he left. His body was discovered fifteen minutes later."

"He left alone?"

"No. With a woman."

"That kind of a bar, eh?"

"That kind of a bar."

"Maybe the killer got the woman to lure him outside."

"You don't think Girotti is a dead end? Somebody else's victim?"

"You saw the photos?"

"I saw the photos. Unlikely, huh?"

"Very. But it won't be long before we know for sure. I should have the ballistics results on those bullets by tomorrow at the latest. Is Babyface back from Rio?"

"Should be by now."

"Send him over to that bar."

Chapter Ten

THE BAR DO ELIAS was a shabby establishment with a sign in the front window offering beer for two reais.

Haraldo Gonçalves wasn't about to miss out on a deal like that. He bellied up to the bar and rapped his knuckles on the wood.

"A Cerpa," he said.

"Beer's only for folks old enough to drink." The bartender grinned.

His attempt at humor failed miserably. "Take a good fucking look," Gonçalves said, flourishing his warrant card in the bartender's face.

"Brahma or Antarctica?" the bartender said.

"I told you. Cerpa."

"No Cerpa. We only got Brahma and Antarctica."

"Antarctica, then."

The bartender reached into a cooler, pulled out a cold bottle, and poured half of the contents into a glass. He set the glass and the bottle on the bar between them.

"You look too young to be a cop," he said.

"No shit. Elias around?"

"Elias sold me this place back in 1997. I never got around to changing the name."

"And yours is?"

"Renato Cymbalista, but nobody calls me that. They call me Gordo." The word meant fatty, and it was appropriate.

"Gordo, huh?" Gonçalves said, eying Cymbalista's vast midriff. "I can't imagine why."

He was still miffed about the fat man's attempt at humor.

"You in my place on business, or pleasure?" Gordo asked.

Gonçalves looked around him with distaste and curled his lip. "What do you think?" he said. "Were you working the night João Girotti was murdered?"

"Yeah."

"How well did you know him?"

"I didn't know him at all. Why he chose my place to drink in, and the alley out in back to get killed in, I couldn't say."

"Did you talk with him?"

"Just to take his orders."

"What was he drinking?"

"Beer with Dreher chasers."

Gonçalves wrinkled his nose. Conhaque Dreher, cachaça flavored with ginger, was just about the cheapest distilled spirit you could buy.

"Got pretty drunk, did he?"

"He got wasted."

"Think back. Did he talk to anyone else?"

"I don't have to think back, on account of I already told the story twice. By now, I got it memorized. First, I told it to the uniformed guys who showed up just after Graça found the body. Then I—"

"Who's Graça?"

"One of the girls."

"She works for you?"

"None of them work for me. We got an arrangement. They use the place to pick up customers, and the customers buy them drinks. Like that, see?"

"How did Graça find the body?"

"The women's toilet is out there." Gordo shot a thumb in the direction of the rear door. "She walked out to use it, and she stumbled over him."

"This was how long after he left?"

"Ten minutes? Fifteen? Not long."

"Back to my question: did he talk to anyone else?"

"Just the girl who was sitting at his table, the one he left with."

"And that would be?"

Gordo shrugged. "Some blond," he said. "I never saw her before. She shoulda come over and talked to me first, but she didn't."

"Why didn't *you* talk to *her*?"

"The guy was buying anyway, and I was busy."

"Seen her since?"

Gordo shook his head.

His eyes now accustomed to the dim light, Gonçalves checked out his surroundings. Standing at the bar, just a few meters away, an old man with bleary eyes was staring straight ahead and nursing a drink.

The other male patrons, seven in number, were distributed between two tables, three at one, four at the other. All of them had given him the once-over when he came in. Since then, they'd lost interest.

The women, on the other hand, were looking at him expectantly. It was still early in the day, and there were only three of them. One, a would-be blond, winked.

Gonçalves turned back to the bartender. "This Graça, is she here?"

The bartender stretched his neck to look over Gonçalves's shoulder.

"No," he said.

"Is there anyone else here now who was here then?"

"Leonardo was." Gordo pointed along the bar. "He almost never leaves."

The old man with the bleary eyes didn't react, even though he was close enough to hear every word.

"But I wouldn't waste your time with him if I was you," Gordo said, not lowering his voice, speaking as if Leonardo wasn't there. "He doesn't recognize his own wife half the time."

"You're exaggerating, right?"

"I'm not. She comes in three or four times a week to drag him home, and he honest-to-God doesn't recognize her. I don't think it's just the booze. Something is screwed up in his head." He pointed at his temple and made a circular motion. Maybe it's that . . . that. . . ."

Gonçalves helped him out. "Alzheimer's?"

"Yeah, that. I figure there's a bright side, though."

"What's that?"

"Think about it. Every time he takes her to bed, it's like he's fucking a different woman. You married?"

"No."

"Then you have no idea what I'm talking about."

"I think I do. There *are* happy marriages, you know."

"So I hear. Never seen one myself. Want another beer?"

"Not yet. So Leonardo was here, but he really wasn't. Who else?"

"None of the guys over there, maybe one of the girls. They're coming and going all the time. It's tough to keep track."

"All right. One more question. After this guy Girotti went outside, did you hear a shot?"

Gordo shook his head.

"No," he said. "And, before you ask, the answer is yes."

"Yes to what?"

"Yes, I know what a shot sounds like. We hear them all the time around here."

Gonçalves picked up his glass and went over to where the women were clustered around a table. Gordo had called them girls, but they were hardly that. They hadn't been girls for a long, long time.

They made for a colorful group: one was a *mulata*, one was black, and one was white.

"Mind if I sit down?" Gonçalves said.

"Your mother let you play with big girls?" the mulata said, sizing him up.

"She lets."

"Then sit," the black woman said. "I'm Dorothy. This is Amalia"—she indicated the youngest—"and this is Ruby."

"Haraldo," Gonçalves said.

Amalia was the one who'd winked at him. She reached out and fingered his necktie.

"Nice," she said. "You a cop?"

"Yeah, I'm a cop."

"I like cops," she said. "Want to go somewhere and show me your gun?"

"Not today, thanks. I'm working."

"Yeah," she said. "Me too."

She took a cigarette from the pack on the table and held it to her mouth, waiting for him to light it.

"Sorry," Gonçalves said. "I don't smoke."

Amalia reached into her purse, produced a cheap plastic lighter, and handed it to him. He held the flame to the tip of her cigarette. She put a hand around his, as if she needed to steady it, which she didn't. When he doused the flame, she released him and took a long drag.

"I hate to break up this little scene," the black woman said, "but you can do me with handcuffs if you want."

Gonçalves shook his head. "I just want some information," he said.

"*Caralho*, you're no fun at all," Amalia said, tipping off some ash.

The white one didn't say anything, didn't even look at him. It occurred to Gonçalves that she might have been pretty once.

"The least you could do is to buy us some drinks," Amalia said.

"What are you having?"

She inclined her head in the direction of the bar. "He knows," she said.

"But I don't," Gonçalves said.

"Champagne," she admitted: part of her deal with the bar's owner, no doubt.

"How much?"

"Has to be a bottle. It goes flat, so Gordo doesn't sell it by the glass."

"How much?"

"Sixty reais."

She blew a smoke ring in his face. The ring was damn near perfect. She must have spent a lot of time perfecting the technique.

"Sixty reais, huh?" Gonçalves said.

The champagne couldn't have been imported, not in a bar like this, not for a price like that. And if it wasn't imported, it was a ripoff. But Gonçalves figured it was worth it to get the girls talking. When he turned in his expenses, he hoped Silva would think so too.

"All right," he said.

The white woman emerged from her stupor to flash him a smile. It was a surprisingly sweet smile, but it didn't last.

The black woman lifted a hand and made a gesture to Gordo.

A minute or so later, he bustled over and made much of opening a bottle of Peterlongo, cheap sparkling wine from Rio Grande do Sul. Gonçalves could have bought it for less than ten reais in any second-class supermarket. The better stores didn't stock it.

He waved off the glass that Gordo offered him and pointed at his own. "Give me another one of those," he said.

"One Antarctica, coming right up."

Gordo hustled off, smiling for the first time since Gonçalves had waved his credentials in his face.

"Wise choice," Amalia said, grinding her cigarette into the ashtray and taking only the tiniest sip of her wine. The butt continued to smolder. "Okay, what do you want to know?"

"You remember that murder a while back? Body found out back?"

"Sure, I remember. Thing like that doesn't happen every day, not even around here. Besides, a friend of mine stumbled over him when she went out to do *xixi*. It scared her half to death. She came back screaming."

"You remember the woman he was with?"

"Sure." Amalia tipped wine onto the butt. It sizzled and went out.

"Do you know her name?"

"I've been working this joint for three years. I thought I knew all the girls, but that one. . . ." She shook her head.

"She been back since?"

"No. You think she had something to do with it?"

"Maybe. Maybe she lured him outside so the killer could get at him."

"Or maybe she was just trying to turn an honest trick, and when the killer showed up she made herself scarce."

"That's possible too. What do you remember about her?"

"She was goddamned fast, for one thing."

"What do you mean, fast?"

"That João, the murdered guy, he wasn't here two min-utes. We're all still looking at him, waiting for him to make

a move. Then she sashays in like she owns the place. She
didn't look around, didn't smile at anybody; she just made
straight for his table and took a seat."

"You think he knew her?"

"Hell, no. He looked surprised. I thought he was going to
tell her to fuck off. But he didn't."

"Then what happened?"

"They talked. He drank. The drunker he got, the louder
he got."

"What did you hear him say?"

"Nothing. Just the same crap, over and over. He was
shitfaced."

"Could you hear anything the woman said?"

"Not a word. But she was trying to calm him down. She
put a hand on him right here."

Amalia laid a hand on Gonçalves's thigh.

"After a while," she said, "she moved it up to—"

Gonçalves crossed his legs.

"Hey," she said, "you don't have to get all fidgety on me. I
was just explaining."

She took another cigarette out of the pack and put it
between her lips. Gonçalves picked up the lighter and lit it.

"So she's got her hand between his legs," he prompted.

"She's grabbing his cock, that's what she's doing. But does
he move? No, he orders another round. And then another
one. He was here for hours. Guy like that, guy who just gets
out of jail, you'd think he'd be crazy for a woman, right? But
no, he just keeps drinking. Around about the time I'm thinking he's gay, he finally pays the bill. When he stands up, his
legs are all wobbly, but I can see he isn't gay at all."

"And then what?"

"And then they left. They went out that way."

Amalia pointed toward the back of the bar. Gonçalves

followed the line of her finger and saw a single door. On the wall next to it was a crudely painted sign. The sign said SENHORAS.

"Why didn't Girotti wait here until she got back from the toilet?"

"Are you kidding? There was no way she was going to let him do that, no way she was going to give anybody else a chance to get their hooks into him. She took him by the hand and led him outside. The lady's toilet opens onto the alley. So does that door. And the alley itself runs between two streets. She never came back."

"What did she look like? Describe her."

Amalia took another puff on her cigarette. Some of the smoke rose past her eyes and caused her to squint. Or maybe she was just remembering.

"She was white, and she was blond. Maybe that's why he let her stay. Guy like him doesn't get many chances with a white woman. And I'll bet he never had a blond in his whole life, probably wanted to know what she looked like down there."

"Tall? Short?"

"Neither. Medium, I'd say."

"How about her eyes?"

"She was wearing sunglasses, big and really dark. She must have had a hard time seeing anything."

"Suppose you saw her in a lineup. Would you recognize her?"

"Not in a million years," Amalia said.

Chapter Eleven

Via E-mail
To: Mario Silva, Headquarters, Brasília
From: Mara Carta, Field Office, São Paulo
Further to your request, please find attached the passenger list for
Transportes Aéreos Brasileiros flight 8101 on the 22nd of
November last year.
Cordially,
Mara

Mara Carta was Hector's intelligence officer. The attachment consisted of six pages. The first was dedicated exclusively to first-class passengers. It added nothing to Silva's knowledge. The last four listed the people in economy class. There, too, he found nothing of interest.

But the second page was a revelation. The third name Silva read caused him to blink; the last three brought him bolt upright in his chair.

TAB Flight 8101 22 Nov. Passenger List (cont.)
Business Class Cabin

	Passenger Name	Nationality
1	Arriaga*, Julio	BR
2	Clancy, Dennis, Fr.	US
3	Cruz, Paulo, Dr.	BR
4	Porto, Lidia	BR
5	Kloppers**, Jan	BR
6	Kloppers, Marnix	BR

7	Mansur, Luis	BR
8	Motta, Darcy	BR
9	Neves, Victor	BR
10	Palhares, Jonas	BR
11	Rivas, Juan	VE

* Dependent of Aline Arriaga, TAB employee
  #13679, traveling on standby.

** Minor child accompanied by parent.

Silva consulted João Girotti's rap sheet and then placed a call to his nephew.

"Have you seen that passenger list for TAB 8101?"

"Not yet," Hector said. "Why?"

"Cruz, Rivas, Neves, and Palhares are on it."

"*All four?*"

"All four."

"That's it, then? That's the connection we've been looking for?"

"Looks that way. On the night of the twenty-second to the twenty-third of November, they were all traveling in the business-class cabin of Flight 8101, TAB."

"Where was Girotti?"

"He was in jail. He'd been there for a week."

"How did he get out?"

"The witness, the only witness, recanted."

"Recanted? Just like that?"

"Just like that. His lawyer was Dudu Fonseca."

"Fonseca? Where did a punk like Girotti get the money to hire Fonseca?"

"Good question. And here's another we should be asking ourselves: if Girotti had the money, why did he elect to sit around cooling his heels in jail? Fonseca could have had him out in a day."

"Maybe Girotti didn't have the money when he went in. Maybe he came into it *after* he got pinched."

"That's the most logical explanation, isn't it?"

"Uh-huh. Fonseca doesn't lift a finger unless he gets a retainer in advance."

"True. He generally needs to bribe some witness or another."

"Or to hire someone to scare the witness off."

"Also true."

"What's our next step?"

"Warn the surviving passengers."

"I suppose it didn't escape you that one of them might be the killer?"

"It certainly did not."

"Who are they?"

"There are seven of them, one female. They're all Brazilians, except for one of the males."

"And he is. . . ."

"An American, Dennis Clancy. There's an 'FR' in front of his name."

"A priest?"

"Either that or a misspelling. There's a 'DR' in front of Cruz's. Maybe they typed an F instead of a D."

"And the others?"

"The woman was Lidia Porto. The men were Julio Arriaga, dependent of an airline employee, probably a kid."

"Airline employee? TAB headquarters is here in São Paulo. Want me to handle that?"

"Would you? His mother's name is Aline Arriaga. She's the employee."

"Got it."

"Next, Kloppers, Marnix and Jan, father and son. Jan is the son, described here as a minor."

"Kloppers? What kind of name is that?"

"No idea. The last two are Luis Mansur and Darcy Motta."

"Names and nationalities, that's all we've got to work with?"

"At the moment, yes."

"There are going to be Mansurs, Portos, and Mottas galore."

"Put Mara on it. Tell her to get into the national identity card database and start sifting. Meanwhile, I'll see what I can find out about the American."

* * *

SILVA'S NEXT call was to the immigration section. He spoke to a clerk who said his name was Cizik.

"Cizik?"

"My old man was a Czech, Chief Inspector. How can I be of assistance?"

Silva explained what he wanted. Cizik told him everything was computerized. It would only take a moment.

A couple of minutes later, he was back on the line. "I've got copies of Clancy's visa application and entry card. First name, Dennis? Occupation, priest?"

"That's him."

"Hmmm."

"Hmmm, what?"

"Unusual case. It appears Father Clancy is still in Brazil."

"And that's unusual?"

"He's been here for almost three months. Most gringos stay for three weeks or less. The few who stick around generally come in on another kind of visa."

"Such as?"

"Study or work."

"Could he have left? Could it be a computer glitch?"

"It's possible, wouldn't be the first time. But frankly. . . ."

"Yes?"

"It's not likely. He listed a hotel in São Paulo. Want me to call them?"

"I do."

"Give me twenty minutes."

***

CIZIK WAS better than his word. Silva's phone rang in less than ten.

"It checked out. He stayed at the Hotel Gloria on Avenida Ipiranga, in São Paulo. But it was only for one night."

"The Hotel Gloria? Why do I—"

"Bobo, Chief Inspector. He used to live there."

"Bobo, the TV star. Of course. I'll get a man over there. Who did you talk to?"

"The manager, a fellow by the name of Vasco."

"I appreciate your assistance, Cizik. Now listen. It's very important we find this man Clancy."

"Because?"

"Because if we don't, and soon, he's liable to kill someone, or someone's liable to kill him. How about you check the passenger lists for domestic airlines?"

"Sure. Glad to help."

"Did Clancy pay the hotel with a credit card?"

"He did, and we have the number. But it's an American card. I've had dealings with those people, Chief Inspector, and they're a pain in the ass. The Americans are too damned afraid they're gonna get sued. They don't cough up anything without legal paper."

"I have a friend who's a cop in Miami Beach. You think he can help?"

"Don't waste his time. They won't give it to him either. We'll get you the information eventually, but we're gonna have to go through channels."

"And how long is *that* likely to take?"

"At least a week, probably more. It's not like we're at the top of any of their priority lists."

Silva told Cizik to do it anyway, thanked him, and placed another call to his nephew.

"The Gloria?" Hector said. "Isn't that the place where Bobo—"

"It is. Listen, I've been thinking about that flight. Something else occurred to me."

"What?"

"We should consider the flight crew as well. Find out who worked the business-class cabin."

Chapter Twelve

BRUNA NASCIMENTO AND LINA Godoy breezed through immigration and followed the rest of the crew to the waiting van. A ten-minute drive brought them to the Caesar Park Hotel. The rising sun was painting the building with gold as they maneuvered their small suitcases through the revolving door and into the marble-floored lobby.

They checked in, sent their luggage upstairs, and then, as they often did after a long flight, the two young flight attendants went to the coffee shop.

Forty-five minutes later, they were on their second pot of hot chocolate and trying to get rid of Horácio Leão. Leão, their copilot, was handsome, single, and on a fast track to captain. He was also vain, shallow, and a crushing bore. His interests, as far as Bruna could determine, were limited to airplanes and sex. Horácio had been trying to get Bruna or Lina into bed for some time, and he'd made it abundantly clear that he'd be equally happy to score with either one.

"I'm just below the penthouse," he was saying. "You can't believe the view from up there. It's almost as good as the one I get from the cockpit."

Bruna toyed with her spoon and glanced out of the window at an A320 on its final approach. Lina looked at the tablecloth.

"So, how about it?" Leão looked from one woman to the other. "One of you ladies want to have a look? I'll get the check."

He turned to signal the waiter; Bruna and Lina exchanged a what-an-idiot glance.

"We have some girl things to talk about," Bruna said as Leão scribbled his name on the check. "What's your room number?"

Leão furrowed his brow. She could practically *see* him decide to be hopeful.

"1607," he said.

"See you later, then."

Later, she thought, would be when they were in the van, on their way to board the return flight.

Leão got to his feet and favored her with a leer before he swaggered off.

"Creep," she said, as soon he was out of earshot.

"Screw him," Lina said.

"Not on your life."

"Figuratively, I meant. Come on, Bruna, come with me. It'll be fun."

Bruna shook her head. "I need sleep."

They were on a seventy-two-hour layover. Lina was going to her uncle's country place in Juquiti, a municipality three hours' drive to the south. The uncle's partner, Franco, was a gourmet cook. And neither man ever talked about airplanes.

But Bruna was exhausted. Her holiday on St. Bart's had been anything but restful. Henri, the diving instructor she'd met on St. Jean Beach, had seen to that.

"I'm going to get into bed," she said, "and I'm going to sleep for twelve hours. Then I'll take it from there."

"Take what where? This hotel's in a dead zone." Lina gestured toward the window where the control tower of Guarulhos Airport towered over some shrubbery and a chain-link fence.

"But in here there's double glazing and room service," Bruna said. She glanced at her watch. "Let's go up to the room. Your uncle's almost due."

"He's always late," Lina said.

***

UPSTAIRS, LINA stripped off her skirt and blouse. Bruna kicked off her shoes and inquired about messages.

There weren't any.

Lina opened her suitcase, took out a shoulder bag, and started stuffing it with things she might need. "Nothing from your Frenchman?" she asked.

Bruna shook her head. "I'll give him another ten minutes. Then I'm going to block incoming calls."

"You? Block incoming calls? You *must* be exhausted."

"I told you," Bruna said, standing up and removing her blouse.

"Why don't you call him?" Lina said and disappeared into the bathroom.

"You have any idea," Bruna said, raising her voice so Lina could hear her over the sound of running water, "how much it would cost to call St. Bart's from this hotel?"

"Probably a lot, but you could make it short, tell him to call you back."

"I told him where I'd be. He's the man, so he's supposed to call. I don't want him to think I'm chasing him."

"Which you are."

"Which I am, but I don't want him to think so."

Lina stepped out of the shower and Bruna stepped in. She'd just turned off the tap when the telephone rang. Lina answered it, but it wasn't Henri. It was her Uncle Eduardo, and he was downstairs.

"Gotta run," she said, coming into the bathroom to give Bruna a peck on the cheek.

Bruna heard the door slam and picked up the hair dryer.

***

IT SEEMED as if she'd barely laid her head on the pillow when something woke her from a steamy dream in which Henri was playing a major role.

She squirmed, stretched, and looked at the clock. Half past eleven. She'd slept three hours, no more. She frowned, rubbed the sleep from her eyes. And then it came again: the sound of someone rapping at her door. She was sure she had hung out the DO NOT DISTURB sign. Once more, the same knock, furtive, as if the knocker didn't want anyone in the neighboring rooms to hear; insistent, as if the intruder knew she was there.

Which, of course, he did. It had to be that damned copilot. He must have seen Lina leaving for her uncle's *sitio*, must know Bruna was alone.

"Who's there?" she said, not bothering to keep the irritation out of her voice.

There was no answer.

"I'm trying to get some sleep," she said. "Whoever the hell you are, come back later. Come back in ten hours."

The reply came in the form of three gentle taps, neither harder nor softer than before.

Furious now, she went to her open suitcase and felt around until she'd found her kimono.

"All right," she said, searching for the sleeves and finding them. "I'm coming. Wait."

And she *did* let him wait. She went into the bathroom, splashed some cold water on her face, grabbed a brush and smoothed her blond hair. Finally, she went to the door and removed the chain. If she'd been more awake, or if it hadn't been the Caesar Park Hotel, with all the security in the world, or if she hadn't been quite sure that it was their copilot, she might have kept the chain on.

But she didn't.

Chapter Thirteen

GUARULHOS, THE LARGEST OF São Paulo's international airports, is viewed with favor by the aviation community. Congonhas, the smallest, is not. The shortest runway at Guarulhos is in excess of three thousand meters; the shortest at Congonhas measures less than fifteen hundred, barely enough for a modern passenger jet. But that isn't the worst of it. The worst of it is that the runways at Congonhas aren't grooved.

Grooving is a technique whereby tiny trenches are cut into the surface of the concrete to drain rainwater. At Congonhas, an airport famous for inclement weather, rainwater on the runways often accumulates to a depth exceeding twenty-five millimeters, which is barely the thickness of a fifty-centavo piece, but it's enough to cause aquaplaning, a fancy word for a skid.

Passenger jets depend on two devices to bring them to a stop: brakes and reverse thrusters. If either fails, and if the runway is as short as it is at Congonhas, skids can be fatal.

Hector approached the airport from the city center, passing on his right the blackened ruins of a warehouse. The area had been closed off by a brand-new fence now lined with flowers and teddy bears. Beyond the fence, bulldozers were demolishing walls and clearing rubble. Thirteen days earlier, a TAB flight from Porto Alegre, landing in light rain and with only one thruster functioning, had skidded off the runway to Hector's left. The runway and the area around it were higher than the road. The Airbus had retained just enough momentum to clear the heavy rush-hour traffic before plunging into the warehouse.

Killed were 187 passengers on the plane, several employees working in the warehouse, and a few passersby, a grand total of 199 deaths. The authorities were still sorting out carbonized bodies, still trying to fix the blame for the disaster.

Hector parked in the underground garage, took the elevator up to the terminal, and asked to be directed to the airline's personnel department.

"Aline Arriaga, Aline Arriaga," the obliging young man repeated to himself, his fingers flying over the keyboard. "Ah, here she is. Works check-in on the noon to eight."

The young man was wearing a red blazer and a name tag identifying him as G. Salcedo, Assistant Manager. He reached out for a telephone without taking his eyes off the screen.

And put it down as quickly as he'd picked it up.

"Sorry," he said.

"Sorry, what?" Hector said.

"She's off today. She works Saturdays and Sundays, takes Thursdays and Fridays off. She'll be here on Saturday."

"She live close by?"

Salcedo consulted his screen, "Not really. Mooca."

The Mooca neighborhood was a long way from Congonhas.

"I'll drop by her place tomorrow," Hector said. He made a writing gesture. "Could you give me her address?"

"Sure." Salcedo grabbed a ballpoint pen and made a note. "Can you tell me what this is about?"

"Sorry," Hector said. "Police business. Confidential. But I

can tell you that she isn't a suspect. It's just a routine inquiry."

Salcedo passed the paper to Hector. Hector slipped it into his breast pocket.

"Something else," he said. "Can you access the flight-crew assignments? Tell me which of your attendants was on which flight and when?"

"Which flights are you interested in?"

"Just one. The 8101 from Miami International to São Paulo on the twenty-second of November, specifically the business-class cabin."

"You're in luck."

"Why?"

"Because the twenty-second of November was less than three months ago, and we only keep that kind of information for three months. Unless there's an incident report, that is. Then we keep it longer."

"Incident report?"

"Yeah, you know, reports on unusual occurrences, like a passenger getting physically abusive."

"Happen often?"

"Not often. But when it does, we keep the records. It's a crime, you know."

"Uh-huh."

"And then there are the subpoenas."

"Subpoenas?"

"First thing a defense attorney does is subpoena our reports, looking for some loophole to get his client off."

"Who makes the reports?"

"The chief steward. Then the captain signs off on it. What was that flight again?"

"The 8101 on the twenty-second of November."

"The 8101 is a daily flight. Are we talking about departure or arrival?"

"Departure. The one that left on the twenty-second, and arrived on the twenty-third."

Salcedo's fingers returned to the keyboard. While he was at it, an older man approached his work station.

"Is there a problem, Gabriel?"

Hector glanced at the newcomer's name tag. He was E. Dornelles, Manager.

"No, Senhor Dornelles. No problem. This man is from the police."

"The police?" Dornelles raised a pair of bushy eyebrows. "How can we be of service?"

Hector told him what he wanted.

Dornelles asked him why he wanted it.

Hector told him the same thing he'd told Salcedo, that it was a police matter, confidential.

Dornelles turned to Salcedo. "The conversation between the two of you is over," he said.

"But—"

"But nothing, Gabriel. It's over. I'm sure you have other duties to attend to."

Salcedo nodded but didn't move.

Dornelles stared at him. "Well?" he said.

"This is my work station, Senhor."

"Take a break. Go have coffee."

When Salcedo was out of earshot, Dornelles turned back to Hector. "You have some kind of identification?"

"I showed it to Senhor Salcedo."

"I'd like you to show it to me."

Hector did.

Dornelles gave Hector's warrant card close scrutiny and

then handed it back. "All right, Delegado, I'm convinced you are who you say you are. But if you don't tell me *exactly* why you want this information, I won't give it to you."

Hector bristled. "I can get a court order."

Dornelles was unperturbed.

"You can," he said. "And we'll comply. Of course, it might take us a while to find the information you need. We have *so* many records. It might take us a week, maybe even two weeks. Do you have two weeks to spare, Delegado?"

Hector opened his mouth to reply, but before he could, Dornelles continued. "On the other hand," he said, "you can back off on the confidential bullshit and, if I'm convinced that what you want isn't something that's liable to cause any damage to this airline, I might be inclined to give it to you."

"Might?"

Dornelles sighed. "Do you have any idea, Delegado, how many lawsuits are launched against this company each year?"

"No, and frankly, I don't care."

"Of course you don't. Why should you? But *I* do." He gestured in the general direction of the devastated warehouse. "What happened just across the street is a prime example. The relatives of those victims are still in a state of grief, and I can't blame them, but they're lawyering up just the same. Pretty soon the civil actions will begin. Are they going to sue the people who make the Airbus 320? You bet they are. Are they going to sue the airport, which means the government? You bet they are. And are they going to sue us? You bet your ass they are. But who do you think, in the end, is going to wind up carrying the can?"

"I don't—"

"Yes, I know. You don't care. But bear with me. Airbus is far away, in France. They've got deep pockets, but they'll also have the data from the flight recorders, the famous black boxes—which, by the way, aren't black, but orange."

"What do the black boxes have to do with—"

"I'm explaining. Hear me out."

Dornelles waited for Hector to nod before he went on:

"The Airbus people will say there wasn't a damned thing wrong with the design of their aircraft. They'll say that an indicator light pointing to a malfunction of one of the reverse thrusters was working perfectly. They'll say the malfunction was detected before the flight took off from Porto Alegre. The black boxes *and* our own maintenance reports will prove them right. Unfortunately for us, the black boxes have been located, and the reports have already been impounded."

"Where are you going with all of this?" Hector said.

Dornelles continued as if he hadn't heard him: "That will leave this airline, and the government, as the only two defendants. The government should have fixed the goddamned runway years ago, but they didn't. They didn't because of corruption in the contracts, and because of incompetence, and because the politicians wanted to show their constituents a shiny new parking lot and a renovated terminal, instead of investing money in something invisible like grooving the fucking runway.

"In a just world, the government would lose the case. But this is *our* government. They're going to appeal, and re-appeal, and in the end the families of the victims might get some money sometime in the next century. That leaves this airline holding the bag. The money bag, I mean.

"The victims' lawyers are going to claim negligence and pilot error, and we're going to fight it, and the odds are we'll lose. Now, granted, there has to be responsibility for a tragedy of this magnitude, but it isn't fair that this airline should have to bear *all* of that responsibility just because a damned mechanic decided to postpone the repair of the thruster, and a damned captain decided to sign off on it."

It had been a long speech, delivered with mounting passion, and Dornelles was winded at the end of it. It could have been *his* money he was talking about, and if he'd stopped there, Hector would have classified him as a company man to his fingertips.

But Dornelles wasn't finished.

"I'm covering my ass here," he said. "If I want to keep my job, I've got to help to keep this airline afloat. Fifteen years ago, the biggest air carrier, the *flag* carrier of this country, was Varig. I put seventeen years of my life into Varig, expected to draw my pension from Varig. Do you know what happened to them?"

"They filed for bankruptcy."

"Exactly," Dornelles said, as if he'd finally gotten his point across. "So you tell me what I want to know, or you can go out and get your court order."

Go out and get your court order came out very much like *go out and fuck yourself.*

Hector weighed his options. It took him less than two seconds.

"You'll keep everything I tell you in the strictest confidence?"

"I will," Dornelles said.

***

As soon as he was out of Congonhas's underground garage and was able to use his cell phone, Hector called Silva in Brasília.

"Aline Arriaga wasn't there. She takes Thursdays and Fridays off. I'll try to catch her at home tomorrow."

"Wasted trip then?"

"Not entirely." He told his uncle about his discussion with Dornelles and finished by saying, "But when I finally got to the records there was nothing to find."

"No incidents?"

"No. But I did discover something a bit out of the ordinary."

"Which was?"

"Two flight attendants called in sick just before the flight was scheduled to depart from Miami. The plane took off shorthanded. Business class, as we already know, had only eleven passengers. Tourist class, on the other hand, was packed. And it was a night flight."

"Day flight, night flight, what's the difference?"

"There's less space in tourist class, so it's harder to sleep. According to Dornelles, tourist-class passengers are up and about throughout the night, going to the toilets, stretching their legs, asking for water and juice. For that reason, and also because there are a lot more of them, they require more attention from the flight crew than passengers in business or first class. So the chief steward took the second flight attendant out of business class and assigned her to tourist."

"I'm sure she was pleased."

"According to Dornelles, she probably was. The tourist class attendants rotate during their shift. The woman who got switched would be able to catch a few hours of sleep, but the one who stayed in business class all by herself would be awake all night."

"And might well have seen something that would throw light on this situation. Did you get her name?"

"Bruna Nascimento. She's in São Paulo on a seventy-two-hour layover. She's staying at the Caesar Park, not the one on Rua Augusta, the one near Guarulhos. I called her room before I left Congonhas. No answer. Dornelles wasn't surprised.

He said there's nothing of interest anywhere near that hotel. The best time to catch her, he said, would be a few hours before flight time."

"Put Babyface on it."

"Will do. How's it going on your end? Anything new?"

"We located Luis Mansur."

"Where is he?"

"São Paulo."

"Have you spoken to him?"

"No, but I hope to later today. I want to show him photographs of that dead thug, Girotti."

"You're coming here?"

"I am. So is Arnaldo. He has a line on the Kloppers, Marnix and Jan. They're from a place called Holambra, a little town near São Paulo. Marnix's parents still live there. Arnaldo spoke to them."

"Marnix is the father of Jan, right?"

"Right. And get this: the old folks say they have no idea how to reach either one of them."

"They don't know where their own son is?"

"Or their grandson. So they say."

"Sounds unlikely."

"Which is why Arnaldo is going there personally."

"Do they know he's coming?"

"He thought it would be better if they didn't."

"What a nasty surprise, opening your front door and finding Arnaldo Nunes on your doorstep."

"I'll tell him you said that."

"I knew you would. That's why I did it. When are you arriving?"

"Tuesday."

"Only on Tuesday? Why not earlier?"

"Sampaio's up to something. He's set a meeting for Monday."

"All right, Tuesday. Congonhas or Guarulhos?"

"Guarulhos. Arnaldo is still going on about that accident, says he's not going to fly into Congonhas ever again."

"I'll arrange it. See you then."

"Wait. There's more. One of the domestic airlines came through on Clancy. It appears he caught a flight to Palmas."

"Palmas? The capital of Tocantins?"

"The very same."

"Why the hell would a tourist want to go there?"

Tocantins was the newest of the Brazilian states, carved out of the much older, and larger, state of Goiás. Palmas was a new city, constructed on what had been, until two decades earlier, a low hill covered with sun-baked red earth and a few stunted trees.

"God knows," Silva said. "And there's no record of him coming back."

"There aren't many hotels in Palmas. If he stayed in one, it shouldn't be tough to locate him."

"We're checking."

"Car rental?"

"Checking that too."

"Credit card records?"

"American. Requesting them through channels."

"How about Motta?"

"Nothing yet. We've placed telephone calls to all the Darcy Mottas in the records, spoken to most, and we're still awaiting callbacks from three. A physical description would help. You should ask the flight attendant if she remembers him. I'll pose the same question to Lidia Porto when I see her."

"When you see her?"

"Sorry. I should have mentioned that. We located her."

"And she's there in Brasília?"

"She is. She agreed to see us at five."

"That's quick. What was she doing in the States? Did she say?"

"She did. She was visiting her daughter and grandchildren. The daughter married an American."

"Have you warned her she might be in danger?"

"Not yet. I thought it best to break the news in person."

"Some of those old grannies can surprise you. Tough as nails."

"This one doesn't sound that way."

"I just had another thought."

"Tell me."

"There may have been a security camera above the boarding gate in Miami. It might have recorded images of the people boarding the flight."

"Where did that idea come from?"

"We were talking about Americans and photos. Sometimes I surprise myself."

"I'll ask Harvey Willis."

"That friend of yours? The Miami Beach cop?"

"Uh-huh. I'll phone him as soon as I hang up."

Chapter Fourteen

THE SINGLE CHIME OF the doorbell was still resonating when frantic barking overpowered it.

"Who is it?"

The woman's voice came from inside the apartment, almost a shout as she strived for audibility over the yapping.

Silva leaned in closer to the door. "Senhora Porto?"

"Yes."

"Chief Inspector Silva, Senhora. And Agent Nunes. We called."

"Oh, yes. Of course. Just a moment."

"Who the hell did she think it was?" Arnaldo growled, looking at his watch. "How many other appointments is she likely to have at exactly five P.M. on a Tuesday?"

In the space of a heartbeat, he'd gone from cheerful to grumpy. They could hear her moving away from the door, calling the dogs. Apparently, there were four of them, and all four had Teutonic names.

"Little bastards," Arnaldo said.

"Since when," Silva said, "don't you like dogs?"

"I like *most* dogs," Arnaldo said.

"But?"

"But *those* dogs are dachshunds."

"How can you tell?"

"Because my sister-in-law, Elisa, has three of them, and no other dog sounds quite like them. You hear the hysteria? The underlying threat in everything they say?"

"Say?"

"Bark."

"Dachshunds are cute."

"They're cute because they have to be cute. It's nature's way of assuring the survival of the species. If their appearance matched their character, mankind would have exterminated them centuries ago. Believe me, those big eyes and adorable little snouts are just a defense mechanism. Inside, dachshunds are dark and twisted."

"I've always liked them," Silva said.

"That's because you don't *know* them," Arnaldo said. "The woman has gone to lock them in another room. Good thing, too, otherwise they'd nip our heels off. You get them in a pack, they're vicious. I'm telling you, Mario—"

The door opened. The dogs were still kicking up a fuss, but now it was coming from a distant corner of the apartment.

"Chief Inspector Silva? Agent Nunes?"

Lidia Porto was a woman in her mid-sixties wearing sensible shoes and a cardigan sweater covered with dog hair. A pair of eyeglasses dangled from a chain around her neck. They gave her a professorial air.

"I'm Silva, Senhora. This is Nunes."

She extended a hand to each of them in turn.

"Won't you come in?"

She led them down the hallway into her living room. There were numerous photos strewn about. But, in the case of *this* grandmother, most of the photos were of dogs. Arnaldo had been right about the breed. They were dachshunds.

She had coffee waiting, and served them each a cup, speaking while she poured. "I'm sorry it took me a moment to answer the door. I thought it best to put my babies in the bedroom. Not everyone likes dogs, you know."

"Hard to believe, isn't it?" Arnaldo said, adding sugar.

"Agent Nunes loves dogs," Silva said, "even more than I do myself. He's particularly fond of dachshunds."

She put down her cup and started to get up. "Well, then," she said, "why don't I just—"

"Unfortunately, though," Arnaldo said hastily, "I've developed a recent allergy to their hair."

"To the hair of dachshunds?"

"Yes," Arnaldo said with a sigh. "I think it came from cuddling them too much. I fear I've stroked my last dachshund."

"You poor man," she said and shot him a look of sympathy.

"If you don't mind," Silva said, putting the interview back on track, "I have a few questions."

"Of course not. Ask away. You wanted to know about my last trip to the United States, isn't that right?"

"Actually, no, Senhora."

She frowned. "No?"

"I wanted to talk about your trip back home. You traveled on TAB flight 8101 on the twenty-second of November, correct?"

"Yes, it was the twenty-second of November. I didn't remember the date when you called, but after we hung up I checked my ticket stub. I always hang on to the stubs. My husband does something with them at tax time."

"Your husband? You're married?"

She cocked an eyebrow at him. "When we spoke by telephone, didn't I tell you I was in the United States visiting my daughter?"

There was nothing wrong with her memory, but somehow, Silva had imagined her to be a widow.

"Uh, still married, I meant."

"Twenty-nine years," she said with satisfaction. "And very happily."

"But your husband didn't accompany you to the States?"

She gave him a censorious look. "Someone had to stay at home and care for the babies."

In the bedroom, the "babies" were still going ballistic.

"A kennel?" Silva suggested.

She made a dismissive gesture. "Goodness, no. People who love their animals never subject them to kennels. Isn't that so, Agent Nunes?"

"Never," Arnaldo agreed, draining his cup.

"Do you recall who sat next to you on the flight?" Silva said.

"He was a famous author. Shortly after we got back, someone murdered him. Is that what this is about?"

"In part," Silva admitted. "So you sat next to Paulo Cruz?"

"I did, and I was thrilled. I've read *all* of his books. They're so . . . *educational*."

"Do you recall the tenor of your conversation?"

"We didn't talk much, I'm sorry to say. I had a thousand questions, of course. As soon as he told me who he was, I started right in. But he'd been attending some conference or other, and he was exhausted."

"So he slept?"

"He didn't even want dinner. He couldn't seem to keep his eyes open. He asked the stewardess for a pillow and drifted off."

"And he slept until. . . ."

"He slept all the way to São Paulo. He didn't even wake up for breakfast."

"So you didn't have much of a chance to form an impression."

"Oh, I wouldn't say that. There were a couple of things I noticed."

"Such as?"

"He looked older, for one thing."

"Older than what, Senhora?"

"Older than he does on the jackets of his books."

"I see. Anything else?"

"He wasn't wearing a wedding ring. I didn't think much about it at the time, but later, in the pictures of his funeral, there were three children who looked just like him."

"Anything else?"

She thought about it for a moment, shook her head, and said, "Have you found out who murdered him? Or why?"

"Not yet, Senhora."

"Such a pity. He seemed like a very nice man. And so . . . *talented.*"

"After he fell asleep, Senhora, did you sleep yourself?"

"I don't really sleep on airplanes, Chief Inspector. I only doze a little. It's not that flying makes me nervous, or anything, but I can't seem to fall asleep unless I'm lying down."

"So you were awake all night?"

She nodded. "All night."

"Did you get up, move around the cabin?"

"No, I didn't. I was in the window seat. Professor Cruz was sleeping between me and the aisle. I didn't want to disturb him."

"Tell me about your fellow passengers," he said. "Who else do you remember?"

"There was a very unpleasant man at the check-in. He sped up at the last minute and pushed in ahead of me. He smelled of whiskey."

"Luis Mansur?"

"I don't know his name. But if you ask the man with the spot on his face, he could probably tell you."

"Man with a spot on his face?"

"Yes. You're speaking to all of the passengers, aren't you?"

"We are."

"Then I guess you haven't gotten to him just yet. He has a mark on his face. Just here." She touched her cheek.

"What kind of mark? A birthmark?"

"A birthmark, yes. A rather large one."

"And why would he be likely to remember the name of the fellow who smelled of whiskey?"

"Because at a given point, the fellow who smelled of whiskey came over and sat down next to him."

"And they spoke?"

"And they spoke. But not for long, only a couple of minutes. Then the man who smelled got up and went back to his original seat."

"Did you hear what they talked about?"

"No. But the man with the birthmark wasn't enjoying the conversation. He looked very displeased."

"Do you remember any of the other passengers?"

"There was a priest; at least I *think* he was a priest. He was wearing a . . . what do you call it?" She pointed to her neck.

"Clerical collar?"

"Yes."

"Did you speak to him?"

"No."

"Who else can you remember?"

"I was reading most of the time. But I do recall a young man, a teenager. He was traveling all by himself in business class, and I thought that was strange. I never traveled business class until I was over forty. Even now, my husband complains about the difference in price; but frankly, he can afford it. And the tourist cabin is just *too* uncomfortable."

"A teenager. Who else?"

She put a finger to her lips, remembering. "A gentleman traveling with his son. Both of them appeared to be very nervous."

"Nervous?"

"Craning their necks to see who was getting on board, muttering to each other in voices just above a whisper. But that was before we took off. Once we were in the air, they settled down and went to sleep."

"Like Professor Cruz."

"Like Professor Cruz, except the two of them woke up for breakfast."

"Who else?"

"A young man with a ponytail. Another young man with a little moustache and a gold earring here." She touched an ear. "I think that was about it. There weren't many people in the cabin. Oh, yes, I almost forgot, there was a fellow in his thirties with a suit and an attaché case. He was one of those people who don't make much of an impression. I forgot about him last time, as well. I wouldn't have remembered him at all, if the woman hadn't prompted me."

Silva glanced at Arnaldo, who raised an eyebrow.

"What last time?" he said. "What woman?"

"Some research person. Doing work for the airlines."

"When was this?"

"Quite some time ago. Not long after I got back. She called and made an appointment. Maybe I couldn't have told you as much as I have if she hadn't taken me through it once already."

"She posed the same questions we've been asking?"

"Her focus was on passenger service, and the experience of flying business class over long distances. But many of the questions *were* similar."

"Did she leave a business card?"

"No, she didn't."

"How about identification? What did she show you?"

"She didn't offer any."

"And you didn't ask?"

"No."

"Why not?"

"I didn't ask *you* for any either, did I?" she said. "I like to be cooperative. This woman already knew, when she called, that I'd been a business-class passenger on the flight. She must have had access to records. I had no reason to be suspicious."

"No, Senhora, of course you didn't. What did this woman look like?"

Lidia Porto put her hands over her head and waved her fingers. "She had frizzy red hair, quite a lot of it. She wasn't young, but she wasn't old either, mid-thirties, I'd say. About my height, maybe a little taller. Not fat, not thin, just . . . normal. I'm sorry I can't be more helpful than that."

"Eye color?"

"I don't know."

"You don't remember?"

"No. I don't *know*. She was wearing dark glasses."

"Dark glasses? Here, inside your apartment?"

Lidia Porto nodded. "She told me she was suffering from conjunctivitis."

"Anything else you can remember about her?"

"Not really. Why?"

"Senhora Porto, if she—or anyone else claiming to be from the airline—gets in touch with you again, don't let her in. Lock the door and call us immediately. Call me personally. Here's my card."

Silva took one out of his case and handed it to her. She looked at it and then looked back at him. For the first time, he saw alarm in her eyes.

"Don't you think," she said, "it's time you told me what this is all about?"

"Yes, Senhora," Silva said. "I do."

And he did.

Chapter Fifteen

THE FOLLOWING MORNING, AT half past seven, Hector called Gonçalves. Gonçalves picked up on the fifth ring.

"Who's this?"

"It's Hector. What are you up to?"

"What the hell do you think I'm up to at this time of the morning?" Gonçalves said testily.

"Kindly drag your tail out of bed," Hector said. "I've got an assignment for you."

Hector told him about Bruna Nascimento

"A stewardess, huh?" Gonçalves said, sounding more awake.

"These days, they're called flight attendants."

"And is this *flight attendant* of the attractive sort?"

"Spoken like a true professional. She's a real looker."

"You wouldn't be misleading me, would you?" Gonçalves asked.

"Not at all. I saw her photograph. The woman is gorgeous."

"That being the case, why haven't you taken this plum assignment for yourself?"

"You have a suspicious nature."

"I do. It comes from being a cop. Answer the question."

"I am happily affianced."

"A fact of which I am aware. But I am also aware that you are not immune to the attractions of the fair sex. Could it be you fear Gilda's sharp scalpels?"

Gilda Caropreso, Hector's fiancée, was an assistant medical examiner.

"I do not fear Gilda," Hector said. "I love her. It's constancy that motivates me, not fear."

"Constancy? What's that?" the Federal Police's Lothario said.

An hour later, he was at Bruna's hotel. As he entered the air-conditioned comfort of the lobby, a team of paramedics was pushing a gurney toward the elevators. At the reception desk, a man with a badge was taking a statement. The cop tried to wave him off, but Gonçalves flashed his Federal Police ID.

"What's up?" he said.

"Simple homicide," the cop said, "nothing that would interest the Federal Police."

"Maybe not. Man or woman?"

"Woman."

"Flight attendant?"

The cop raised his eyebrows. "Yeah."

"Bruna Nascimento?"

"How the hell did you know that?"

"Just a bad feeling I had. And now it *does* interest the Federal Police."

***

ACCORDING TO the time stamp on her registration, Bruna Nascimento had checked in at six twenty-seven in the morning of the previous day. The reception clerk remembered her well; remembered, too, that she'd sent her luggage upstairs. Then she and her companion, another flight attendant, had headed off in the direction of the coffee shop.

The homicide cop let the clerk finish his story and then filled Gonçalves in on the other things he knew. The two women had taken a table near the door and ordered hot chocolate and croissants. They'd been joined by a man in uniform. The waiter, no expert on airline uniforms, was unable to say whether he was a flight attendant or a pilot. The airline guy left before the women did.

There'd been a DO NOT DISTURB sign on her door all day long. That wasn't unusual. Sometimes the people on flight crews liked to laze their time away in their rooms.

The next day, when the sign was still there, a chambermaid had knocked. There'd been no answer, so she'd let herself in. And left screaming.

That had been just over an hour ago. The captain and the copilot had already been located. The captain hadn't slept in the hotel at all. He had family in town. The copilot said he'd been in the coffee shop on the previous morning, but, since then, he'd had no further contact with the women.

The homicide cop went off in search of other people to interview. Gonçalves went upstairs.

The assistant medical examiner was already there.

"How's it going, Babyface?" the AME said. It was Plinio Setubal, a friend of Gilda Caropreso's. Gonçalves had met him once, at a party.

"Haraldo," Gonçalves said. "Haraldo, not Babyface."

Setubal looked puzzled. "I thought everybody called you Babyface."

"Only a few ballbusters," Gonçalves said, "and I don't like it."

Setubal shrugged and changed the subject. "You ever see anything like that?" He pointed at Bruna's body. The once-beautiful girl was a frightful mess.

"Was she, by any chance, also shot?" Gonçalves asked.

Setubal did a double take. "Once. In the lower abdomen. How did you know?"

"She's not the first," Gonçalves said. "You already take the body temp?"

Setubal shook his head.

"Can't. Not until Janus Prado gets here. He gets antsy if we start messing with the bodies before he's had a look. I can tell you a couple of things, though."

"What?"

"Rigor is diminishing, so she's probably been dead for at least twenty-four hours. And some of those wounds are post-mortem. The guy who did it just went on beating her and beating her."

"After she was dead?"

"You have another definition of postmortem?" Setubal said.

***

TWENTY MINUTES later, just when Gonçalves was concluding that there was nothing to be learned by hanging around any longer, Bruna's friend showed up. Her name was Lina Godoy.

They put her in a vacant room, and Gonçalves went to talk to her. He knew Janus Prado wouldn't like his questioning her alone, but Prado, São Paulo's head of homicide, was one of those people who'd been spreading the "Babyface" nickname around. Gonçalves delighted in irritating him.

Lina was sitting on one of the beds, staring at the wall and clutching a handkerchief. She looked up when he opened the door, started talking even before he'd introduced himself.

"I can't believe it," she said. "I can't believe she's dead."

Lina was pretty, a brunette, his type. But then, most women were Gonçalves's type.

"I'm sorry," he said, and told her he was a cop.

"Who did it?" she said. Her eyes were a grayish green.

"We don't know. Not yet."

"Was she . . . raped?"

"We don't know that either. I'll have to ask you some questions."

"Anything. Anything I can do to help."

He took a chair from in front of the desk, placed it against the wall, and sat down. There wasn't much room on that side of the bed. Their knees were only centimeters apart, which suited Gonçalves just fine. He took in a deep breath of her perfume. Something floral.

In a few short minutes, she took him through the events of her last morning with Bruna: the coffee shop, the copilot's clumsy advances, and her departure for the country. Then she asked a question of her own. "Have you told her parents?"

"I don't handle that end of it, but I'm sure someone is trying to get in touch."

"I don't know what to do," she said. "I don't want to be the one to tell them, so I'm scared to call. But if they already know, and they know that I know, and I don't call. . . ."

"Best to give it a while," Hector said. "When we're done here, I'll give you the name of someone to talk to, someone from the civil police. They're in charge of notifying relatives."

"I thought you said *you* were from the police."

"I am," he said. "But I'm federal. We do . . . other things. Did Bruna have a romantic interest? A boyfriend?"

"Yes. A new one. He lives on St. Barts."

"The island?"

"Yes."

"He's there now?"

"As far as I know."

"Name?"

"Henri, with an i."

"Henri what?"

Lina shrugged. "She always just called him Henri. His number must be in her address book. The book is red. It's about this big." Lina held up a thumb and forefinger. "It'll be in her purse if. . . ."

"If what?"

"If her killer didn't take it. My God, I don't believe all of this. It's like some bad dream."

"I wish it was, Senhorita. What can you tell me about your copilot?"

"Horácio?"

"Him."

"He's a creep."

"But harmless?"

"How can you ever be sure about anyone?"

"True. Look, the guys from the homicide squad are going to be here any minute, and they're going to ask you all the same questions. Just be patient with them and run through it again, okay?"

She wiped her eyes and nodded. "Okay," she said.

"Something else," he said. "I was trying to get in touch with Bruna to ask her a few questions about another case we're looking into. Maybe you can help."

"If I can. Sure."

"Bruna was on the 8101 on the twenty-second of November."

"That's our usual run."

"Were you aboard as well?"

She reached for her purse and took out a diary with a black plastic cover. "The twenty-second of November, you said?"

He nodded.

She turned pages, found the date, looked up. "Yes," she said.

"On that flight," he said, "she was, initially, one of two flight attendants assigned to business class. There were only eleven passengers in there, but the economy class cabin was full. The chief steward changed the assignment—"

"I remember," she said. "That was me. I got pulled out of business and put into economy."

"Can you recall if Bruna told you anything about that night? Told you anything unusual that might have happened to her?"

Lina frowned, remembering. "She mentioned a couple of things," she said. "First of all, there were some unwelcome advances."

"Unwelcome advances?"

"That's the training manual talking. It means someone coming on to you. She had *two* of those. One was from this creep who came up behind her when she was making coffee. He put his hands around her waist. She had to brush them off."

"You don't, by any chance, remember the man's name?"

She shook her head. "He told Bruna he sold lubricants, and that he traveled back and forth from São Paulo to Miami all the time. Maybe so, but. . . ."

"She didn't recall having seen him before?"

"Neither of us did."

"So you saw him?"

"Bruna pointed him out, told me to watch out for him, but . . . well, it was a while ago."

"Would you recognize him? In a photo?"

She frowned. "I'm not sure. I could try."

"A couple, you said, a couple of unwelcome advances. Tell me about the other one."

"Bruna was dozing. Someone touched her hair and she woke up with this character breathing bad breath into her face. He was only a few centimeters away. Can you imagine?"

"Must have given her a start," Gonçalves said.

"It did. He claimed he wanted to know where the ice was, but you don't have to get right into somebody's face to ask a question like that."

"No, you certainly don't. Did she point him out as well?"

"She did. And that one I'm sure I'd remember. He had a brown mark right here."

She touched her cheek.

"Brown mark? Like a liver spot?"

"Yes, like a liver spot. This whole business is right out of a crime novel. What did you say your name was?"

"I didn't. It's Haraldo. Haraldo Gonçalves."

"Call me Lina." She extended a hand and Gonçalves took it. Her palm was moist, no surprise after the shock she'd been through.

"Lina," he said, "you suggested that something else happened as well, aside from the . . . what did you call them?"

"Unwelcome advances."

"Unwelcome advances. What was it? What else happened?"

"In the middle of the night, Bruna heard somebody moving around in the cabin. She was on her guard by then. She stuck her head around the corner of the galley, and there he was, the one with the mark on his cheek, messing around in one of the overhead compartments. When he spotted her looking at him, his eyes got all round, and his mouth dropped open. It was like she'd caught him with his hand in the cookie jar, she said."

"Did she speak to him?"

"She did. Asked him, sarcastic like, if he needed any help."

"And he?"

"And he told her no. But she could see he wasn't happy. Looked furtive, was the way she put it."

"Furtive?"

"That's the word she used. Furtive. Bruna was always using words like that. She had two years of university, you know."

"No, I didn't. Did she report the incident?"

"Right away. She went to first class and talked to Leandro, the chief steward."

"And?"

"And he asked her if the guy took anything, and she said not as far as she knew."

"So the chief steward didn't take any action?"

"Leandro has fluent Japanese. He mostly works that Tokyo run."

"So?"

"I guess what I'm trying to say is that Bruna wasn't an alarmist. She was a good judge of character. But Leandro never had a chance to learn that about her. They only worked together a few times. Oh Jesus!"

"Oh Jesus what?"

"Oh Jesus, what am I going to say when I talk to Bruna's mother?"

Chapter Sixteen

"ALINE ARRIAGA?" HECTOR ASKED.

The woman who'd opened the door nodded. She had eyes as blue as aquamarines, was moderately tall, had medium-length black hair, and her figure wouldn't attract a second glance. But her eyes were beautiful. They were also bloodshot and underlined with dark circles. The woman had been doing a good deal of crying and getting very little sleep.

"What is it now," she said glumly.

"Now? I'm sorry, Senhora. I don't—"

"The guard downstairs said you were from the police."

"I am," Hector said. "The Federal Police. I'd like to talk to you and Julio."

"Julio?"

"Your son."

"Junior," she said. "Not Julio. Julio is my husband. My son is Julio Junior. And if you want to talk to him, it means you're not here for the reason I thought you were. It means you don't know."

"Know what, Senhora?"

"You'd best come in," she said and stepped aside. After he'd entered, she closed the door behind him and leaned against it as if she needed the support.

"Junior's dead," she said.

"Dead?"

She narrowed her eyes. "They said he fell, but I don't believe it. Not for one minute."

"My sympathy for your loss, Senhora. When? When was this?"

"Almost three months ago," she said. "He was on his way back from the United States. My husband, Julio, lives there. Junior was visiting him. They arrested Junior at the airport."

"Arrested him? For what?"

"Drug smuggling, they said. And I don't believe that either. They dragged him off to a delegacia and put him into a shower with a bunch of perverts. Junior was only fifteen years old. What could they have been thinking? Tell me that! What could they have been thinking?"

"Senhora, I'm sorry to hear all this. Truly sorry."

"Spare me your pity. I don't want pity."

She pointed toward the small couch. Her outstretched finger was trembling. Hector, wishing to avoid an outburst of hysteria, sat. She took a seat facing him and then a deep breath.

"Now," she said, "tell me."

"The flight Julio—"

She cut him off. "Junior. It's Junior. You say Julio, you're talking about his father."

"Junior, then. The flight he was on, 8101, the one that arrived on the morning of the twenty-third of November—"

"Yes?"

"There were some . . . incidents, things that happened to some of the other passengers."

"What kind of incidents?"

"Senhora, I—"

"Tell me. What kind of incidents?"

"Murders. One of the victims was the son of the foreign minister of Venezuela. We've been asked to investigate."

"The death of the son of the foreign minister of Venezuela rates an all-out investigation by the Federal Police, but the death of my son doesn't matter to anyone but me. Is that what you're telling me?"

"No, Senhora," Hector said. "That's not what I'm telling you."

"Well, it sure sounds like it. It sounds exactly like what you're telling me."

"Senhora, believe me—"

She held up a hand to silence him, stood up, walked to a table near the door. "I want you to hear something," she said.

She started pushing buttons on an answering machine. Her movements were very rapid. Whatever she was doing, she'd done it many times before. There was a final click, and she turned up the volume on a young and frightened voice.

"Mom? Where are you? Mom? For God's sake, Mom, pick up the phone." Some indistinguishable words were growled in the background. "Mom, they say I have to be quick. It's like this: they opened my backpack when I was coming through Customs. There were pills in there, drugs, they said. And now they say I need a lawyer, but I didn't *do* anything. I swear. Those pills weren't mine. They weren't—"

The boy's plea came to an abrupt end followed by a beep.

Aline pushed another button and scoffed, "Drugs! My Junior with drugs!"

"You don't believe it?"

"I never believed it! Not for a moment. I still don't."

"What kind of drugs?" he asked quietly.

"Ecstasy."

A drug teenagers favored. Hector had seen kids as young as twelve using the stuff. Junior might well have been carrying it; in fact, Hector couldn't think of any other reason why the boy might have been arrested. But he wasn't about to say that to his overwrought mother.

Aline Arriaga walked to the windowsill, picked up a picture frame, and handed it to him.

"Junior," she said.

Julio Arriaga—Junior—a good-looking kid with his mother's black hair and a lopsided smile, wore a gray shirt with blue piping. A baseball bat, gripped in one hand, was resting on his shoulder.

"His last photo," she said, "taken in Florida. Julio sent it."

"His father lives there?"

"I already told you that."

"Yes, I'm sorry. You did."

"And I live here, but not for long. I want to get out of this country, wanted to get out even before what happened to Junior . . . happened. Julio's saving money. He's going to send for me."

"I'd like to speak to him," Hector said.

"Julio? Why? Why do you want to talk to Julio?"

"He took your son to the airport, didn't he?"

"Yes."

"Then he might have spoken to one of the other passengers, seen something that would be significant for our investigation."

"Julio moved recently. I don't have his new phone number."

"An address perhaps?"

"I don't have an address either. I'll have to get back to you."

She wasn't meeting his eyes. And there was something else, too. Something he couldn't put his finger on. He suddenly had the feeling she wanted to get rid of him. He looked back at the photo in his hands, made a point of admiring it. "A handsome young man," he said.

The tactic was successful.

"Sit right there," she said. "I have lots more."

She went into another room and, seconds later, came back with a thick album.

She put the heavy book on his lap and took a seat next to him. "This one," she said, "was taken on the same day as that one." She pointed to the picture in the frame.

Junior was looking over his shoulder. There was a baseball cap on his head, a number on the back of his shirt. She started leafing through the pages, going slowly, so he could admire the pictures. "Up there, in the United States, they called him Jule. Julio wasn't 'cool' enough; neither was Junior." She paused at a photo that took up a full page. "That's his father," she said, tapping the image with her forefinger.

Julio wore combat fatigues and looked every inch the soldier: lean, hard, not the sort you'd like to tangle with.

"That was taken about four years ago," she said, "in Manaus. Before Manaus, we were in Belo Horizonte, and before that it was Porto Alegre. We spent two winters there. Do you have any idea how *cold* it gets in Porto Alegre in the winter? That was some change, I'm telling you, Porto Alegre to Manaus."

Hector leaned in for a closer look. Julio was turned slightly away from the camera, and his shoulder patch was clearly visible: CIGS.

CIGS is the acronym for the *Centro de Instrução de Guerra na Selva,* the Brazilian army's elite training corps for jungle fighting. They were the best of the best, a unit exclusively composed of career men.

Hector felt his pulse quicken. "Why did Julio leave the army?"

Again, she avoided his eyes. "It was a problem with one of his officers."

"What kind of a problem?"

"I couldn't say."

Can't, or won't, Hector thought.

"When he was here for Junior's funeral, did—"

"Julio didn't come to Junior's funeral," she interrupted quickly.

"No?"

"No. He . . . doesn't have a work visa for the States. He's there illegally."

"What's that got to do with—"

"If he leaves, they won't let him back in. Then I'd never get out of here either. And what would have been the point? To see Junior's body in a box? To see the box being put in the ground? Junior wasn't here any more. Junior was gone."

But his grieving mother wasn't. And a husband who loved her wouldn't let her go through the funeral alone. Or would he?

A tear dropped from her cheek. She took a paper handkerchief from a box on the coffee table, dried the photo, and blew her nose. "Sorry," she said.

More to calm her than for any other reason, Hector said, "Tell me about that day. Did you go to the airport to meet your son?"

"I *always* went to the airport to meet him. Sometimes I had to take a day off to do it, but I always went. First, I'd call to make sure the flight was on time. We have two flights a day, both in the morning. He was on the early one. It arrived just a little after six."

"So you called to check the flight's arrival time. . . ."

"And I took the shuttle to the airport. When I'm on my own, I use the company shuttle. It doesn't cost anything, and it's convenient. One of them leaves every hour, day and night. I stood waiting for him to clear Customs, waited for two and a half hours after the flight landed. By that time I was frantic. I went to the TAB counter and spoke to a woman I know. She has a pass."

"A pass?"

"You need a pass to get into the Customs area. She came back and told me they'd taken him away."

"What did you do then?"

"I called my answering machine to see if he'd left a message. He had. You heard it."

"He didn't say where he was calling from, did he?"

"No," she said. "He didn't."

"And next?"

"I opened the yellow pages, looked for criminal lawyers."

"And picked the lawyer with the biggest ad?"

"Yes."

"Dudu Fonseca?"

She raised her head and looked at him. "You know him?"

Hector nodded. Not every cop in São Paulo knew Dudu Fonseca, but those who did hated his guts.

"I got him on the second try. It was just after nine. He asked for ten thousand. A 'nonrefundable retainer,' he called it."

"You paid him *ten thousand?*"

She hung her head. "I was desperate. Over the telephone he told me he'd only take cash. I went to the bank and got it. Then I went to his office. The first thing he asked me was if I'd brought the money. I said I had. He told me to give it to him, and I did. Then he made one telephone call. *One telephone call.* He put it on his speakerphone so I could hear the whole thing. Whoever he called, and I have no idea who it was, told him my son had been in a shower at the Fifteenth Delegacia, the one out near Guarulhos. He'd fallen. That was the story. He'd fallen when he was in the shower, and he'd hit his head, and it had killed him. Fonseca just sat there, saying uh-huh, uh-huh. They're telling him my son is dead and he's saying uh-huh, uh-huh."

"And then?"

"I don't even know how the call ended. I'd broken down by that time; I was crying my eyes out. That didn't affect him either. He sat there looking at me like an ugly toad. It must happen to him all the time, people getting hysterical in his office."

"I expect it does," Hector said. "How about your money?"

"He kept it. All of it. It was nonrefundable, like he said. I really didn't care. For years, Julio and I have been saving for Junior's education, and Junior wasn't going to need it any more. I left Fonseca's office in . . . oh, I don't know . . . a kind of trance, and I took a cab to the Fifteenth Delegacia to see my baby. They'd stretched him out on the floor in a storage room, *a storage room*, and covered him with a sheet of black plastic. They'd closed his eyes, stuffed cotton wads into his nose and ears. He looked fine from the front, like he was sleeping. But there was a horrible wound here." She put her hand to the back of her head. "I couldn't see how anyone could get a wound like that from a fall. I told them that. They said he must have hit it on one of the fixtures."

"They hadn't bandaged the wound?"

"No, there was no bandage, nothing. And his body was already cold. Finally, an ambulance showed up. The paramedics were the only ones who showed me any kind of sympathy at all. One was a man. He said he was sorry it had taken them so long, but they had to give priority to the people they could help. The woman looked at me, looked at Junior, and started to cry. She hugged me before she left."

"And then?"

"They brought him to the *Instituto Médico Legal*. It took them three days to release his body. God knows why. The story didn't change. They're still saying he fell. Lots of his friends came to the funeral, almost his whole class from school. He had sixty-three people in all."

"And no one, at any time, suggested that what happened might have been anything other than an accident?"

Aline gave him a bitter look. "No one, at any time," she said. "The cops in that delegacia must have thought I was really stupid, that I'd never read about the sort of things that happen in jails, that I never picked up a newspaper. Afterward, after the funeral, I went back to the place where they'd been holding him. The delegado didn't want to see me."

"Why not?"

She shrugged. "Sergio Bittencourt, that's the little bastard's name. He tried to sneak out the back door."

"He *what?*"

"I'd been crying. There was a sergeant, an older man, not like a policeman at all. He kept giving me paper handkerchiefs, offering me coffee. Then another policeman came in and whispered something in the sergeant's ear. As soon as he left, the sergeant said the delegado had gone out the back door and was on the way to his car. The car was a gray sedan. Bittencourt was wearing a brown suit. If I was quick, I could catch him in the parking lot, but I wasn't to tell the delegado he'd told me that. I took off like a shot."

"And you caught up with Bittencourt?"

She nodded. "I got between him and his car. When he spotted me, he looked like he'd just taken a mouthful of sour milk, then he turned solicitous."

"And what, exactly, did he tell you?"

"He said there were two dozen men taking their showers along with Junior, but no one saw him fall. Can you believe that? Two dozen men in the same shower, and no one saw him fall?"

"No," Hector said. "I can't."

"Bittencourt said he was looking into it, he said he was questioning everyone. He promised he'd get back to me."

"And did he? Did he get back to you?"

She paused for a moment. "No," she finally said.

And that's something else she isn't telling me, Hector thought.

"I think I've troubled you enough," he said.

"Wait," she said. "You'll be looking closely into everything that happened on that flight, correct?"

"Correct, Senhora."

"If, in the course of your investigation, you happen to discover who planted those drugs on my boy, will you tell me?"

"Senhora, I—"

"It's not that I don't believe every word Junior said. It's not that, but . . . well, there's always a bit of doubt, isn't there? It would set my mind at rest to know that he didn't lie to me."

She was staring into his eyes. There was something manic about her look. "Will you?" she said. "Will you do it?"

Hector nodded. *What harm could it do?*

She continued to search his eyes. "I have your word?"

"You have my word," he said.

"Good," she said and got up to lead him to the door.

***

THERE WAS a *padaria* just across the street from Aline's apartment building. Hector went in, sat down at the zinc-covered counter, and ordered a cachaça neat. It was eleven o'clock in the morning. If the girl behind the counter thought it was early to be drinking straight cane spirit, she didn't show it.

Hector had surreptitiously switched off his mobile phone

while Aline was showing him the pictures. Now he turned it on. He intended to call his uncle, but the phone rang before he could hit the speed dial.

Haraldo Gonçalves's name was on the caller ID.

The conversation that ensued prompted Hector to order another cachaça. He was still sipping it when the phone rang once again.

"Why couldn't I reach you?" Silva asked.

"I switched my phone off."

"Why?"

Hector told him about his disturbing conversation with the bereaved mother.

Silva was silent for a moment. He knew what it meant to lose a child. Then he said, "Completely different MO."

"And it happened in a jail," Hector said. "No way it could be connected."

"Maybe not. But the boy was in that cabin with the others, and that's too much of a coincidence to ignore. Did you hear about the flight attendant, Bruna Nascimento?"

"Just now. Babyface called."

"Call him back. Tell him to turn around, go to international arrivals and try to talk to the customs agents who nailed the kid."

"How about Bittencourt? That delegado?"

"Take him yourself. He's liable to pull rank with Gonçalves. And don't call him first. Surprise him."

Hector looked at his watch. "Not even noon. I should catch him easy."

"Who did the autopsy on the Arriaga boy?"

"I don't know. I'll find out."

"From Gilda?"

"From Gilda. I'll call her straightaway. That it?"

"No. One more thing: call Mara and ask her to see what she can find out about the kid's father."

"You think—"

"I don't think anything. I'd just like to know."

The guy behind the counter picked up Hector's glass and gave him a questioning look. Hector shook his head and pointed at the coffee pot.

Chapter Seventeen

Luis Mansur's first phone call from the Federal Police initially provoked curiosity, then irritation.

A woman who identified herself as Senhorita Mara Carta asked if he was the Luis Mansur who'd flown from Miami to São Paulo on the twenty-second of November.

"Yes," he'd said. "What's this all about?"

"That was on TAB flight 8101, is that correct?"

"Yes. Why do you want to know?"

"Are you acquainted with a man called Juan Rivas, or a man called Jonas Palhares, or a man called Victor Neves?"

"No. And why the fuck are you asking?"

She sniffed. "I've given you no cause to be offensive, Senhor Mansur. I'm just doing my job. Did you make the acquaintance of any of the other passengers on that flight?"

"What is this? The Spanish Inquisition?"

"No, Senhor, it's the Federal Police, and I advise you to answer the question."

"I *never* speak to people on airplanes."

That was not, strictly speaking, true. The two times Mansur had been seated next to an attractive woman, he'd tried very hard to strike up a conversation.

"If you didn't speak to anyone," the voice on the line went on, "what *did* you do on that flight?"

This was really too much. Mansur was tempted to hang up on her, but it *was* the Federal Police.

"What does anybody do on a flight? I had a drink. I ate my dinner. I watched a movie. Then I put on a sleeping mask, stuck in some earplugs, and slept all the way to São Paulo. Now, I want to know—"

She didn't let him finish. "That's all for the moment. Someone will be contacting you soon."

She hung up, without so much as a thank you.

Bitch!

Mansur had interpreted "soon" as sometime within the coming days. But the second call came less than an hour later, and at a most inconvenient time. He was in the process of firing Jamile Bastos and had made it clear to Rosa, his secretary, that he was not to be disturbed. But he hadn't locked the door to his office and that, in retrospect, proved to be a mistake.

Jamile possessed an ample bosom and very long legs. Mansur had made a play for her, and she'd brushed him off. He wasn't about to let her get away with this simply because she showed up on time and was good at her job. She was a single mother with two children to feed. She had *obligations*. She should have known better.

He'd been expecting tears, got them, and was handing Jamile a third paper handkerchief when Rosa barged in without waiting for a response to her knock. Luis raised his chin and glared at her, expecting her to back out again. But she didn't. Instead, she took a deep breath, closed the door behind her, and came over to whisper in his ear.

"I'm terribly sorry to interrupt, Senhor Mansur, but I have a chief inspector from the Federal Police on the line. I told him you weren't to be disturbed, but he insisted. He says it's vital he speak to you."

Mansur was about to tell his secretary that the federal cop could wait until he was damned good and ready to call him back. But at that moment, Jamile rose to her feet, called him a *canalha*, and stormed out, the tears still running down her cheeks. He'd been only seconds away from explaining, in detail, exactly what she had to do to keep her job, and he had a full erection. The cop's timing couldn't have been worse.

"What's this cop's name?" he snarled.

"Silva. Chief Inspector Silva."

"Put him on," Mansur said.

*   *   *

THE FIRST thing the São Paulo businessman said was, "What's so goddamned important?"

Silva took the telephone away from his ear and looked at it, as if it was the instrument itself, and not the man, who had offended him.

"Am I speaking to Luis Mansur?"

"You are."

"Senhor Mansur, I'm—"

"Chief Inspector Silva of the Federal Police. So my secretary told me. I repeat, what's so goddamned important?"

Silva suppressed a brusque retort. "There is a chance, Senhor Mansur, that your life is in danger."

"What?" Mansur said. "What the fuck are you talking about?"

"You traveled business class aboard TAB flight 8101 from Miami to São Paulo on the twenty-second of November, correct?"

"I already answered that question the last time you people called. What's this 'life in danger' crap?"

"Someone has murdered five of the people who traveled with you."

"Five people on the same plane?"

"Five people who were in the business-class cabin."

Silva elected not to mention young Julio Arriaga. Five killings were, he thought, quite enough to make an impact; gauging by Mansur's response, he was right.

"You're shitting me," Mansur said.

"I can assure you, Senhor Mansur, that I am not, as you put it, shitting you."

"*Caralho*. What happened to them?"

"They were shot and subsequently beaten to death."

There was silence on the other end of the line.

"Senhor Mansur?"

"I'm here. Who's doing this and why?"

"We have, as yet, no idea. The murders took place in four different cities."

"Then how can you be sure they're connected?"

"The method of killing was the same, a single shot to the abdomen followed by beating with a blunt object. And the bullets were all fired from the same gun."

"Who was killed?"

"The flight attendant, Bruna Nascimento."

"I remember her all right. Arrogant bitch. Lousy service. Who else?"

"Juan Rivas—"

"Sounds like a fucking Argentinean."

"A Venezuelan, actually."

"Almost as bad. Who else?"

"Victor Neves."

"Never heard of him."

"Jonas Palhares."

"Him either."

"And Paulo Cruz."

"The professor? The writer? That Cruz?"

"That Cruz."

"His funeral was in the paper. I didn't know he was on the same plane."

"He was. What were you doing in Miami, Senhor Mansur?"

"Huh?"

"I asked you what you were doing in Miami."

"Business."

"What kind of business?"

"I deal in petroleum-based industrial lubricants. Let's cut right to the chase. You're *telling* me I could be a victim, but you're *thinking* I could be a murderer, right?"

"You're a perceptive man, Senhor Mansur."

"You're goddamned right I am. Well, Senhor Chief Inspector Silva, let me tell you this: I didn't kill anybody."

"Then you could be in danger yourself."

"Who else was in that cabin? Remind me."

"Would names have any significance for you?"

"Probably not."

"Then it would suffice to say there was a fifteen-year-old boy, the son of an airline employee—"

"I remember him. I wondered why he was traveling alone in business class. They must have upgraded him because of his father. I guess we can rule him out. Who else?"

"An American."

"Aha."

"Aha?"

"You can't trust Americans."

"You're entitled to your opinion, Senhor Mansur."

"What does this American do for a living?"

"He appears to be a priest."

"What do you mean, 'appears to be'?"

"We're awaiting confirmation on that."

"Priests don't murder people."

"I have to differ with you. Occasionally they do. I've known one who did."

"Who are the other—dare I say—*survivors*?"

"Three Brazilians. We haven't located any of them either."

"So let me add this up. You got the American priest, the

woman, a teenager, four dead guys, a dead stewardess, three other people, and me. That's twelve altogether."

Whatever else Mansur might have been, he wasn't stupid. And he had a good memory.

"Correct," Silva said.

"Well, I sure as hell didn't kill anybody. The old lady probably didn't, and the teenager ditto. That brings you down to four suspects."

"One of the four is a child."

"Oh, yeah. I remember him too. Traveling with his father. Waste of money, taking a kid into business class. His old man should have popped him back in coach and let the stewardesses take care of him."

Silva was beginning to develop a healthy dislike for Luis Mansur.

"So, let's see who we have left," Mansur said. "There's only the priest and those two other guys, right? Maybe you'd better give me their names after all."

"The father of the boy is Marnix Kloppers."

"What the fuck kind of a name is that?"

"It's of Dutch origin, I believe."

"And the priest?"

"Dennis Clancy."

"And the last guy?"

"Darcy Motta."

"Oh, yeah, Motta." Luis Mansur chuckled.

Silva picked up on the reaction. "You know him?"

"Know him? Hell, no."

"You didn't sit down next to him?"

Mansur bristled. "He tell you that? Tell you I sat down next to him? If he did, he's lying."

"He hasn't told us anything. We're still looking for him."

"You found *me*. How come you haven't found *him*?"

"His ticket was purchased with cash. We've been unable to uncover any credit cards. He has no driver's license, no telephone, no cell phone, no criminal record. It's possible that Darcy Motta is an alias, that his real name is something else."

"Hmmm," Mansur said. He sounded pensive.

"Is there something you want to tell me?" Silva asked.

"No."

"Does the name Girotti mean anything to you? João Girotti?"

"Not a thing. Why?"

"He, too, was murdered. The method of killing, and the bullet used, matched the others."

"But he wasn't on the plane?"

"No, he wasn't. Listen, Senhor Mansur, I'd like to speak to you personally. Could we meet on Tuesday morning? About ten?"

Mansur did a noisy flip through of his desk calendar.

"Make it nine," he said. "I've got a busy day, but I'll shuffle my schedule around."

"Nine, then. In the meantime, be careful."

"Let me tell you something, Senhor Chief Inspector Silva. I've got a Taurus .38 and, before you ask, yes, I *do* have a permit to carry it. I was robbed one time on the street; a little punk threatened me with a knife. I gave him my wallet, and my watch, and the little fucker cut me anyway. It took six stitches to close the wound, and if I'd raised that arm up a fraction of a second later, I would have gotten it right in the face. I'm not about to let anything like that happen again. Anybody, man, woman, or child, who threatens me is gonna eat a bullet."

Chapter Eighteen

THE CUSTOMS AGENTS WHO'D nabbed Junior Arriaga were Fausto Mainardi and Douglas Caetano. Mainardi, who seemed friendly enough, was a veteran in a baggy suit. Caetano, new to the service, was surlier but a better dresser. They brought Gonçalves to the windowless room where they'd interrogated the teenager.

A television camera was mounted high in one corner, a monitor in another. A microphone protruded from the ceiling. The only source of illumination, a fluorescent tube, was protected by a metal grate.

Gonçalves, preparing to take notes, tried to move his chair closer to the table. It wouldn't budge. He looked down and saw it was bolted to the cement floor.

"Why are we interested in this kid?" Mainardi said.

The *we* was a reminder. The Customs Service was a division of the Federal Police. Mainardi and Caetano fell into the category of colleagues. They expected Gonçalves to tell them the whole story.

Which he did, starting with the murder of Juan Rivas and emphasizing the director's personal interest in the case. When he told them about young Arriaga's murder, neither man seemed shocked—or even interested.

"Sounds unrelated," Mainardi said.

"Probably no connection at all," Gonçalves agreed, "but my orders are to follow up on it. Tell me what you remember."

"Start with the old system," Caetano said to his partner.

Mainardi nodded and leaned back in his chair. "Time was," he said, "we asked people with taxable goods to fill in a form. Those that didn't, they'd go straight to nothing-to-declare. There was this button they had to push, and a sign right next to it, all in lawyer's language: *By pushing this button I affirm* yadda, yadda, yadda and so forth and so on. If an arrow in front of the pusher went green, it would be pointing left and they were home free. But if the arrow went red and pointed to the right, and a loud fucking buzzer went off, they'd have to go to the tables and start opening their bags. Way I heard it, some cousin of some higher-up sold us this system and cut a nice deal for doing it. Way I heard it, it was the most expensive buzzer-and-light system in the history of the world."

"Not to be impolite," Gonçalves said, "but what's this story got to do with—"

"Hold your horses. I'm getting there."

"You gotta hear the whole thing," Caetano said. "Otherwise you're not gonna get it."

Mainardi waited until Gonçalves nodded. Then he continued. "A lot of us were pissed off about the changes. We figured we were better than any random system. We lobbied for an override, a little transmitter we could keep in our pockets and use to buzz anybody who looked suspicious. In the end, the higher-ups agreed."

"Uh-huh," Gonçalves said. He started to drum his fingertips on the table.

"Almost there," Mainardi said. "So we used the hybrid system, random and override, for a couple of years, until the guy who had it installed retired to his villa on the French Riviera, or some such place, and the new regime took over. That's when we switched."

"To what?"

"Now *everybody* has to fill in the form, whether you have goods to declare or not. We stand there and collect them. Anybody looks suspicious, we shake 'em down. Back to square one, you know what I mean? But it wasn't square one, because working with the other system taught us something."

"Which was?" Gonçalves said, still drumming.

"Which was that no matter how good we think we are, we're still gonna make mistakes. The random system picked up people we would never have expected. And we chose to stop people who, no matter how shifty they looked, weren't trying to get away with a thing."

"And that's what happened on this flight, the one the kid was traveling on?"

Mainardi pointed a finger at Gonçalves as if it was a gun. "You got it," he said. "There we were, young Douglas and me, working the flight in question and collecting the forms. First thing that happens is, I pull a guy name of . . ."—he consulted the file he'd brought with him—"Darcy Motta."

"Why did you pick on him?" Gonçalves asked, his interest quickening.

"Same reason I pick on anybody. He looked shifty. But no, I'm wrong. The guy's carrying hand luggage and a small suitcase, that's it. Inside the suitcase there's a pair of pants, a couple of dirty shirts, ditto underwear. In the hand luggage, there's a carton of cigarettes, a pack of chewing gum, some condoms, and a couple of girlie magazines. Meanwhile, young Douglas here decides to shake down Arriaga, an innocent-looking fresh-faced kid, somebody you wouldn't suspect in a million years."

"But if you wouldn't suspect him, why—"

"Let me finish. Turns out the kid is carrying three plastic containers. They're pretty big, about the size of a jar of mayonnaise. On the outside, it says they're multiple vitamins.

Under the caps are foil seals. At least there are on two of them. The seal on the third one is broken. And what's inside that one really *are* vitamin pills."

"Kid's eyes got real big," Caetano said, "and he started to stammer. Claimed he'd never seen those containers before in his life. I picked up one of the sealed ones and rattled it. It sounded like it was full of pills, just like it's supposed to be. But then I ask myself what kind of pills. I break the seal, and guess what?"

"Not vitamins."

"Ecstasy. Branded, no less. Little dollar signs on every pill."

"Again, why did you pick on the kid?"

"You're gonna laugh."

"I doubt it."

"No, really, you're gonna laugh. It wasn't because I suspected him at all. I just wanted to bust his chops."

"Why did you want to bust his chops?"

"Because he was an arrogant little punk who pissed me off, that's why," Caetano said.

"Let me get this straight. You chose to make trouble for him because he rubbed you the wrong way?"

"What good is power if you don't abuse it, right?"

"What did he do to annoy you?"

"It was the way the little bastard looked at me, like I was beneath him."

Julio Arriaga, a fifteen-year-old kid, was dead because of a few Ecstasy pills and because this prick hadn't liked the way he'd *looked* at him.

Gonçalves tightened his jaw, but Caetano didn't seem to notice and went blithely on. "'What's this?' I said, when I pulled the first container out of the kid's bag. 'I got no idea,' the kid says. 'It's not mine.'"

"Not mine," Mainardi said, joining in. "You have any idea how often we hear that?"

"A lot, I suppose," Gonçalves said.

"You bet your ass," Mainardi continued, "a whole lot. We took him here, cuffed him to the table, let him stew while we ran the tests. We needed the results to make the case."

"We came back here," Caetano chimed in, "told him he was good and busted, and guess what? He's not so arrogant any more. You want to see the tape?"

"In a minute. What did you do next?"

"Did what we're supposed to do." It was Mainardi again. "We called the civil police. They took him away."

"To the nearest delegacia? The one where Bittencourt is in charge?"

"The nearest. The Fifteenth. I don't know what the chief honcho's name is."

"Tell me more about this Darcy Motta."

"What's to tell?"

"Physical description?"

"Forty, maybe forty-five," Caetano said after a moment's thought. "Maybe a meter ninety, maybe ninety kilos. Got a brown spot right here." He touched his right cheek. "Like one of those things old people get." His eyes shifted to his partner's hands. There were liver spots on the backs of both.

Mainardi took them off of the table and folded them in his lap.

"Anything else you remember?"

Mainardi shook his head.

Gonçalves turned back to Caetano. "And you?"

"No," Caetano said. "That's it. The little fucker practically pissed himself. The tape's a gas." He pointed at the television monitor. "Want to see it now?"

Chapter Nineteen

"Major Funchal isn't available at the moment. Who's speaking?"

It was a woman's voice, and she wasn't happy.

Jealous wife, Mara thought. "Agent Mara Carta of the Federal Police," she said.

The woman's tone softened. "Sorry. He's sleeping."

"Sleeping?" Mara glanced at the clock on the wall of her office. It was two thirty in São Paulo, one thirty in Manaus.

"I know what you're thinking," the woman said. "He walked in here this morning stinking like a pig and looking like death warmed over. I doubt if he's slept more than two hours in the last forty-eight. People who call here generally know how it goes when he's on a mission. They don't want to wake him up. You probably did just that."

"Sorry," Mara said. *A protective spouse, not a jealous one.* "Who am I speaking to, please?"

"Beth."

"His wife?"

"The only one, as far as I know. What did you say your name was?"

"Mara."

"It's like this, Mara. He always comes back from one of these things flat-out exhausted. The officers feel they have to set an example, so they push themselves harder. He's only thirty-six, but this jungle survival stuff is a young man's game. I'm trying to talk him into getting out of it, but he loves it.

And I love him. So what am I going to do, huh? What do you want to talk to him about?"

"I need some information about a man who served under him, a certain Julio Arriaga. It would have been three or four years ago, maybe a little more."

"The name doesn't ring any bells. But I'll have him call you back. You're here in Manaus?"

"No. São Paulo."

Mara recited her telephone number. Beth read it back. "If he runs true to form," she said, "he'll get up in a few hours, eat something, and then crash for the night. If that happens, I'll have him get back to you. Otherwise, he'll call tomorrow morning."

But Mara didn't have to wait that long. Major Funchal called back less than half an hour later.

"Julio Arriaga?" he said, his voice hoarse. "Yeah, I remember him. He was a good soldier, but that temper of his. . . . What's he done now?"

"His son was murdered. We're investigating."

"Junior? Somebody murdered Junior?"

"I'm afraid so."

"Jesus. Arriaga loved that kid with a passion. I sure as hell wouldn't want to be in the murderer's shoes."

"What's that supposed to mean?"

"What I said. Julio is a dangerous guy to cross. You know what his specialty was?"

"No. What?"

"Stealth killing."

"You think he'd be capable of practicing that specialty of his on someone who killed his son?"

"He'd sure as hell know *how* to do it if he wanted to."

"How come he left the service? His file lists him as resigned. But it doesn't say *why*."

"No. It doesn't," Funchal said. And stopped there.

"Are you going to tell me?"

"Is it important?"

"Very important. Lives might depend on it."

"All right, then. The fact is, he struck a superior, a lieu-tenant. He should have gotten a prison term and a dishonor-able discharge, but. . . ."

"What?"

"Well, frankly, we cut Arriaga some slack. The lieutenant was a prick, an incompetent, and, worst of all, he was wrong. Arriaga was good at what he did, and right. But we can't have enlisted men going around beating up officers. Julio had to go. He took it hard. As to the lieutenant, the poor bastard had no idea how lucky he was. If Julio had wanted to go all the way, he certainly could have, and some of us thought he should have. I'm not going to tell you any more than that."

"You people work with silenced weapons?"

"We don't just sleep rough and eat snails."

"Which handguns do you use?"

"Just one. The M975."

"Which is?"

"The military version of the Taurus PT92."

"Then it's a single/double action 9x19 Parabellum, a copy of the Beretta 92?"

"Nice to talk to a woman who knows her handguns. Our M975s are so quiet, somebody fires one in the next room, you hardly hear it."

"And I suppose Arriaga had lots of experience with that particular pistol?"

"Lots. And he was an expert marksman. There was this trick he used to do with an ax head and balloons. He'd shoot at the sharp edge of the ax. The ax would divide the bullet in two. He'd burst a balloon on either side of the ax with a single shot."

"Impressive."

"More impressive was that he could do it seven or eight times out of every ten."

"Those M975s of yours, do you lose one every now and then?"

"Some of the guys get pretty attached to their handguns. We don't make a fuss if one disappears. We're all professionals here, and we figure lost weapons are ultimately gonna be used in good causes."

"You think Arriaga might have taken one with him when he left?"

"I didn't say that."

"No, Major, you didn't."

"Can I tell you one more thing?"

"Sure."

"I know Arriaga pretty well, and I like him. He's not unjust. He's not a thug. He's got a clearly developed sense of right and wrong. I hope to hell he isn't the guy you're looking for, but if Julio did this thing, the guy who messed with his kid would have deserved everything he got."

"Thank you, Major. You've been very helpful."

"What do you think should happen to a slimeball that kills a kid?"

"I'm not prepared to say."

"Understandable, you being from the Federal Police and all, but my feeling is that we understand each other perfectly."

Chapter Twenty

"I GOT GOOD NEWS and I got bad news, Mario."

"Good news first, Harvey. I need some cheering up today."

"Then this should help do it," the Miami Beach cop said. "Those cameras you asked about? They exist. You're gonna get a copy of a DVD showing everybody who boarded that flight."

"Everybody?"

"Including the crew. They all board through the same door. The camera mounted above it runs continuously."

"You are a prince among men, Harvey Willis."

"Don't lay it on too thick. Now for the bad news: we haven't been able to track down this Arriaga guy. You sure he's here in Florida?"

"No, I'm not. But he's supposed to be."

"Well, we came up with what we think is his address, but he doesn't answer his door. And we got what we think are his home and cell numbers, but he doesn't pick up his phones and, up to now, he hasn't responded to our messages. His car, if it is his car, isn't in the driveway, and his neighbors have no idea where he is. They're all Anglos, and Arriaga, they say, doesn't speak much English."

"All Anglos? In South Florida?"

"Hard to believe, isn't it?"

"No fixed place of employment?"

"Nope. He floats."

"As what?"

"A handyman. One of those neighbors had him in to do some work. Apparently he's good."

"And I guess it's tough to find gainful employment if your specialty is killing people."

"Not at all. Like you said, it's South Florida."

"You think maybe he's still at it? Killing people? On the side, I mean?"

"If he is, there's nothing in the records. And I mean nothing. No arrests, not even a speeding ticket. He appears to be squeaky clean."

"No Social Security number? No credit card?"

"He has both."

"How did he manage that?"

"Manage what?"

"Social Security. Credit cards. He's not a legal resident."

"Who told you that?"

"His wife."

"You mean his ex-wife."

"No. His wife."

"And this wife you're talking about lives there in Brazil?"

"She does."

"Two possibilities then: either we got the wrong Arriaga, or she's lying. And I'm pretty sure we've got the right Arriaga."

"Interesting."

"Arriaga won a green card in one of those lottery things. He's married to a woman whose maiden name was Inez Bocardo, also a legal resident, and has been for over a year."

"How easy would it have been to marry a second woman without divorcing the first?"

"Not easy. He would have been required to list his marriage status on his visa application. That would have shown him as married. So he'd need proof of divorce if he wanted to marry again."

"We were told he couldn't come to Brazil for his son's funeral because he was in the States illegally."

"Again, if we've got the right Arriaga, that's bullshit. He could have gone, and come back, any time he wanted to."

"Can you get a copy of those divorce papers?"

"Sure. Public records."

"Check them, will you? Confirm that the ex-wife's name is Aline."

"Okay, and if it is?"

"I can only think of one reason why she'd want us to believe he wasn't in Brazil when the murders were taking place."

"Like she still loves him?"

"And is covering for him."

"Well, duh," Harvey Willis said.

Chapter Twenty-One

WHEN SUMMONING STAFF, NELSON Sampaio expected them to appear before him instantly.

"Where have you been?" he demanded of Silva.

"Ana only called me five minutes—"

"Five minutes is five minutes. Sit down. You've got a lot of explaining to do."

Sampaio could have been displeased about any number of things, past and present. Saying anything at all would have been unwise. Silva took the indicated seat in silence.

"You *knew*," Sampaio said, pointing an accusing finger at his chief inspector's face, "that Tomás Garcia was a pederast."

"I knew nothing of the kind, Senhor."

"What?"

"A pederast, Director, is a man who has sex with boys. Juan Rivas was not a boy. I recall you telling me that he was thirty-two years old. That was on the day when you assigned me to the case. I called him a 'kid,' and you—"

Sampaio held up a hand. "I want a straight answer. Did you, or did you not, know that Tómas Garcia was buggering Juan Rivas?"

"I'm not sure who was buggering who, Senhor."

"Stop that! Stop splitting hairs. Do you deny you were aware of what was going on between Tomás Garcia and Juan Rivas? Do you deny you were aware of their sexual relations? Answer yes or no!"

"No, Senhor."

"Aha! And you saw fit to conceal that information from me?"

"I didn't consider it relevant, Senhor. Many times, you've asked me not to burden you with details."

"You didn't consider it relevant? *You didn't consider it relevant?*"

"No, Senhor."

"All right, Chief Inspector. I'm listening. I want you to tell me *why* you didn't consider it relevant. But before you do, I want to give you a small inkling of the trouble you've put me through."

"Yes, Senhor."

"Goddamn it! Haven't you got anything else to say other than yes, Senhor and no, Senhor?"

"If you'd only tell me—"

"Last night, Chief Inspector, those two old pals, Jorge Rivas and Tomás Garcia got good and drunk together."

"Last night? Rivas is still here?"

"He's still here. He stayed on for talks with the president and the foreign minister. Stop interrupting."

"Yes, Senhor."

"And stop that, I already told you to stop that. Now, while in his cups, Garcia admitted to Juan's old man that he'd been fucking his son—*fucking the foreign minister of Venezuela's son*, which was news to the Foreign Minister of Venezuela, and was news to me, and was news to the minister of justice and was news to the president of this republic—but wasn't news to *you* because *you* already knew all about it. Garcia said so just before Rivas punched him."

"Yes . . . I mean, as you say, Senhor."

"Goddamn it, I told you to stop that. After Senhor Rivas finished giving Senhor Garcia a few well-earned punches in the face and kicks in the groin, Garcia went on to admit that

Juan had ditched him for somebody younger. That's grounds for murder right there. So what do you suppose Jorge Rivas did then?"

"I don't—"

"He picked up the goddamned telephone and called the foreign minister, that's what!"

"He did, did he?"

"Yes, he damned well did. And who do you think the foreign minister called? The president. That's who! And who do you think the president called?"

"The minister of justice?"

"Exactly! And who do you think the minister of justice called?"

"You?"

"You're goddamned right it was me! And his question to me, and my question to you, is: *why haven't you arrested the filho da puta?*"

"Because he didn't do it, Senhor."

"And just because he didn't do—" The significance of Silva's words suddenly sunk in, bringing Sampaio up short. "What did you say?"

"He didn't do it."

"What makes you think he didn't do it?"

Silva rubbed his chin, wondering if the time had finally come to brief Sampaio on their progress. He decided it had. "We're sure," he said, "because we quickly discovered that similar murders preceded the death of Juan Rivas, murders that were committed with the same MO. An MO, short for modus operandi, is a criminal's characteristic pattern—"

"I know what a goddamned MO is! Get to the point."

"The victims were all shot in the abdomen and then violently beaten to death with a blunt instrument."

"The same gun?"

"Yes."

"What's the instrument?"

"We don't know. The killer takes it with him."

"And why can't the killer be Garcia?"

"One of the murders was in Brodowski. That's a small town near—"

"I know where Brodowski is. It's Pignatari's birthplace. What do you think I am, some kind of goddamned philistine?"

"The painter's name was Portinari, Senhor."

"Stop beating around the bush, goddamn it, and get to the point."

"The other murders were in São Paulo, Rio, and Campinas. We've interviewed the doormen at Garcia's building and we've spoken to people in his office. Various witnesses are willing to swear that Garcia was here, in Brasília, when those four killings took place."

"Damn. Why the hell didn't you tell me this before?"

"As I said, Senhor, I didn't want to burden you with details."

The director sat back in his chair. "I want a full report," he said, "and I want it right now. What else is going on?"

Silva told him about their discovery of the passenger list; the murder of Bruna Nascimento, the flight attendant; the death of the thug, João Girotti.

"What's the significance of other victims having shared that cabin with Rivas?" Sampaio asked.

"We don't yet know."

"And Girotti? What's he got to do with it?"

"We don't know that either. It's part of the puzzle. Bear with me. There's more to tell."

"Out with it."

Silva told him about the death of Julio Arriaga, Junior;

about the boy's father, his background as a soldier, his short temper, the fact that he might own a silenced pistol, the fact that he'd gone missing, the fact that his ex-wife had lied about their still being married.

"Why are you wasting my time?" Sampaio said when he was done.

"Wasting your time, Senhor?"

"What do the kid and his father have to do with the murder of Juan Rivas? Not a damned thing, as far as I can see."

"Maybe not, Senhor."

"No maybes about it. Who else have you got?"

"We're looking at four other people."

"Who are they?"

"Other passengers who traveled in the business-class cabin. Their names are Luis Mansur, Marnix Kloppers, Dennis Clancy, and Darcy Motta."

"What's suspicious about them?"

"Mansur knows something he's not telling us."

"You know that for a fact?"

"No, I just have a feeling."

"A *feeling*, huh? Very scientific. How about the other three passengers?"

"Clancy is an American priest. He went to Palmas."

"Tocantins? That Palmas?"

"Yes."

"Well, *that's* suspicious. Why the hell would anybody, particularly a gringo, want to go to Tocantins?"

"Add to that the fact that Clancy has dropped off the map. So has Kloppers."

"Kloppers? What the hell kind of name is that?"

"Dutch. But he carries a Brazilian passport."

"Born here?"

"Born here. He was traveling with his son. We've spoken

with his parents by telephone. They claim they have no idea where he is. Or his son either."

"Their own grandson? How likely is that?"

"Not very. Arnaldo Nunes is going to speak to them."

"All right. That leaves one."

"Darcy Motta."

Silva related the story that Lina Godoy, Bruna's friend and fellow flight attendant, had told Gonçalves.

Sampaio rubbed his chin. "So Motta may be the one who framed the kid?"

"It seems likely. And I should add that he, too, has disappeared."

"Using an alias?"

"We think so."

"So what are you sitting around here for? Get back out there and find the killer. And be quick about it. I can't hold off the whole damned Brazilian government for much longer."

Silva nodded and stood up.

"And, Mario?"

It was Mario again, no longer Chief Inspector, a sign that the storm had blown over—at least for the moment.

"Yes?"

"Make sure you're here for the meeting."

"I'll be here. But since you brought it up, would you mind telling me what it's all about?"

"All right. But keep it under your hat."

Silva nodded his assent.

"It's about next year's budget," Sampaio said. "I'm going to explain why none of you can count on any raises."

Chapter Twenty-two

WHEN HECTOR WAS USHERED in, the window behind Sergio Bittencourt's desk was framing an Airbus 320. As it sank out of sight behind some shrubbery, the office was suddenly filled with the roar of reverse thrusters being engaged. The racket precluded conversation.

Junior Arriaga's mother had been right when she called the delegado little. He didn't quite come up to Hector's chin. She'd also called him a bastard. Bittencourt went on to prove it.

"I hope this isn't gonna take long," he said. "I got better things to do than waste my time on a little punk of a dope smuggler, much less a dead one."

"A dope smuggler, is it?" Hector said. "Guilty, was he?"

Bittencourt shrugged. "Caught with the goods, wasn't he?"

"Arriaga was fifteen. You should have taken one look at him and transferred him."

"It happened early in the morning, before I got in," Bittencourt said. "I never even saw him, not until he was dead. And what makes you think you got the right to barge in here and tell me how to run my delegacia?"

Before Hector could reply, an oncoming roar built to a crescendo. Another aircraft sailed into view, the heat from its turbines distorting the air behind it. He watched it disappear, waited until he was sure the delegado could hear him, and said, "I'm here because the minister of justice wants a full investigation. Take it up with him if you've got a beef. I'll even wait until you have him on the line."

Bittencourt's mouth tightened. Then he seemed to realize Hector might be perfectly serious, and he forced a smile.

"Sergeant Rocas gave me your name," he said. "I forgot it."

"It's Costa. Hector Costa."

"Okay, Hector, let's start this conversation all over again. Maybe we got off on the wrong foot. You call me Sergio, okay?"

"Sure, Sergio. Now, about the kid?"

"First time I saw him, he was on the shower-room floor."

"You told his mother you were going to investigate. Did you?"

Bittencourt squirmed. "You know how many prisoners this place was built to hold? Fifty! You know how many I got back there right now? Hell, *I* don't know how many I got, but it's more than two hundred. You got no idea of what I have to put up with."

"No, I don't. And you know what, Sergio? I don't care. I'm here to talk about the kid."

"I *am* talking about the kid. He wasn't the first person to die in here, and he wasn't the youngest either, and he sure as hell won't be the last. Only difference is, most of them get stabbed."

"Stabbed, huh? Where do they get the weapons?"

"The walls in this place are concrete, like sandpaper. These guys got nothing to do all day, so they sit around and scrape away on spoons, and bedsprings, and anything else they get their hands on. They keep scraping, and sharpening, until they have a weapon. Once a week, we do a search, but you can't imagine the places they think of to hide things in. We got cases in here that're always on the lookout for tender young ass, but they steer clear of kids raised in the shantytowns. First thing that kind of kid does is arm himself. The perverts don't want to get stuck, so they wait for the ones like Arriaga. And when one comes along, they settle on him like flies on honey. We don't get many of them, so the competition is fierce when we do."

"You're telling me your people *knew* Arriaga would be attacked?"

"Hey, it's easy for you to take the high moral ground. You don't have to deal with it. First thing people learn when they come to work here is that, if they get between the flies and the honey, *they're* the ones who get stuck. You think I can find guards who're willing to lay their lives on the line for eight hundred reais a month? Give me a break!"

"So these guards of yours, they just let it happen?"

"It's like this: a lot of prisoners really look forward to their showers. Washing, fighting, fucking. It's recreation for them. Hell, I don't know why I'm wasting my breath explaining this. I really don't expect you to understand."

"You're right. I don't."

"As far as that kid is concerned, if I'd known he had somebody's juice up his ass, I woulda been on it in a flash. I don't want any more trouble than the next man. Last thing I want to see on my record is a reprimand. And juice up his ass, coupled with the time that's gone by without me doing anything about it, is sure as hell gonna get me a reprimand. But those pricks at the medical examiner's office never told me a goddamned thing. They kept me in the dark. First thing I heard about it was when those two guys from homicide showed up to take samples."

"Which was when?"

"Yesterday. Up to then, we had it down as an accident. We thought the kid fell."

"Sure you did. So between the time the kid was killed and yesterday, you did absolutely nothing?"

"Look, even if I'd suspected something, which I'm not, for

one minute, about to admit I did, there wouldn't have been any point. You know how felons think. Nobody sees anything. Nobody knows anything. Why bother to ask? But now it's different. Now we've got DNA and we'll be able to nab the son of a bitch. I got no problem with that. It's what he deserves. No, my problem is different. My problem is I shoulda been kept in the loop. Then I could have filed as murder, instead of accidental death."

"The DNA samples, did they get one from everybody?"

"Everybody who was still here. Some had moved on."

"Some? How many?"

"Two, I think. Yeah, two."

"Was one of them a punk by the name of João Girotti?"

"Why are you asking?"

"Just answer the question, Sergio."

"I don't remember. I got people going in and out all the time."

"And the name doesn't ring a bell?"

Bittencourt shook his head.

"Do me a favor, Sergio. Get me those two names. And while you're at it, get me their jackets."

Bittencourt grunted and picked up his phone. Five minutes later, two folders were on the desk. One was João Girotti's. The other belonged to a man named Ubaldo Spadafora.

Spadafora's mug shot showed a mild-looking man with mousy brown hair and moustache. He looked like anything but a hardened criminal. The written material confirmed the visual impression. Spadafora was a bookkeeper, arrested for embezzlement and larceny. It was a first offense. He wouldn't have spent a single night in jail if his employer hadn't caught him leaving the office with a briefcase full of cash.

"This address," Hector asked, "is it current?"

Bittencourt shrugged. "It's the only one I got."

"The homicide guys get a copy of this?"

"They got a copy. But they're gonna be wasting their time. The guy's a wimp."

"And only real *machos* rape fifteen-year-old kids, right? I want a copy of this."

"Copier's broken."

"Then I'll borrow it and return it."

"You want the other one too?"

"No. I already have everything I need on Girotti." Hector stood up. "I might be back," he said.

Bittencourt didn't seem pleased at the prospect.

* * *

UBALDO SPADAFORA lived in a small house with a vase of dead flowers on the porch. The bookkeeper opened his front door to find Hector looking down at the dried leaves and stalks. If he was surprised to see someone he didn't know standing on his doorstep at six o'clock in the evening, he didn't show it.

"My wife left when I got home from jail," he said. "I kept forgetting to water them."

Hector looked up. "You normally start a conversation by admitting you've been in jail?"

"I do if the conversation is with a cop. You're a cop, aren't you? You look like one."

Hector held up his badge.

"Okay," Spadafora said with a sigh. "Come on in. You want coffee?"

"I wouldn't mind."

"All I have is instant. It's not bad if you make it with milk."

"Good enough."

Spadafora led the way to a small kitchen, where he

popped two cups of milk into the microwave. Next, he opened a tin of cookies and began to arrange them in a circular pattern on a plate.

"They're not homemade," he said. "I don't cook any more. There doesn't seem much point to it, cooking for one person."

"You cooked before?"

"Serena said she had a full-time job taking care of her garden. She used to grow flowers: no fruits, no vegetables, just flowers. She'd have a fit if she saw it now. Most everything is dead."

The microwave beeped. Spadafora removed the two cups, spooned in instant coffee, and began to stir.

"I'd do the shopping on my way home and then cook dinner. I'd call her away from the TV so she could join us for the meal. Afterwards, she'd go back to her *novelas*, leave me to do the cleaning up and the rest of the housework."

"You had your hands full."

"I did. I took care of the kids, too, when she was glued to the TV. But none of it was enough. Serena had her heart set on buying a weekend place at the beach, somewhere near Ubatuba. She loves Ubatuba. Take your cup and come along."

"Is that why you stole the money?" Hector asked.

"I stole it," Spadafora said, "because she wanted that house, and I wanted to get it for her. Then, when it all went wrong, she left and took the kids. She's taking this place too. Got a good lawyer, Serena did; cleaned out our bank account to hire him."

"No chance that she'll forgive you, that you can make a fresh start?"

"You wouldn't ask that if you knew Serena. Enough about me. Why are you here?"

"The Arriaga boy. Remember him? The one who died in the shower?"

"How could I forget? Most brutal thing I ever saw."

"You *saw* it?"

"Only the aftermath. I was at the other end of the shower room, and I had soap in my eyes. I heard a commotion, washed out the soap, saw him lying on the floor, bleeding from the head."

"So you didn't see him being struck?"

"No, but I saw the rape. They propped him up on all fours. Two men held his thighs so they wouldn't collapse. Another pushed the nape of his neck so his head went down to the concrete floor. Then he buggered him."

"*Who* buggered him? João Girotti?"

Spadafora shook his head.

"Girotti was in line. He would have been third. Except. . . ."

"Except what?"

Spadafora winced, the memory painful. "He never got a chance. Somebody said the guards were coming. Girotti gave it up. He turned around, went under one of the showers, turned on the cold water to get rid of his erection."

"So who was it raped the kid?"

"Castor Salles; Big Castor, they call him. And it's an apt description. When he saw Arriaga, the first thing he said was, *He's mine.* I heard him say it. The boy did too. He backed up against the wall. I went to the other end of the cell and turned my face away. Five minutes later, they were herding us into the shower. Less than five minutes after that, the boy was dead."

"You think Delegado Bittencourt is aware of what he's got in Castor Salles?"

"How could he not be? You know, before I went to prison,

I was against the death penalty. I used to look down my nose at primitive societies that execute people."

"Primitive societies, huh? Like the Americans?"

Spadafora smiled a thin smile before he went on. "But now I think differently. People like Castor Salles, they're . . . purely evil."

The bookkeeper shivered, as if he could see Big Castor Salles right there in the room with him. Then he looked Hector full in the face. "You're a cop. You must see people like Salles all the time, primitives with no regard for other people and no respect for human life. What do you think should be done with them?"

Hector didn't answer, not because he didn't *have* an answer. He did. He had very firm convictions about what, in a land with no death penalty, should be done with animals like Big Castor Salles.

But he'd never share those convictions with a man like Ubaldo Spadafora.

Chapter Twenty-Three

GILDA'S HOUSE KEYS RATTLED when she tossed them onto the counter. She hung her purse on the back of one of the kitchen chairs and sank heavily into another.

"Sometimes," she said, "people make me sick."

Hector had a spare glass waiting. He filled it from the open bottle of Chilean red and handed it to her.

She took a healthy gulp, sighed, and leaned back in her seat. After a moment, she went on.

"I know you were annoyed when I wouldn't talk to you," she said, "but when you called everybody was standing around, waiting for me to cut."

"I wasn't annoyed," he said, "I just—"

She continued as if she hadn't heard him.

"It was a double autopsy, a married couple, murdered in their bed. They'd been asleep when the killer came in. The husband died instantly, one shot to the temple. His wife took two in the chest. Neither shot hit her heart."

She took another sip of wine. For a moment, Hector thought she was finished. But she wasn't.

"She must have awoken in pain," she said, "awoken to see the person who was killing her."

Hector put down the spoon he was using to stir the spaghetti sauce and leaned against the sink. "And that was?"

"Her daughter. Fourteen years old. Because her parents wouldn't let her go to a party."

Gilda took another swallow of wine, put down the glass, and rubbed her eyes. She'd been crying.

"Where did she get the gun?" Hector asked.

"Does it matter?"

"No. No, I suppose it doesn't."

"It was her father's. That Arriaga case, the one you called about, that makes me sick too."

Hector picked up his spoon. She took a paper towel from the roll and blew her nose.

"The boy didn't fall," she continued. "Not unless they held him on their shoulders so he could fall from a height of at least two and a half meters. There was semen in his rectum. The rape was postmortem."

Hector poured himself another glass of wine and sat down.

"Postmortem? How can you tell?"

She looked at the sauce bubbling on the stove. "You really want me to tell you that? Before dinner?"

Hector shook his head. "You didn't, by any chance, bring me a copy of the autopsy report?"

"It isn't finished."

"After all this time? Why not?"

"The mother came to the morgue and wanted to know all the details. Paulo didn't have the heart to tell her. And he didn't want her getting her hands on any report. But he wouldn't falsify it either. So he put off finishing it until the cops could complete their investigation. He told the mother her boy died from a severe cranial trauma, which was true, and he put a sample of the semen out for DNA analysis."

"In order to provide evidence for the homicide guys? So they could bust someone before the report became available?"

"Exactly. But without that report, there was no justification for DNA analysis. Paulo asked the lab to do him a favor. They said they would, but not as a priority."

"So it's still not done?"

"Oh, it's done, all right. It arrived the day before yesterday. One rapist only. Paulo briefed the civil police. They're getting samples from the men who were in the shower with Arriaga."

"Has the delegado in charge of the jail been informed?"

"I have no idea. Why?"

Hector topped up his glass. "He reported it as an accident."

"He must have known otherwise."

Hector got up to stir the sauce. "Probably did, probably saving himself the trouble of investigating. I doubt he would have done it if he'd known there was semen in the kid. He'll get a reprimand at the very least."

"The bastard should be fired."

"True. When is Paulo going to finish his damned report?"

She raised an eyebrow at the adjective. "Paulo will finish it," she said, "when they identify the rapist. He believes it will bring the mother some degree of closure if she knows that the man responsible for her son's death is going to pay for it."

Hector put down the spoon and returned to his seat. An image of Aline Arriaga's tear-stained face popped into his mind. There would be no closure for her. Not ever. He took a sip of wine, looking at Gilda over the rim of his glass. "You agree with what Paulo did?"

Gilda crossed her arms across her chest. "I wasn't consulted."

"I didn't ask you if you were consulted. I asked you if you agreed."

"Don't use that tone of voice with me, Hector Costa."

He put down his glass. "I'm going to call Paulo right now."

"If you pick up that phone," she said, steel in her voice, "you can sleep on the couch."

"Goddamn it, Gilda—"

"Paulo Couto is a kind, caring man. He did what he did to spare that woman grief. Can you get that through your thick skull?"

"So you *do* agree with him."

"I've had just about enough of this. I didn't come home to subject myself to an interrogation. Go question some criminal and leave me alone."

Gilda got to her feet, stormed into the bedroom, and slammed the door.

Chapter Twenty-Four

"YOU NEED ANYTHING ELSE?" Rosa asked. Mondays were slow days, and this Monday had been even slower than usual. It was only 7:00 P.M., not late as far as Mansur was concerned, but Rosa was already wearing her tennis shoes, a sure sign that she was on her way out the door.

Mansur shook his head, didn't respond when she wished him a good evening, and waited until he heard the ping of the elevator before opening his refrigerator. The damned thing wasn't big enough for more than a couple of six-packs, and the ice cubes were tiny, tinier still when Rosa didn't fill the trays as, once again, she hadn't.

Mansur gritted his teeth. There was enough ice for three drinks, maybe four. Three drinks was nothing, just enough to get a taste. One more mistake like that, just one more, and he'd fling Rosa out on her ass. That would mean he'd have to hire his third secretary since August, but so what? Secretaries were expendable.

He harvested what ice there was, twisting the plastic trays, letting it clink into the little crystal bucket with the silver top. Then he fished out a handful, put it in a glass, and wiped the wetness from his hand on the seat of his pants. The tongs were for visitors.

Mansur kept his whiskey under lock and key; had to, otherwise the cleaners would get at it. One time, he'd found the deep amber of his Black Label watered down to the pale straw of his J&B. Right after that, he'd put the lock on the cupboard. He took out a bottle and checked the tiny mark he'd made on the label. The level hadn't lowered since last time. Thing was, Rosa had a key to that cabinet too—and he really didn't trust anyone when it came to his whiskey. Or much else, for that matter.

The whiskey came from Scotland via Paraguay, all smuggled in, all delivered directly to the office. That not only provided him with cheaper alcohol, it also concealed the extent of his consumption from Magda. He knew damned well she wouldn't give a shit if he drank himself into an early grave, but the money it cost was something else. She'd bitch about that.

And bitching, when it came right down to it, was about the only thing he *did* get from Magda. Bitching about where he spent his evenings, bitching about the occasional perfume she smelled on his clothes. Bitch, bitch, bitch— and no sex.

Magda didn't drink, either; but Magda could go fuck herself, because he could always find someone to drink with. He could also find women to have sex with, so her attitude on that score didn't bother him either. The glue that held their marriage together was his hard-earned money. Magda would strip him to his underwear if he gave her half a chance.

He uncorked the bottle and poured himself a generous dose. Swirling the ice with a forefinger, watching it dissolve, he leaned back in his chair and put his feet on the desk.

The door to his office was open and the whiskey bottle in plain sight. The odds were someone would show up before long.

But no one did. And today, of all days, he had a great story to tell. As he sipped, he tried to put names to the faces on that airplane.

The uppity stewardess was the first one who came to mind. And as he was thinking about her, he remembered

Juan Rivas too. With a name like that, it had to be the arro-gant little prick with the dark skin, earring, and moustache. He'd kept the stewardess busy, practically monopolized her. Every time he'd wanted a refill, the little fairy seemed to sense it and get his finger on the call button first. One of the enduring impressions Mansur had of the flight was lots of sucking on ice in otherwise empty glasses.

And then there was Motta. Motta of the birthmark. Motta, the dumb fuck. Mansur had good reason to remember him. *How could he talk to Silva about Motta without getting his ass in a sling?* Short answer: he couldn't. But it really didn't matter. It wouldn't change anything, wouldn't contribute to solving the cop's case. Motta, that little weasel, didn't have it in him to kill anybody. No, if anybody on that flight was a murderer, it was the guy who was posing as a priest. A hard case, that one, steely gray eyes, black hair, nose in his book all the time, none of that "love thy neighbor" stuff you'd expect from a clergyman.

Mansur got up, dropped more ice into his glass—not much left now—and poured another drink. While he was on his feet, he decided to take a stroll around the floor, find some company.

***

EMERSON CUNHA wasn't at his desk. Cassio Zannoto was, but he didn't have time for a drink: he was meeting some-body for dinner. That's the way he said it. Somebody. Not his wife. Not a friend. Not a client. Somebody.

Which meant he was being discreet. Which meant it was probably somebody who worked in the office. Maybe that new receptionist, the blond. Sneaky bastard, Zannoto. Nice piece of ass, the blond.

He went back to his office, picked up the phone, and tried calling Gilmar Pedroso down on the second floor.

No answer.

His glass was empty again and he refilled it. He drank quickly, cracked the last vestiges of ice between his teeth, locked away the whiskey, and dumped the empty trays on Rosa's desk along with a nasty note.

It was almost a quarter to eight, and he was still alone.

He went down to the garage, nosed his black Corolla up the ramp, and plunged into the rush-hour traffic. It took him fifteen minutes to go three blocks. If he'd known it was going to be that bad, he would have drunk a couple of whiskies neat, given the traffic time to die down. But it was too late now. He was in the gridlock, committed to moving forward.

Running on alcohol, his thoughts took flight: *It's Magda's fault. If she'd gone along with buying an apartment in town, I'd be living within walking distance of work. But no. Goddamned Magda had to have a house out in Alphaville with a garden, and a swimming pool, and two maids to sit around and drink coffee with. That's when she wasn't at the hairdresser's, or playing cards, or—*

He screeched to a halt, narrowly avoiding a white BMW that jumped the light. He hit the horn. The driver of the BMW, pulling away, opened his window and stuck out an arm to make an obscene gesture.

His sudden stop had put him on the crosswalk. Pedestrians were moving all around him. He crept forward for another three blocks. He glanced at the clock on the dashboard.

Eight sixteen now. Getting dark.

The traffic showed no sign of thinning. Half an hour out of the office, and he hadn't moved eight blocks.

The Jockey Club! No races tonight, but the bar is open. Just a small detour.

He turned left at the next corner, got onto Avenida Europa, made it by fits and starts over the bridge, and turned right. On nights when the nags weren't running, it was dark under the trees, and the long street was lined with girls. Black girls, white girls, *mulattas*. Blond girls (they usually got the color from a bottle), red-haired girls (ditto), black- and brown-haired girls. Girls with short-shorts and no panties, girls with dresses cut down to their navels. Girls with hemlines that rose above their thighs. Girls who wore only short bathrobes, or sarongs.

There were a few cars pulled over to the curb, men on their own, leaning toward open passenger windows, doing some negotiating. Mansur felt a stirring in his groin. Instead of leaving his car with the valet, he took a left at the corner and circled the block.

When he appeared again, and the girls saw him for a second time, they started strutting their stuff in earnest, pouting their lips, lifting their skirts to crotch level, plunging their hips forward, flashing what they had (or didn't have) under their short bathrobes and sarongs.

Mansur swelled to full erection, painful in the confinement of his trousers.

By the time he'd reached the end of the line, he'd made his choice, but she was back at the beginning of the queue, so he had to circle the block a second time before he could stop. Her voice was deep, deeper than that of most women. If he'd been more sober, he might have paused, thought twice.

He and his Chosen One cut a deal. She hopped aboard and directed him toward one of the high-rotation motels that lined the Raposo Tavares.

Sometimes the girls worked scams with the motel's owners. When the happy couple got to their room, the john would find a man or two waiting for him. Instead of getting laid, he'd be relieved of his watch and wallet. If he was a married man, and wanted to keep it that way, who could he complain to? The cops? Creating a risk that his wife would get her hands on the statement? Leaving her in a position to be able to prove, with a legal document, that he was picking up whores? And then have her divorce him and take all his goddamned money? No way!

Mansur *did* go to the Raposo Tavares, but he drove right past the establishment his girl had suggested and went to the Bariloche, a motel he'd used before, a place he trusted. He was too smart, too experienced, to fall for some cheap scam.

But he wasn't smart enough, or experienced enough, to spot the Ford Escort that followed him from his office all the way to the front gate of his nice, safe motel.

Chapter Twenty-Five

IN ONE OF THOSE rare moments in Brazilian aviation, Tuesday morning's first flight from Brasília to Guarulhos arrived early. The undercarriage hit the ground in São Paulo a full seven minutes ahead of schedule.

Silva turned on his cell phone as soon as the airplane came to a stop. It began ringing almost immediately.

"Forget about your chat with Mansur," Hector said. "It's never going to happen."

"Dead?"

"Dead."

"Shot?"

"In the gut."

"Beaten?"

"To a bloody pulp."

"Damned fool! He said he had a revolver."

"He did. It was in his briefcase, but he left the briefcase in his car."

"Where did they find him?"

"In a motel room. The homicide guys know we're interested in the MO. They called us right away."

"How do I get there?"

"It's on the right-hand side of the Rodovia Raposo Tavares. You know that big supermarket, the Carrefour?"

"I know it."

"About a kilometer farther on. Call me when you get close."

"Transport?"

"Babyface for you, Samantha for Arnaldo."

Samantha Assad was one of the director's appointments. She had a law degree from Rio Branco, a black belt in jujitsu, and a chip on her shoulder the size of Nelson Sampaio's ego.

Arnaldo couldn't stand her.

"Call her on her cell phone," Silva said. "Tell her I've determined that Arnaldo will be the point man on this one. He's the one who's going to question Marnix Kloppers's parents. She's not to pull rank."

As a delegada, Samantha stood above Arnaldo in the pecking order. He had no law degree and was simply a senior agent.

"I already told her," Hector said. "She said she wouldn't, but you know Samantha."

"Unfortunately, yes," Silva said. "I do know Samantha."

* * *

THE TWO cars were in the no-parking zone in front of the terminal. A couple of uniformed cops were staring daggers at them. It went against the cops' grain to have *anyone* occupying the no-parking zone, even the Federal Police.

Silva hopped in next to Gonçalves.

"Morning, Babyface."

"Don't you think this Babyface stuff is getting a bit tired, Chief Inspector?"

Silva made a point of studying Gonçalves's unlined face.

"Not yet," he said.

* * *

"YOU'RE DRIVING," Samantha said, tossing aside her copy of *Vogue*.

"No 'Good morning, Senhor Nunes'?" Arnaldo said. "No 'How are you, Senhor Nunes?'"

"My morning went out the window when I heard I'd be spending it with you. And I really don't care how you are. Get in and drive."

"Did it ever occur to you, Samantha, why you're not married? Is it perhaps because you're so damned bossy?"

"Fuck off," she said and flounced to the passenger side.

"Tick, tick, tick," he said, opening the door.

"What's that supposed to mean?"

"Biological clock. It's ticking."

"My biological clock is none of your business, Nunes. Get your fat ass into the car."

He did and slammed the door.

"We're taking the Anhangüera," she said as he started the engine.

"Holambra is near Campinas," he said, adjusting the mirrors. "Bandeirantes will be quicker."

"Bandeirantes isn't as pretty. I'm into pretty. We're taking the Anhangüera."

"See what I mean? Bossy."

"Shut up. I've got a date tonight, and I don't want to be late, so get moving. The Dutra to the Marginal to the Anhangüera."

"You don't have to tell me how to get to the Anhangüera," he said. "I've lived in this town for more years than you've been alive."

"Wait," she said, holding up a hand. "What's that?"

Arnaldo cocked his head to listen. "What? I don't hear anything."

"Retirement clock," she said. "Tick, tick, tick."

"I don't get it," Arnaldo said, after a few minutes of not-so-companionable silence.

"What?" she said.

"Holambra."

"Oho," she said. "So the Great Expert on São Paulo doesn't know what Holambra means."

"And you do?"

"I do. Holambra is composed of the first three letters of Holland, the first two letters of America, and the first three letters of Brazil. Hol-Am-Bra, home of the Expoflora."

"What's the Expoflora?"

She said, "How could I forget? You're Arnaldo Nunes. Beauty and art are beyond you. You wouldn't know anything about the Expoflora."

"Enlighten me."

"It's *only* the biggest flower exposition in all of Latin America, that's all. Three hundred thousand visitors last year."

"What do they do the rest of the year?"

"They grow flowers and bulbs and seeds for the national and export trade. And they sit around and marvel that someone like you can live in this country and be unaware of the existence of their Expoflora."

"I don't live in this country," Arnaldo said. "I live in Brasília. It's kind of like Oz, with politicians."

A little later, he said, "So how come a gang of Dutchmen decide to come and live in Brazil?"

"Economic refugees," she said. "Came after the Second World War when their country was still a wreck."

"And we were the land of the future. Funny how things change."

"I can't believe you're such a cynic. That's another thing I dislike about you."

"How come you know all this? About Holambra, I mean?"

"Because I, unlike a certain Neanderthal I could mention, am aware of my surroundings. I am also a curious person—"

"You can say *that* again."

"—who is always interested in finding out things about other people."

"Nosy, I'd call it. And while we're on the subject, did Hector tell you I'm to take the lead with the Kloppers?"

She looked out the window.

"Did he?" he insisted.

"Yes," she sniffed.

And the silence descended again.

Chapter Twenty-Six

SILVA CALLED HECTOR WHEN they were passing the Carrefour.

"Just keep coming until you see the sign," Hector said. "It's blue and white, and it flashes. You can't miss it."

Indeed, they couldn't. The huge sign was on a concrete pillar ten meters high. Sky blue and white are the Argentinean national colors. The Bariloche for which the motel had been named is an Argentinean winter resort where much of the architecture appears to be Swiss, or German. The motel, doing its best not to look out of place on a subtropical hillside, and failing miserably in the attempt, consisted of about thirty small chalets surrounded by a cinder-block wall. They went through the untended main gate and found themselves surrounded by uniformed cops, technicians, detectives with badges dangling from lanyards, gawkers, and the ladies and gentlemen of the press.

Silva got out of the car. Gonçalves went off to face the challenge of finding a place to park.

Silva was immediately set upon. Hector, springing forward to rescue his uncle from the gang of reporters, took him by the arm. A uniformed cop lifted the yellow crime-scene tape so they could pass under it. That brought them out of the crush, but not beyond the cacophony of shouted questions. The journalists wanted to know who the victim was, whether there was more than one of them, how he, she, or they had been killed, when Silva was going to be available for comment.

The tenor of their questions indicated that they were being kept in the dark, for which Silva gave silent thanks.

"Show me," he said.

"That's the garage," Hector said, pointing it out.

Most high-turnover establishments had garages. Clients didn't want to run the risk of having their vehicles spotted by spouses, acquaintances, or private detectives.

Brazilian motels, by and large, are not places where one stops with one's family to spend a night. You can do so in a pinch, but you're still going to have to pay by the hour and put up with a lot of squeaking, banging, and groaning from your neighbors.

The higher-class places offered such amenities as in-room saunas and whirlpool baths. The Bariloche was at the other end of the scale, a no-frills establishment, designed to provide the basics and appeal to the frugal.

"The ME has only been here for about twenty minutes," Hector said. "He's still at it."

"Paulo?" Silva was hoping it would be his friend, Paulo Couto, São Paulo's chief medical examiner.

Hector shook his head. "Plinio Setubal, a friend of Gilda's."

"Don't know him."

"Young, but good."

"Who's here from the civil police?"

"The man himself."

"Janus Prado?"

"Yes."

"Good."

Unlike Gonçalves, both Silva and his nephew liked São Paulo's head of Homicide.

"He's agreed to keep it quiet," Hector said, "until we can tell Sampaio. But he wants it to be soon."

"Understandable. Let's get to it."

* * *

INSIDE THE ersatz chalet, a couple of uniformed cops were watching a video on the TV. The sound were turned down, but you didn't need sound to follow the action. It was that kind of video.

Near the far wall, a guy in green scrubs had Luis Mansur's pants down to his ankles and was removing a thermometer from the corpse's rectum.

Between the body and the door, Janus Prado was talking to a man with an unruly mop of hair, wire-rimmed glasses, and a paunch.

Prado spotted Silva and came over to extend a hand. The other man trotted along behind, as if he were Janus's pet.

"Mario," the civil cop said, nodding agreeably.

"Janus. How's life?"

"People ask me that all the time. You know what I tell them? Life is fragile. Life is a question of luck. Some *filho da puta* could come along and snuff you just like that." He snapped his fingers.

"If Arnaldo was here," Silva said, "he'd call you a philosopher."

"No," Prado said, "he wouldn't. If Nunes was here, he'd call me a bullshit artist. I ever tell you I threw a party when he left São Paulo?"

"*You* threw a party for Arnaldo?"

"*He* wasn't invited. The party was for the *rest* of us. I still owe you one for hauling him off to Brasília and getting him out of my hair."

"I'll tell him you sent your regards."

"I didn't." Prado took the arm of the man behind him and brought him forward. "This is Gabriel Rocha," he said. "He has a story to tell. Gabriel, this is Chief Inspector Silva of the Federal Police. Tell the nice man what you saw."

Rocha, who wasn't sure how he was supposed to react to

the preceding exchange and consequently had kept his eyes on Silva's left earlobe, now looked him full in the face.

"I tried to tell him," he said, his Portuguese thick with the cadences of the Northeast, "but he wouldn't listen."

"Tried to tell who what?" Silva asked.

"That dead guy,"—Rocha inclined his head in the direction of Mansur's body—"I tried to tell him. But would he listen? No, he wouldn't. 'You got room?' he says. 'Yeah,' I says, 'I got plenty of room. But are you sure you want to come in here with *that?*' And I point at Eudoxia. And she puts out her claws and damned near spits at me. 'And what the fuck business is it of yours?' the dead guy says. 'You got any idea,' I says, 'what she—' I was gonna say what she is, but would he let me explain? No, he wouldn't. Too fucking drunk, that's what. He wanted two hours, and he wanted to pay cash. So I took the money and I gave him the key. That's it. That's all I know."

"Wait," Silva said. "Slow down. Go back to the beginning. The guy over there drove up to the gate, and he had this girl in the car, and—"

"No. No! That's just the point. He didn't have no girl in the car. He had Eudoxia!"

"And if Eudoxia isn't a girl, what is she?"

"She's a man, that's what she is! A whaddayacallit."

"Transvestite?"

"Yeah, a transvestite. Anybody who isn't a complete asshole, or who isn't completely smashed, is gonna spot it right away. We got bright lights over there at the entrance. Eudoxia uses lotsa powder on her face, and she shaves close, but you can still see her beard. And that voice of hers! Deep, really deep, not a bass, mind you, but certainly not a tenor, more like a baritone. Hey, you like opera?"

"You're saying she doesn't sound like a woman?"

"I guess you didn't hear me the first time, so I'll say it again: Eudoxia has a voice like an opera singer, a male opera singer. I guess you didn't hear my question either: you like opera?"

"Yes, I like opera, but—"

"Listen to this, then," Rocha said. And then, to everyone's amazement, he sang the first stanza of "La donna é mobile." He could have passed for the Duke of Mantua in a second-rate company, which was still pretty good for a guy who kept the gate in a motel.

When he finished, there was a slight pattering of applause from everyone, including the two cops who'd been absorbed by the video.

Basking in the attention, he opened his mouth to continue. Before he could, Silva put a hand on his arm.

"Very nice," he said, "but we're investigating a murder here. Tell me more about this Eudoxia. You've obviously seen her before."

"Lotsa times," Rocha said, not pleased to have been cut off in mid-performance. "She hangs out with all those whores near the Jockey Club. It's like camouflage, being surrounded by real women. It helps fool the guys who pick her up. Mind you, they're generally drunk or they wouldn't be taken in so easy. Like I say, you don't have to be a rocket scientist to figure out she's really a man."

"It must be disconcerting when they find out."

"It's funny, that's what it is. They're all hot to trot, and they can't wait to get into the room and get her clothes off. Then, generally about two minutes later, they're outside again, the guy all red-faced and nervous and Eudoxia with a smile on her face. I guess she makes them pay her in advance. Most whores do. Must be a shock, reaching down between her legs and finding a cock. Sometimes, though, sometimes they stay for a while. Those are the sick bastards. But I didn't peg the dead guy for one of those. You think she killed him?"

"Do you?"

"See? That's what I can't figure out. Eudoxia's weird, but I don't think she's violent. One time, a john beat her up pretty bad. He was a single guy, and he didn't give a damn who found out she'd fooled him. He just wanted to make sure nobody thought he was a fag. He kicked the shit out of her, and then he called us to clean up. Eudoxia was lying there on the floor all black and blue. She'd just curled herself up into a ball and let him beat her. We asked her if she wanted us to call the cops, and she said no, just call a cab. It arrived, and off she went."

"Maybe this time she decided to fight back."

"Maybe she'd fight back," Rocha said, "but she'd never do it like that." He pointed at the body. "Look at that poor bastard."

Rocha had a point. Luis Mansur was a mess, every bit as much of a mess as Juan Rivas had been.

"Who discovered the body?" Silva asked.

"I did," Rocha said. "I told you, he only paid for two hours. Part of my job is to make sure nobody gets something for nothing. When he didn't leave, I came over here. There's this sign I put on the gate, 'Back in five minutes,' it says. If the guy who owns this place wasn't such a cheapskate, he'd hire somebody else. Friday and Saturday nights I have to work my ass off running between the gate and one chalet or another. The chambermaids won't do it. They say people give them too much lip. It has to be a man that does it."

"The customers complain when you remind them their time is up?"

"What am I telling you? You speak Portuguese?"

In fact, Silva's Portuguese was a good deal better than Rocha's; but all he said was, "Go on."

"People give me lip, I don't take it personal. I mean, there you are, humping away, and some guy knocks on the door and asks you when you're gonna be done. I wouldn't want it happening to me either. Kinda breaks the mood, you know what I mean?"

"I can imagine," Silva said dryly. "What happened when you knocked?"

"No answer. I did it again. Still, no answer. I called out, said I was from the *portaria*, told the guy his two hours were up. Nothing."

"And then?"

"And then I used my passkey and opened the door."

"You do that often? Use your passkey?"

Rocha shook his head. "Hardly ever. People can get out of this place by climbing over the wall. It's not so high, comes down to less than two meters where the ground rises out there at the back. But they can't rent a room unless they drive in with a car, and they can't get the car out without driving through the gate. Makes no sense to pretend they're not in the room, so they generally don't."

"What do you normally expect to find?"

Rocha blinked. "Whaddya mean?"

"Just what I said. When you use your passkey, and you go in, what do you expect to find?"

"I expect to find people asleep. Sometimes I get a shot of some hot broad's crotch. Sometimes I get an earful from her boyfriend, or client, or whatever. I never found a body before."

"How about Eudoxia?"

"What about her?"

"Where was she?"

"Gone."

"Gone where?"

"How the fuck should I know?"

"Was the door to the bathroom closed?"

Rocha considered for a moment. "Yeah," he said, "yeah, it was."

"But you didn't look inside?"

"I took one look at that mess over there and ran off to call the cops. I didn't even get halfway across the room."

Silva turned to Prado. "Any blood in the bathroom?"

Prado shook his head. "Not a drop," he said.

Chapter Twenty-Seven

THE RESIDENTS OF HOLAMBRA were either proud of their heritage or good at setting a tourist trap. Access to the town was through a gate three stories high. The gate was fashioned of red brick and featured Dutch-looking gables. Beyond it towered an even higher structure, a fake windmill housing a café on the ground floor. They went into the café.

"Town this small," Arnaldo said, "everybody knows everyone else."

"Every now and then," Samantha said, "you say something that isn't completely stupid. Let me do the asking. Kloppers, right? Marnix and Jan?"

"Marnix and Jan were the two on the flight. We drove out here to talk to Marnix's parents. She's Greetje, he's Hans."

"Don't ask them a thing until I get back," she said and headed directly for the ladies' room. Arnaldo passed a display selling wooden shoes and took a seat at a table. A woman in pigtails, wearing a starched white cap with wings, came over with a menu.

"This thing work?" Arnaldo asked, immediately violating Samantha's instructions and pointing upward.

The waitress shook her head. "The motor's broken. Want to eat?"

"Just coffee, thanks. Motor? The windmill runs on a motor?"

"Ran," she said. "For one?"

"For two."

"Milk?"

"Separately."

"We've got some nice *koekjes*," the woman said, dropping the word without hesitation and with no trace of an accent in her Portuguese. "*Speculaas*, they're called, kind of like gingerbread, but crispy."

"Bring 'em on," Arnaldo said.

"These are really good," Samantha said a few minutes later. She was talking about the speculaas, addressing the lady in pigtails and doing her best to exclude Arnaldo.

"Want some to go? We sell them by the box."

"Bring two boxes and put them on the bill," Samantha said. "This gentleman is paying."

The waitress came back a few minutes later with a bag and the check. Samantha snagged the bag. Arnaldo took out his wallet.

"Lived here long?" Samantha asked the woman in pigtails.

"All my life."

"I'm looking for a couple, Hans and Gretel Kloppers."

"Greetje," the woman corrected her.

Arnaldo rolled his eyes, but said nothing. Samantha gave him a dirty look. "Yes," she said. "That's right. My mistake. Greetje."

The woman took a napkin from the table and a pen from her pocket, and started making a map.

* * *

SETUBAL, THE same assistant medical examiner who'd performed the postmortem on Bruna Nascimento, estimated that Mansur's death had occurred between eight P.M. and midnight. He was struck by the similarity between the two corpses.

"Shot in just about the same place," he said, "and, for my money, he used the same club."

"Tell me more about this club," Silva said.

"Looks to be a little over twice the diameter of a cop's baton," Setubal said, "and long enough for him to build up a considerable degree of momentum. An unusual weapon."

While the crime-scene people were still giving the motel room a thorough going-over, Prado, Hector, Gonçalves, and Silva left by the back door and set out to examine the grounds.

The property was roughly rectangular in shape, about three times as deep as it was wide, flanked by a furniture factory and a shop that sold gardening supplies. The rear wall was set flush with that of the buildings on either side. Standing on a little rise, turning around, and peering over the wall to the rear, Silva could see a vacant lot. Beyond it, at the bottom of a steep grade, a dirt road paralleled the highway.

The cops took Prado's vehicle, a van that could carry eight, honked their way through the gaggle of reporters, and drove out the main gate. They weren't followed.

Two minutes of driving took them to the dirt road. They got out and walked up the hill.

Against the outside perimeter of the motel's wall, they found imprints of bare feet.

"Jumped," Prado said. "Look, the first impression is deeper than the others." He followed the footsteps for a few paces, comparing the interval between them to his own. "Running," he said. "Running like hell."

"Could have been Eudoxia," Silva said.

Gonçalves was dispatched to follow the footprints. The rest of them moved on. They came to a second set of footprints made by what appeared to be a pair of tennis shoes. The footprints pointed to the wall and then, a little farther on, pointed away again. The closest set was only about a meter from where the barefoot person had crossed.

"Scuff marks," Prado said. "He clambered over the wall, and here"—he pointed at two deeper footprints pointing in the opposite direction—"he jumped down on his way out. It rained the day before yesterday. These are fresher than that."

"And look at this," Silva said.

On the white-painted surface of the wall, directly above the point where the retreating footprints first made contact with the soil, were some reddish-brown drops.

"Could be blood," Prado said, leaning in for a closer look. "Could have dripped off the murder weapon." He picked up his radio and called the chief of the crime-scene techs up at the chalet. "Get down here," he said after telling her where he was. "We're going to need casts of footprints, and I want some blood samples lifted. Make sure you aren't tailed by any reporters."

Prado was signing off when Gonçalves came back up the hill, breathing hard from the climb. "Those bare footprints become women's high heels down at the road," he said. "Then they move off to the right, toward the city, but I lost them among tire tracks. If I keep going, maybe I can pick them up again."

"Try it," Silva said, not holding out much hope.

Gonçalves trotted off.

"And as soon as the techs get here," Silva continued, "I suggest we follow these." He pointed down to the other set of retreating footprints.

"Not very large impressions," Prado said. "He isn't a particularly big guy. I think the time has come for you guys to share the things you know and that I still don't."

"Why don't we follow these first?" Silva said, pointing at the footprints. "Then we'll go get some coffee?"

"No, Mario, no coffee. Information."

"We've unearthed quite a lot. Don't you want to go somewhere and sit down?"

"What I want is for you to come clean. One hand washes the other in this business. You, of all people, should know that."

"As you wish," Silva said.

Fifteen minutes later, when Silva finished talking, Prado said, "All right, let me see if I've got this straight. All the victims were on that flight, and killed with the same MO, except for two: the kid, Julio, *was* on the flight, but he was killed with a different MO; the thug, Girotti *wasn't* on the flight, but he still got shot in the lower abdomen and was beaten to a pulp. And the only apparent connection between Girotti and the others is that he shared a cell with the kid."

"So it appears," Silva said.

"Something happened during that flight," Prado said, thinking aloud. "Something the murderer did, or said, and wanted to keep secret. The kid was a witness. He told Girotti what it was, so Girotti had to be killed as well."

"Someone else has expressed that opinion," Hector said.

"Yeah? Who?" Prado asked.

"Gonçalves."

"Babyface? I'm glad you mentioned that name. I got something I want to say about him."

"Which is?"

"I'll come back to that in a minute. You know who I like for this?"

"Who?" Silva said.

"The last guy you mentioned, the eleventh passenger."

"Motta?"

"Motta. The stewardess saw him slinking around the cabin, right?"

"Correct."

"So he's the one who had something to hide. He's a man with a secret."

"Maybe he had a secret," Silva said, "but it doesn't necessarily follow that he's the killer. I'm not excluding Julio Arriaga, or Clancy, or Kloppers. Arnaldo has gone to Holambra to talk to Kloppers's parents, and I have people working on the other two."

"Arriaga is a long shot. You don't even know if he's here in Brazil."

"My boss, Sampaio, agrees with you. He thinks it's a long shot too."

"That idiot? Then maybe I should reevaluate."

"What did you want to come back to?"

"Your boy over there"—Prado pointed at Gonçalves, who was climbing the hill again—"went ahead and questioned Lina Godoy before I got to her. They told him I was coming, but he didn't have the courtesy to wait until I got there. That pisses me off."

"I'm sure it wasn't intentional, Janus," Silva said. "He's young and inexperienced."

"Don't try that one on me, Mario. I know he looks like he's about twenty, but I also know for a fact that he's well over thirty."

"An ugly rumor," Silva said. "I can't imagine who could have started it."

* * *

GONÇALVES HAD been unable to follow the trail of the high heels. The marks from the tennis shoes, they soon discovered, began and ended at a set of tire tracks. The car, quite a small one by the look of it, had been parked for a number of minutes or even hours. The crime techs couldn't be sure how long, but they did assure Prado it had been removed before dawn, before the sun began to bake the ground. When the driver left the scene, he'd steered into a U-turn. Within three hundred meters, the dirt turned to asphalt and the tracks vanished.

The area around the chalets was almost entirely paved and provided no further clues. The gardening-supply shop and the furniture factory had both been closed at the time of the murder. Neither one had a night watchman.

It had been a weeknight, and most of the motel's guests had already checked out, but not the pair inhabiting the chalet closest to Mansur's. That particular couple had remained in their room, avoiding the cops and reporters, apparently waiting for an opportunity to leave without being questioned. But the investigation continued, and the reporters stayed on. Eventually, the couple hazarded a discreet departure. At that point, they were detained.

The woman was wearing stylish clothing. She neither looked nor sounded like a prostitute. Silva also thought she was too old to be a high-class call girl. The man, also well-dressed, was driving an Audi. Their national identity cards confirmed that they were who they said they were. They gave the cops separate addresses, both in very good neighborhoods. Reluctant to be questioned, and terse in their responses, they claimed to have heard nothing, seen nothing. The woman kept glancing at her Rolex.

A husband at home, Silva concluded. And that thought triggered another one. He drew Janus Prado aside.

"Has anyone spoken to Mansur's wife?"

"I sent a man out there about two hours ago," Prado said. "Should be hearing from him any time now."

"Where's 'out there'?"

"Alphaville."

Alphaville, a series of upper-middle-class residential

communities spanning two municipalities, was some twenty kilometers outside the city of São Paulo.

"The guy I sent was Manoel Dias," Prado said. "Old Dias isn't the brightest bulb in my chandelier. Matter of fact, he's downright lousy at clearing cases. I don't even let him ask questions any more. They're always the wrong questions, and he never gets any useful answers."

"So why do you keep him on?"

"Because Dias has one thing he does better than anyone else: he's everybody's favorite grandfather, a master at breaking bad news. And in this town, I've got a lot of bad news to break."

Just then, Prado's cell phone rang. He held up a palm, put his hand over the microphone, and mouthed the word "Dias."

He uh-huhed his man three or four times, then said, "Check with the guys at the gate on your way out. They'll have records. If she left during the night, call me. I want to talk to her personally. Tell her she can expect a visit in about an hour."

He flipped his phone closed and said to Silva, "Dias. Calling from Mansur's house. I'm going out there."

"Why? What happened?"

"Dias is prepared for the usual tears and hysteria. He puts one hand on the package of paper handkerchiefs he keeps in his pocket, keeps the other hand ready to break her fall in case she faints. Then he hits her with the news. She looks at him for a couple of seconds and then, instead of turning on the waterworks, all she says is, 'Where did they find the bastard?'"

"Hard," Silva said.

"Harder, even, than my mother-in-law," Prado agreed. "Want to come along?"

Chapter Twenty-Eight

WHERE THE WAITRESS FROM the windmill had told them to expect a road, they found a rutted track, half-hidden behind a stand of bamboo.

"You think?" Arnaldo said.

"Take it," Samantha said. "We can always come back."

They bounced along through potholes, coating the car with red dust. Farther on, a sprinkler system was irrigating green shoots. Drops peppered the windshield. Arnaldo switched on the wipers and caught his first glimpse of the house through streaks of red mud.

No faux-Dutch architecture here. The place looked like most other farmhouses in the state, whitewashed walls surmounted by a roof of red tiles. The windows and doors were trimmed in blue.

Arnaldo parked between a tractor and a dusty pickup truck.

"Somebody's coming," Samantha said.

Arnaldo turned his head and saw a man emerging from a little outbuilding. He was tall, in his late fifties or maybe early sixties. When he saw them looking toward him, he doffed his broad-brimmed hat in a curiously old-fashioned gesture. His smile of welcome showed good teeth.

Samantha rolled down the window.

"We're looking for Hans Kloppers," she said.

"That's me." Kloppers clapped his hands and rubbed them together. "Like to have a cup of coffee before we get started?"

"We're not the people you think we are," Samantha said.

The smile faded.

"You're not the brokers from São Paulo?"

"Federal Police," Arnaldo said, taking charge. "I'm Agent Nunes. I spoke to you on the phone. This is Delegada Assad, who is going to leave all the questions to me."

Samantha glared at him. Kloppers simply looked glum.

"What do you want?" he said.

"For starters," Arnaldo said, "I want that cup of coffee you just offered."

"Follow me," Kloppers said, no longer making an effort to be cordial.

Inside, he called out something in Dutch. A woman answered and fluttered into the living room. She looked at Arnaldo and Samantha with big eyes.

"My wife," Hans said. "Greetje." And to her he said, "They'll have coffee."

Arnaldo was struck by the multitude of family photos. They were on the piano, on the television set, on both of the bookshelves, on the end tables flanking the couch, on the walls; they were everywhere.

"Why are you here?" Kloppers said.

Apparently, they'd come to the end of the social chitchat.

"Let's wait for the coffee—and your wife."

Silence fell, punctuated only by the regular ticking of a mantelpiece clock. Liars, Arnaldo had often observed, became uncomfortable with silence. Over the course of the next few minutes, Kloppers didn't stop fidgeting, cleared his throat at least five times, and assiduously avoided Arnaldo's eyes.

Greetje Kloppers came back with a tray and served them very decent coffee, the rich odor of which filled the room. Arnaldo took an appreciative sip and zeroed in on one photo in particular.

"Nice-looking boy," he said. "Is that him? Is that Jan?"

"Yes," Kloppers said, and swallowed. "Yes, that's our grandson."

"Uh-huh," Arnaldo said. "And that's another picture of him. And so's that one over there. The man with his hand on Jan's shoulder, that's your son, Marnix?"

"Marnix, yes."

"And there, and there, and there too."

Kloppers let Arnaldo's words hang in the air. The silence continued until Greetje broke it.

"If you don't mind," she said, "I've errands to run." She stood up. "You don't need me. Hans can answer for us both."

Samantha started shaking her head from side to side.

"Nice to have met you, Senhora Kloppers," Arnaldo said. "Have a good day."

Greetje picked up a purse from a side table and left the room.

Arnaldo waited for an exasperated snort from Samantha, reveled in it, and turned back to Hans. This time, he put an edge in his voice. "How stupid do you think I am, Senhor Kloppers? Do you expect me to believe that a man who has as many pictures of his son, and grandson, as you do has no idea of their whereabouts?"

"It's the truth."

"Like hell it is! Where are they?"

"I told you. I told you on the telephone. They went to the United States."

"You know what you're doing, Senhor Kloppers? You're obstructing justice. There are penalties for obstructing justice."

"I'm not—"

"How about you take me on a tour of the house?"

"What?" Kloppers gaped like a fish.

"A tour. Of your house. I want to have a look in the bedrooms."

"No."

"Why not? You have something to hide?"

"No. I simply don't want you poking around my home. Now I think it's time for you to leave."

He stood up and pointed at the front door.

Arnaldo, without a search warrant, had no other choice but to stand up and walk through it.

***

"WHAT NOW, wiseass?" Samantha said when they were off the rutted dirt track and back onto the tarmac.

"I'm thinking," Arnaldo said.

"Thinking? Is that what you call it? Don't make me laugh. Hey, goddamn it, what are you doing?"

Arnaldo had stepped heavily on the brakes. Now he was pulling onto the shoulder of the road.

"Look at that," he said as they came to a stop.

"Kids kicking a ball around," Samantha said. "So what?"

"Towns of this size, how many teams have they got? My guess is one. Those kids are all about Jan's age. Go and talk to them."

Samantha stood on the sidelines for a while, long enough for them to get used to her, and then sidled over to the bench. A minute later, she was talking to one of the kids, a boy of nine, maybe ten, with red hair and freckles. At a given point, he turned around and pointed.

A minute after that, Samantha was back at the car.

"Drive," she said. She couldn't keep the excitement out of her voice. "I'll tell you where to turn."

"Jackpot?"

"Those are the Holambra Juniors, and Jan Kloppers is their best striker. Five minutes ago, the kid was there, kicking ass, and his father was watching him do it. Then his grand-mother, the old biddy *you* allowed to leave the house, drove up. They called the kid in from the field and took off, all three of them. You screwed up, Nunes. You should never have let her out the door."

"If I—"

"Shut up. I'm talking. Fortunately for us, Greetje made a mistake. She told Jan she was taking him to his aunt's place, and then let him say a quick good-bye to his friends."

"And he told them where he was going?"

"Exactly."

"And one of them told you how to find the place."

"Uh-huh. And now that we're no longer talking to the old folks, my orders from Hector no longer apply. I'm gonna take the lead. So kindly keep your mouth shut when we get there."

"You're a vengeful person, Samantha, a vengeful person. Maybe that's why the other girls in the office don't like you."

"They're not girls, they're women, and I couldn't care less about whether they like me or not. I can't wait to get back to São Paulo and tell everybody how you screwed up."

"See what I mean?" Arnaldo said. "Vengeful."

Arnaldo caught sight of it first: the same dusty pickup they'd seen at the Kloppers' house.

"There," he said.

The truck was nosed up to the garage of a modern villa. He pulled into the driveway behind it.

They tried the doorbell. There was no response.

"Knock," she said.

"They heard us. They're just not coming to the door."

"Knock anyway."

He did. There was still no response.

Samantha opened her shoulder bag, produced a Glock, and took a stance to the right of the door.

"Break it down," she said.

"What?"

"You got a hearing problem, Nunes? I said break down the goddamned door. Then get out of my way."

Arnaldo shook his head and sighed. Then, leaning into the door and raising his voice, he said, "Listen to me, Kloppers. We need to talk, and we know you're in there. You want to get your mom and dad in trouble? If you do, just keep on doing what you're doing."

Samantha put her mouth next to his ear and hissed: "Are you out of your mind? You think a guy who's going to all this trouble to avoid us cares about—"

He didn't let her finish. "Come on, Kloppers," he said, "play it smart. I'm not kidding. If you don't open this door *right now*, I'm gonna have your parents up on a charge of obstruction of justice. Is that what you want? Huh?"

Samantha pursed her lips and shook her head.

And Marnix Kloppers opened the door.

Chapter Twenty-Nine

MAGDA MANSUR LIVED IN Alphaville Nineteen. Like the other twenty Alphavilles, Nineteen was surrounded by a high wall surmounted by fragments of broken glass. The glass was anchored in concrete and crowned by electrified razor wire. Situated to either side of a low brick guardhouse were two gates. The one on the right was for visitors.

When Prado rolled his van to a stop, a guard with a revolver on his hip approached the vehicle. "Here to see Magda Mansur," Prado said.

The guard nodded.

"Police, right?"

"Right."

"She's expecting you. Still gonna have to see some ID."

Everyone reached for their credentials. The guard went through them, making notes on a clipboard as he went. When he was done, he lifted his arm and signaled to another guard behind the bulletproof glass. That one picked up a telephone. Seconds later, the gate in front of them was opening and a security car was rolling up to lead them to the Mansur home.

"Seems pretty tight," Hector said.

"Believe me," Prado said, letting out the brake and putting the van in gear, "they pay for it."

The gate closed behind them and they started rolling through the streets of the community. The security car kept the speed down to a little less than twenty-five kilometers an hour. Even without the car, they wouldn't have been able to go much faster: there was a speed bump every fifty meters or so.

"Once you're in here," Prado said, "you're safe. The problem is getting here. The bad guys cover the approach roads like old-time highwaymen, put out sharp stuff to perforate tires and make people stop. And that's just one of their ploys. Another one is they dress whores in designer clothing, make 'em look like housewives, put 'em next to a car with a flat tire, and then—ah, this is it."

A hand protruding from the security vehicle was pointing at a red brick house set between two tall palms. Prado pulled into the driveway. The rent-a-cops made a U-turn and drove off.

Senhora Mansur was an attractive woman in her mid-to-late thirties, casually dressed. Pale blue jeans were topped by a baggy sweater. Her hair was drawn back in a severe bun, making a no-nonsense impression. She did not appear to be in any way devastated by her husband's death. Once they were all seated inside, Prado kicked off the interrogation.

"I apologize, Senhora, for intruding on you at a time like this."

It was a formula. Every one of the cops present had said it to a bereaved person at one time or another. Silva had probably said it over a hundred times. But he'd never gotten a response like the one Magda gave Prado.

"No, Delegado, *I'm* the one who should apologize. I'm afraid I shocked that nice man you sent. Tell me, do you think I murdered my husband?"

Silva found her forthrightness refreshing.

"It did cross our minds," he said, making a bid to take over the interview. Prado sat back in his chair, a sign that he had no objection.

"Of course it did," she said.

"And did you?" Silva asked.

She shook her head. "No," she said. "But I thought about it often enough."

Silva had come prepared to dislike the woman. Instead, he found himself warming to her.

"So you're not terribly displeased that someone else did it for you?" he said.

"I should have left him years ago. If he was still beating me, I would have. But after I walloped him with one of his golf clubs, a seven iron as I recall, he stopped. We have no children. I've got money of my own. So why did I stay with him?"

"Indeed. Why did you?"

"I'd become little more than an object to Luis, something he owned, like a car or a house." She leaned forward, folded her hands and put her elbows on her knees. Evidently, it was important to her that Silva fully understand what was coming next. "But he didn't abuse me any more. He paid the bills. He wasn't jealous. He let me do the things I wanted to do. He was almost never home, and the time he *did* spend at home he mostly spent sleeping. When I'd tell the women around here that I was considering leaving him, they'd look at me like I was insane."

"They didn't think it was important that you no longer loved him? Or that he no longer loved you?"

She smiled and leaned back in her chair. "You don't know my neighbors, Chief Inspector. Most of the people who live in Alphaville, men and women alike, have another perspective. For them, earning money isn't a necessity of life, it's the purpose of life. Love doesn't enter the equation. The husbands, by and large, are workaholics, and the wives are work widows. They see each other on weekends and not always then. Mind you, I'm not saying all the men are like Luis. They could be loyal husbands, for all I know."

"Luis had other women? That's what you're saying?"

"Yes, Chief Inspector, Luis had other women. Luis chased skirts like dogs chase cats. He couldn't help himself."

"You weren't jealous?"

"You've got to feel attraction, or love, or . . . something to be jealous. What I felt for Luis was disgust. It's viscerally repulsive to have your husband come home smelling of another woman's perfume, smelling of sex. He could at least have had the decency to take a bath before he got here. But he never did. He wasn't a decent man."

"You were . . . estranged?"

"I suppose that's a delicate way of asking me whether I was still sleeping with him. The answer is no. I have my own bedroom now, and I lock the door at night. But he didn't start whoring around because I'd stopped sleeping with him; I stopped sleeping with him because he was whoring around. And I didn't want to catch anything worse than the dose of gonorrhea he gave me once."

"Did he ever mention any of his women by name?"

"He denied they existed. When I was diagnosed, he said I must have picked it up from a seat in a public toilet. I told him it didn't work like that. So he got his cousin, a medical doctor, to call me up and assure me it was common. I believed him for a while. That was back when I cared, and I *wanted* to believe it. Now, Chief Inspector, can I ask you a question?"

"Go ahead."

"Why would a prostitute want to kill him?"

"You've been frank with us, Senhora Mansur—"

"Magda."

"Magda. So I'll be frank with you. There is a possibility that the person he brought to that motel room murdered him; but that person wasn't a woman."

"A man? I don't believe it. Luis was a lot of things, but he wasn't a homosexual."

"The person was a transvestite. By all accounts, your husband was drunk. He took her for a woman."

A smile creased her face, but she immediately repressed it.

"What a surprise for Luis," she said.

"Do you think your husband would have reacted violently?"

"It's hard to say. He had a fear of ridicule. He wouldn't have wanted to make a scene."

"But if they were alone in a motel room? Just the two of them?"

"Provided the transvestite was considerably smaller and weaker, Luis would have beaten the crap out of him. The operative words, Chief Inspector, are smaller and weaker. My late husband was a coward."

"There is another possibility," Silva said. "If you'll bear with me for a moment, I'd like to tell you about it."

"By all means. Please, go ahead."

"Over the last several weeks, there have been other murders, all committed in essentially the same way. The victims were first shot and then beaten to death. The same weapons, as far as we can determine, were used in all cases. Yesterday, I called your husband. I told him about the other killings, and I warned him that he might be in danger."

"He had a gun. He always carried it. One time he got robbed on the street—"

"He told me about that. The gun was in his attaché case. The case was in his car when the attack took place. He couldn't get at it."

"What brought you to Luis? What did he have in common with the other victims?"

Perceptive woman, Silva thought.

"Most," he said, "were fellow passengers on a flight from Miami to São Paulo. One was a stewardess on that same flight. The flight arrived here early on the morning of the twenty-third of November. Does that date ring any bells?"

She shook her head. "Luis was always going back and forth between here and Miami. He had some clients there, probably a girlfriend or two as well."

"Let me try some names on you."

"The other victims?"

"Yes. Bruna Nascimento?"

"She was the flight attendant?"

"Yes."

"No. I've never heard her name."

"Paulo Cruz?"

"*Professor* Cruz? The one who wrote those pseudo-studies on sexuality?"

"Yes."

"I read about his murder, which is more than I can say for the trash he wrote. But, no, I didn't know him, and I know nothing else about him."

"Victor Neves?"

"No."

"Jonas Palhares?"

"No."

"Juan Rivas?"

"I've heard of a Jorge Rivas."

"Juan's father. He's the former ambassador to Brazil from Venezuela, currently his country's foreign minister."

"He must have his hands full, what with that idiot running his country. No, I never heard of his son."

"Dennis Clancy?"

"No."

"Darcy Motta?"

"Yes."

"Excuse me?"

"I said yes. Luis mentioned a man by the name of Darcy Motta."

"When and in what context?"

"He got home from the airport two or three flights ago, maybe on the twenty-third of November, but I'm not sure. He came into the house very pleased with himself, saying he'd closed a deal with a patsy on the plane. That's the term he used, a patsy."

"But you're sure this patsy was a man."

"Yes, because later in the conversation, he used that name."

"Darcy Motta?"

"Yes. He said the deal didn't amount to much, but it more than paid for his ticket."

"And?"

"And that was it. I knew he wanted me to ask him more, to give him a chance to show how smart he was, but I wouldn't give him the satisfaction. I told him I was on my way to play tennis, which I wasn't, and I left."

"Did he describe this Motta fellow?"

"No."

"Ever return to the subject?"

"No. May I ask another question?"

"Ask away."

"You said Luis was beaten."

"Very badly."

"I'll have to arrange the funeral. Open casket?"

"Under no circumstances," Silva said.

Chapter Thirty

KLOPPERS WAS A SLIGHT man with a hollow chest and stooped shoulders, the antithesis of a healthy farmer. When he caught sight of the pistol in Samantha's hand, his eyes bulged.

"There's no need for that," he said.

"Shut up," she said. "Step back."

Kloppers swallowed and moved out of the doorway. His mother was standing a meter behind him.

"Hello, Senhora Kloppers," Arnaldo said. "Nice try."

Greetje Kloppers sniffed. She didn't look frightened; she looked angry.

"Where's the kid?" Samantha said.

That got a rise out of Greetje. "You leave him alone! He didn't do anything."

"Please, *Moeder*," Kloppers said. "Don't make them angry. You can't help me now, you can only hurt yourself."

"Where's the kid?" Samantha repeated.

"Jan's in the bedroom at the end of that hallway," Kloppers said. "He's hiding in a closet. Please let my mother fetch him. I don't want you to frighten him any more than he already is."

"Who else is in the house?"

"No one."

Samantha nodded, put her Glock back in her shoulder bag, and took out a pair of handcuffs.

"Are you going to use those on me?" Kloppers said.

"Who else would they be for? Turn around."

But he didn't. Maybe, Arnaldo thought, he wasn't quite the wimp he appeared to be.

"I don't want my son to see me in handcuffs," he said. "I'm perfectly willing to let you use them after you've taken me away. Not now."

"I really don't care if you're willing or not," Samantha said. "You're going to wear them. Turn around."

"Hang on just a minute," Arnaldo said. "I don't know about you, Samantha, but I'm beginning to wonder if we've got the right guy."

"Oh, you've got the right guy," Kloppers said. "I admit it. I'm guilty, and I know you're going to take me away. But I'm not a violent man, and I'd really appreciate it if you didn't use those handcuffs."

"Now I'm confused," Arnaldo said. "You say you're guilty, and in the next breath you tell us you're not a violent man. What, exactly, are you guilty of?"

"Shut up, Nunes, and get out of my way."

"No, Samantha, this time *you* shut up. Tell me, Kloppers. What did you do?"

Their prisoner looked from one to the other in confusion.

And then he told them.

***

ON THE way back to Hector's office, with Samantha still fuming on her side of the front seat, Arnaldo called Silva.

"We found Kloppers and his kid. It's a dead end."

"You kill Samantha yet?"

"Not yet. Any time now. I'm still devising the most painful method."

"If Kloppers was a dead end, who's he hiding from?"

"His ex-wife."

"Tell."

"She's American, a wholesale flower buyer in Florida. Marnix is an office drone who used to work in Holambra's export division. They met at some flower show. A year later, they're married. A year after that, Jan comes along. A year after that, she's throwing dishes at Marnix's head. According to him, he never laid a hand on her, but she used to beat him up a couple of times a week. He moved out."

"Two sides to every story, especially in divorce cases."

"True. But I believe his side."

"Why?"

"I'm getting there; bear with me. He filed for divorce. She got custody of Jan. Marnix claims she only took the kid to spite him. He pays alimony, he pays child support, says he never missed a payment. Five years later, she decides to get married again. Two years after that, she's throwing dishes at the new husband. But he doesn't move out, he hits her back. Then they have a few drinks and make up. Pretty soon, they're drinking and fighting every day."

"If it's true, it's no environment for a kid."

"Wait. There's more. The new husband has two kids, and they're both bigger and stronger than Jan is. So while their father is beating up on his mother, the kids are beating up on Marnix's son. Marnix, who goes up there four times a year to spend time with his kid, gets the whole story. Jan wants to move out and come down to Brazil with his father. The ex-wife, who's got more important things in her life than her kid, agrees to let him go. So Marnix goes over to the consulate and gets all the paperwork: a Brazilian passport for Jan and the authorization for him to travel without his mother. Then, just when he thinks the whole thing is settled, a done deal, the ex-wife tells him she wants money."

"She *what*?"

"She tries to hold Marnix up for money. Tells him he can

have the kid, but he'll have to give her fifty thousand dollars."

"She wanted to sell him his own kid?"

"Uh-huh. And Kloppers said he would have paid it. But he didn't, because he couldn't."

"And?"

"And she told him to get it from his parents, who she thought were well off."

"And?"

"And Marnix knew they weren't as well off as all that."

"So he kidnapped the kid?"

"He did. Took him straight to Miami International and got on the first flight to Brazil. The only thing available was business class, so he maxed out his credit card and bought that."

"You talk to the kid? Alone?"

"Samantha did. He backs up his old man's story. Says he doesn't want to go back to the States, no way. He loves his grandparents, they love him, and he's having a ball. Here's the clincher, though, the thing that makes me think Marnix is really telling the truth."

"What?"

"I called Mara Carta and got her to run a check. There's no complaint against Kloppers. He thought there was, but there isn't. So I started thinking why not."

"Because the mother doesn't really care about getting her son back; she's still hoping to hold Kloppers up for all or part of that fifty grand."

"That's my guess."

"If there's no complaint, we're not under any obligation to do anything."

"I told him that. And I told him to keep away from anybody who isn't from Holambra until we get this thing sorted out."

"He know anything that throws light on the case?"

"Not a thing. They didn't pay attention to anyone else on the plane. And they were scared until they got off the ground. Once they were in the air, though, the adrenaline rush wore off. They were both exhausted and slept like babies until breakfast time."

Chapter Thirty-One

FIFTEEN MINUTES AFTER HANGING up with Arnaldo, Silva got another call from his friend in Miami.

"You are *so* lucky to have my brilliant expertise at your disposal," Willis said.

"I have never thought otherwise, Harvey. What have you got for me?"

"Luca Taglia is an old friend of mine. With a name like that, I keep telling him, he should be a *capo* for the mafia. Actually, he works intelligence for the Boston PD. He not only ran Clancy's records, he sent a couple of guys over to the address you fed me, the one from Clancy's visa application."

"Uh-oh. Sounds like I owe somebody another lunch."

"No."

"No?"

"I sent Luca two tickets to a Red Sox game. You're gonna buy me two for the Hurricanes."

"Gladly."

"Okay, here's the dope on Clancy. First of all, the priest bit checks out. The address you fed me is a soup kitchen for winos. Clancy lives in a little room at the rear, puts in long days doing God's work. His neighbors say he's a really good guy. The records say he's never had a brush with the law. The diocese says he's been doing his current work for three years. His credit cards say that when he got to Brazil, he spent a night in a hotel in São Paulo. Then he moved on from there and spent another night in a hotel in Palmas, wherever the hell that is."

"Up north. Capital of the state of Tocantins."

"Whatever. Then he went to Miracema, again wherever the hell that is, and spent another night. While he was in this Miracema place, he used the same credit card to take money from an ATM. He did it three times, took the maximum he could get every time."

"And then?"

"And then nothing. That's it."

"Strange."

"Taglia thought so too. So he decided to dig a little deeper. He went over for a personal conversation with the people at the diocese. They refused to talk."

"Refused?"

"Refused. It's their right."

"How about Clancy's family?"

"They don't want to talk about him either."

"They don't want to talk about their own son?"

"Taglia sent two of his best men over there. The Clancys serve tea. Tea, mind you, not coffee. Mom and Dad are from the old country. They have shamrocks and leprechauns all over the place. Dad's wearing a ring from the Ancient Order of Hibernians."

"The what?"

"Skip it. It has no significance to the case, only a bit of local color. Mom's got a crucifix around her neck. There's a portrait of the Virgin Mary on one wall, a portrait of the Pope on another—"

"All right, all right, I get the picture."

"Okay. So their son Dennis, they tell Taglia's boys, is the youngest of four. The cops tell them they know their son is in Brazil, and they want to know what he's doing down there. Ma and Pa Clancy look at each other. Then Pa Clancy says, 'We don't want to talk about it.' Just like that. 'Whaddya mean?' Taglia's boys say. 'Whaddya mean you don't want to talk about it?' 'Just that,' Pa Clancy says. 'We don't want to talk about it.' And that was it."

"That was it?"

"Yup. They kept dishing up the tea, but they refused to say anything more about Dennis."

Silva scratched his head. He couldn't think of anything to say other than "Huh."

"Huh is right," Willis said. "You get any information on Dennis, you let me know, okay? Because now I'm curious."

***

"ALL RIGHT, how about this then?" Fabio Pessoa snapped, making an adjustment to his sketch.

Pessoa, the Federal Police's forensic artist, and Rocha, the opera buff from the motel, were seated side by side at a battered wooden table. The table was in a conference room adjoining Hector's office.

"Hmmm," Rocha said, studying the screen on Pessoa's notebook.

"Hmmm, what?" Pessoa said testily. He was running out of patience with this guy.

"Hmmm, maybe."

"Maybe?"

"Maybe. Can I go now?"

"No, you can't. If *that*"—he pointed to the screen— "doesn't look like Eudoxia, we're gonna keep at this until we got a face that does."

Rocha shook his head. "Waste of time. I go to a family reunion, I keep my wife next to me all the time."

"And that's relevant to what we're doing here because?"

"She's like, 'You remember Cousin Carlos, don't you?' She's like, 'Hello, Carolina,' saying 'Carolina' so I'll get it. She has to feed me clues all the time so I won't embarrass her. I have no memory for faces."

"You know what? You're absolutely right."

Behind them, the door opened. Both of them turned their heads.

"Any progress?" Silva said.

Pessoa shook his head. "The guy's hopeless," he said.

"Hopeless is you," Rocha said.

"Hopeless is unacceptable," Silva said. "I need a likeness." He turned to Pessoa. "What else can you suggest?"

"Photos. We're going to look at photos."

"No, we're not," Rocha said. "You can't make me. I'm sick of this whole business. I want to go home."

"Tell me one thing," Silva said. "Would you recognize Eudoxia if she was standing in front of you?"

"Sure. Eudoxia? I see her twice a week at least."

"Okay," Silva said.

"Okay what?"

"Go home."

Rocha raised a suspicious eyebrow.

"How come?"

"Because that's where we're going to pick you up at eight o'clock this evening. And you'd goddamned well better be there."

* * *

ROCHA WAS. They decided to try the area around the Jockey Club first and got lucky immediately.

"That one right there," Rocha said, pointing to a tall dark-skinned figure in a miniskirt, a platinum wig, and high heels.

He sounded surprised it had been so easy.

Hector dropped Gonçalves three hundred meters up the street, well beyond the long line of girls and maybe-not-girls. Then he took a left turn and circled the block. As soon as he was out of sight of the flesh market, he pulled over to the curb, hopped out, and Silva took the wheel. Rocha moved to the front.

Minutes later, they had Eudoxia in a box. The Jockey Club's high concrete wall was behind her. A continuous string of gated houses lined the opposite side of the street. The cross streets were cut off by Gonçalves and Hector, who were converging on Eudoxia from either side.

Certain now that their prey couldn't flee in any direction, Silva pulled the car up in front of her. Hector arrived and gripped the transvestite by the arm. Gonçalves, still panting from his run, opened the back door of the car. They were about to push her into the backseat when Eudoxia screamed.

Eudoxia's colleagues reacted immediately. Cans of pepper spray were produced. So were cell phones. One woman, a brunette in shorts, took a little nickel-plated semiautomatic out of her handbag and pointed it at Hector. "Let her go, you filho da puta," she said.

Rocha cowered down in the seat and covered his head. Silva got out from behind the wheel. Shielded by the car, he rested the butt of his Glock on the roof and pointed it at the brunette. His weapon was at least twice the size of hers.

The shouting stopped. No one wanted to attract the attention of the man with the gun, but no one wanted to back down either. Into the silence, Silva said, "We're federal cops. We need Eudoxia to help us with our inquiries."

"If you're cops," the whore with the pistol said, lowering her arm, "you've got to show us ID." The uncertainty in her voice telegraphed that the threat, from her direction at least, was over.

"Yeah, show us ID," someone else shouted.

And then they were all shouting it. "ID, ID, ID."

Without taking his aim off the woman with the pistol, Silva used his left hand to produce his gold badge. He held it up, high, so all the whores could see it.

"Show them your badges," he said to his companions.

Hector and Gonçalves held theirs over their heads, slowly rotating their wrists so people pressing around them could have a look.

Two tough-looking guys appeared from nowhere and pushed their way to the front of the crowd. One of them, an oaf with a short forehead and a single gold earring, waved at Silva as if they were old friends.

"I know this guy," he said, lifting his voice so the crowd could hear. "He is what he says he is, and I don't want any trouble with him. Anybody who doesn't back off is going to have trouble with *me*."

The brunette put her pistol away, took a few steps backward, turned, and ran. Prostitution isn't a crime in Brazil. Being a transvestite isn't a crime either. But carrying a concealed weapon without a permit is.

Silva nodded his thanks to the thug with the earring and got a nod in return. Then he put his Glock away and got back behind the wheel.

Eudoxia's identity card identified her as Alvaro Moura, twenty-seven years old, male, one meter sixty-two in height, seventy-seven kilos, black hair, brown eyes, and a native of Caxias, a town in the state of Rio Grande do Sul.

He was still one meter sixty-two, but he'd adopted a Carioca accent, looked a good deal older than twenty-seven, had put on weight since he'd gotten his card, and was using green contact lenses. Under the platinum wig, his hair had been tinted to a dirty blond.

He was high on adrenaline and crack, so before interrogating him, they put him under a cold shower and plied him with coffee.

When Moura finally started talking, he was well-spoken and seemed to have total recall of the events. He'd been standing in front of the Jockey, he said, for quite a while when he'd spotted Mansur.

"That was his name, huh? Luis Mansur? Told me he was Raul Chiesa, but, hell, who am I to talk, right? Far as I'm concerned, anybody can call themselves anything they want. What's in a name, anyway?"

"A rose by any other. . . ." Arnaldo said.

"What?"

"Ignore him," Silva said. "The rest of us do."

"Hey!" Arnaldo said.

Silva kept his eyes on Moura. "How long were you out there trolling before he picked you up?" he said.

"More than an hour. And I had to piss like a stallion. That's the first thing I did when I got to the motel. Good thing he wasn't one of those guys who gets his jollies from watching girls peeing. I couldn't have stopped him. He was much bigger than me, and the bathroom door was flimsy."

"He still thought you were a woman at this point?"

"Must have."

"Why 'must have'?"

"The way he was talking dirty while we were in the car. It was sorta . . . explicit. And I kept thinking *brother, have I got a surprise for you.*"

"So you went into the bathroom, and. . . ."

"And I was sitting on the toilet when I heard knocking on the door. Not the bathroom door, the door we'd both come in by. I figured it had to be that asshole from the gate, the one who was with you when you picked me up, figured there might be something wrong with the john's credit card or something. Anyway, I'd already flushed and was turning around to wash my hands when I heard him open the door. Not the bathroom door, the one to the room."

"'Him' being your customer?"

"Yeah."

"And then?"

"And then there was a sound."

"What kind of a sound?"

"Hard to describe."

"Try."

"Sort of halfway between a pop and a spit."

Silva took that to be a silenced pistol.

"And then," Moura said, "the john, what's his name again?"

"Mansur."

"Mansur starts to scream, but he doesn't finish it because it's cut off by this other noise."

"What kind of a noise?"

"Like a crunch, but squishier. Maybe like a hard splat."

"What did you do then?"

"I bent over and looked through the keyhole."

"What did you see?"

"Nothing. I couldn't see Mansur, and I couldn't see the person who'd come in. But by that time, I was convinced that someone was beating him."

"Why? Why were you convinced?"

"The sounds. Thwack, thwack, thwack. Like that. They went on and on."

"No voices?"

"The john screamed a couple of times, begged whoever was doing it to stop."

"And before that?"

"He said something when he first opened the door, and the person outside said something back, but I couldn't hear what it was."

"Can you remember Mansur's words?"

"He said, 'What the fuck is it?' or something like that. He wasn't at all polite."

"How about the voice of the person who knocked on the door. Any accent? Any speech defect?"

"I told you. I couldn't hear him."

"What did you do then?"

"I got the hell out of there, that's what! I grabbed my shoes and purse, climbed through the bathroom window, jumped the wall in back, ran down to the road, and hightailed it back to town."

"How? How did you get back to town?"

"Stuck my leg out and my thumb in the air and hitchhiked. The guy who picked me up was interested in a program, but my head was all fucked up by what had happened. I gave him a quick blow job, and he dropped me where I could get a taxi."

"Why didn't you call the police?"

"Me? Call the police? Just because somebody got beat up? Get real."

"When did you find out Mansur was dead?"

"When I got up this afternoon. I saw it on the news."

"And you still elected not to come forward?"

Moura squirmed in his chair.

"No," he said. "You got it all wrong."

"How so?"

"A beating is one thing. Murder? That's like, like *really* serious. I was going to do it. I was going to talk to the cops first thing tomorrow morning."

"Sure you were," Silva said.

"You don't have to take that tone with me, Chief Inspector. I'm not a criminal. You may disapprove of my lifestyle, but what I do isn't illegal, and I'd never, ever hurt anyone."

Moura was indignant, and if he wasn't sincere, he was a damned good actor.

Chapter Thirty-Two

WHEN THE VIDEO DISC arrived from Miami, Gonçalves was at Guarulhos airport waiting for it. It was almost two in the morning by then, but Mainardi and Caetano were there, too, working the midnight to eight shift. By two thirty, they were all huddled in front of a television screen.

"Nope," Mainardi said, after the first group of passengers filed by the camera.

"I backed it up to the previous flight," Gonçalves said. A new group of travelers started passing in review. "This is it. Pay attention."

Half a minute later, Mainardi sat bolt upright in his chair.

Gonçalves reacted by freezing the image.

Caetano put his finger on the screen, pointing out a man with a brown birthmark on his cheek. "Motta," he said.

The image was sharp and clear, ideal for lifting a photo. Gonçalves made a note of the timecode so he could locate it again with ease. "All right," he said, "now let's find the priest."

***

SILVA, ANXIOUS to see the video, got up at six in the morning. By seven, he was at the São Paulo field office, where a yawning Gonçalves was waiting for him.

"You look like you could use some sleep."

"I'll get my second wind any time now," Gonçalves said.

Silva believed it. Gonçalves, he knew, could spend an entire night clubbing and put in a full day thereafter.

"Ah, youth," he said.

"Practice too," Gonçalves said.

Silva rubbed his hands in anticipation. "All right," he said, "let's get to it. Who's first?"

"Motta."

"Play it."

Gonçalves did, freezing the image as he'd done with the Customs agents.

"I had time before you got in," he said, "so I lifted the best frame. No hits on the database."

"Damn. You put it in circulation?"

Gonçalves nodded. "Every border control point, every field office, and every delegacia."

"Good. Who's next?"

"The kid." He unfroze the image. They watched in silence for a while, then: "There. That's him."

"Doesn't look nervous at all," Silva said. "Why did they pick on him?"

"One of them took a dislike to him," Gonçalves said.

"Just that? No good reason at all?"

"No good reason at all."

Silva ran a hand through his hair. "*Canalhas,*" he said. "Where's the priest?"

"Coming up. I didn't bother with the timecodes. All the business-class people boarded together. It's just as fast to let it run."

They went through an eerie parade of the dead: Juan Rivas, Professor Paulo Cruz, Victor Neves, Jonas Palhares, Luis Mansur, and then. . . .

"Clancy," Gonçalves said.

The priest was a handsome man, young, with an open face, dressed entirely in black. A sweater was draped over his shoulders; a small valise was clutched in his right hand.

"You give him the same treatment?" Silva asked.

"Same treatment. The e-mails went out about two hours ago."

"Let's keep our fingers crossed," Silva said.

***

They got lucky.

The first call came in at three minutes past nine and by then Hector was there to take it. The call was from a delegado in Santo André, a satellite town southeast of the capital.

"You one of the guys who's looking for Abilio Sacca?"

"Who?" Hector said.

"You got him tagged as Darcy Motta, but that's wrong. His name is Abilio Sacca. I got a rap sheet on him as long as my arm. Better yet, I got his ass in a cell. All you gotta do is come over here and pick him up."

"Where are you?"

"Got something to write with?"

"Go ahead."

"Avenida Duque de Caxias, 384, in Santo André. It's a gray building. You'll be able to park right in front. Ask for me. In case you didn't get it the first time, the name's Carillo, with two l's. I'm the delegado *titular*."

"With two l's. Got it. I really appreciate the call, Delegado."

"Don't mention it. You have something on him you can make stick? I got enough problems in this district without Abilio Sacca running around loose."

***

Fifteen minutes later another call came in. This one was routed to Gonçalves.

"Agent Gonçalves? Ricardo Vasco speaking. I'm the day manager at the Hotel Gloria. You dropped by a while back—"

"Yes, Senhor Vasco. I remember you."

"The guest you asked about? Dennis Clancy?"

"Yes?"

"He's back. He and his wife just checked in."

"His *wife*? Clancy is a priest!"

"Yes, I know. Distressing, isn't it? I regret to say it happens quite often."

"Tell your people to stay away from the room. Where will I find you?"

"At the reception desk."

"I'll be there as soon as I can."

Gonçalves hung up and dialed Hector's extension. Silva answered.

"Don't go alone," Silva said when Gonçalves finished talking.

"You don't want to be in on the bust?"

"Hector and I have a line on Darcy Motta. We're going to Santo André. Take Arnaldo and bring in the priest."

***

IN THE days when the Avenida Ipiranga was the jewel of São Paulo's thoroughfares, the Hotel Gloria was the jewel of the Avenida Ipiranga.

But those days were long gone.

The lobby still boasted silver-plated chandeliers and faux-Aubusson carpeting, but brass had begun to shine through the silver and the carpeting had worn thin.

The Gloria's restaurant had never managed to find quite the right chef or maitre. It had closed for renovation in the late eighties. More than two decades later, it was still closed, and the renovation was no further along than the sign on the door. Management put up a new one every six months (sooner if someone swiped it), to sustain the illusion of a future reopening.

All the rooms in the Gloria were, with one exception, small. Smaller, certainly, than they should have been in a hotel that charged the prices the Gloria did. The exception was the private suite designed for the owner's personal use. That particular accommodation occupied the entire top floor of the hotel and featured an open-air terrace as big as a parking lot. Their first look at that terrace never failed to engender squeals of delight from the impressionable young ladies the owner had been fond of entertaining there. And that, of course, had been the purpose behind its construction in the first place.

When the owner died in the early seventies, the suite had been taken over by a personality whose real name was Meyer Katz, but whom all of Brazil knew as Bobo.

The television program that made Bobo a household name billed itself as a talent hunt. But in reality, performers were chosen not because they *had* talent, but because they *lacked* it. Bobo, dressed in a clown suit and a stovepipe hat with a flower pinned to it, would receive them with great fanfare and give them a big buildup. Then they'd sing, or dance, or tell jokes, or do whatever they thought they could do well—and generally did very badly—until the studio audience would begin to groan and boo. At that point Bobo, feigning surprise and disappointment, would squeeze the rubber bulb on his horn. Honk. Honk. Honk. And the unfortunate performers would be forcibly removed from the stage with a long hook resembling a shepherd's crook. The mere sight of that crook creeping in from offstage was enough to throw the five hundred people in the studio audience, and millions more watching throughout the country, into paroxysms of laughter.

Add to the formula the occasional performer who introduced an element of surprise by demonstrating true talent, add seven scantily clad women who danced to canned music, and you had a recipe that made Bobo a household name for a generation.

And things might have gone on for still another generation if fate hadn't cancelled Bobo's act. One night, returning from dinner with one of the more lissome of his dancers, Brazil's most famous clown had had a fatal heart attack. He collapsed and expired right there in the Gloria's lobby.

This lent cachet to the hotel where he'd lived and died. Many were the tourists who wanted to spend a night in the same place Bobo had spent *his* nights. And many were the tourists who wanted to see the spot where he'd breathed his last.

The widow of the Gloria's original builder, the woman who'd become the hotel's sole proprietress, recognized that Bobo's fading fame wouldn't sustain the place forever. But at the moment it still did.

And thus it was that the Hotel Gloria went on, providing small, relatively clean, overpriced rooms at an occupancy rate that sometimes exceeded eighty percent.

***

THE TWO cops followed each other through the revolving doors, skirted the easel with the black-bordered photo of Bobo, and headed for the hotel's reception desk.

Ricardo Vasco, as promised, was there to meet them. He was a white-haired gentleman in his mid-sixties, somber and thin. Gonçalves introduced Arnaldo. Arnaldo took the lead.

"We appreciate your call, Senhor Vasco."

"I'm pleased to be of service. You don't intend to take Senhor Clancy and his wife out of here in handcuffs, do you?"

"Hopefully not."

Vasco looked relieved. "I'm glad to hear it. It wouldn't be a scene we'd relish. Such things have a way of upsetting the guests."

"You sound like it's happened before."

Vasco smiled a sad smile. "The Gloria has been here a long time. For that matter, so have I."

"Where's our man?"

"Sixth floor. Room 666."

"Six sixty-six," Gonçalves said. "But that—"

"Is the number of the beast," Vasco said. "Yes, I've heard that one before. Silly, isn't it?"

But Gonçalves didn't think it was silly at all. He was already turning pale.

Chapter Thirty-Three

ABILIO SACCA'S CRIMINAL HISTORY was such that it
would have caused even the most dedicated of social workers
to throw up her hands in defeat.

Still only forty-two, Sacca had a criminal record going
back thirty-three years, more than two thirds of them spent
behind bars. First arrest: age nine. Shoplifting. Charges dis-
missed. First conviction: age eleven. Armed robbery. It was
Sacca's debut in that particular specialty—and his last performance in it.

He'd the misfortune to choose a plainclotheswoman for
his victim. When she'd drawn her gun, the woman reported,
the kid had dropped the shard of broken glass he'd been
threatening her with and started to cry.

Since he either didn't know, or wouldn't admit to, the
whereabouts of his parents, Abilio was committed to the
FEBEM, a reform school where no reform ever took place.
The judge gave him five years, partly to get him off the
streets, partly in the hope he'd get an education. The judg-
ment was successful on both counts. It kept him away from
honest citizens, and it taught him a great deal about breaking
the law.

It was true that he'd never become a *successful* criminal, but
that stemmed from Abilio's own shortcomings and had nothing to do with the excellent instruction he'd received from his
fellow delinquents. He was a pathetically bad liar, and he *liked*
people, commendable attributes in an honest citizen but two
major drawbacks for a criminal. He was, furthermore, a

practicing alcoholic. Of all things in life, he was most fond of getting drunk with a few convivial companions.

São Paulo's underworld being what it was, it stood to reason that not all of those convivial companions had Abilio's best interests at heart. Sometimes they were police informers; sometimes, even, cops. That had led to a number of charges, some proven, some not, but Abilio never seemed to learn. Within a week of being released, he would be back in one bar or another, shooting his mouth off all over again.

Abilio's most recent arrest hadn't stemmed from indiscretion, but it had been monumentally stupid all the same. His objective had been a jewelry store, and jewelry stores, because of their alarm systems, were invariably hard targets. A wiser crook would have picked something easier, or would have planned better. A wiser crook wouldn't have undertaken the enterprise dead drunk. And a wiser crook certainly wouldn't have chosen a shop where the owner lived upstairs and was known to possess a firearm.

Sacca's record contained another indication that he wasn't among the brightest: other than the time he'd spent at the cost of the state, Sacca had never lived anywhere except in Santo André. He was, by now, one of the "usual suspects," one of the first people the cops would look for whenever a burglary was committed.

Burglary. Burglary. Burglary. As Silva scanned Sacca's record the word kept repeating itself. No murders, no assaults, nothing but burglaries.

And that, Silva thought, was inconsistent with the personality of a murderer. Sacca may not have been good at what he did, but it *was* a specialty. And that specialty was nonviolent. After his single youthful indiscretion Sacca had never again been accused, or suspected, of threatening someone's life, much less of taking it.

Silva studied Sacca's most recent likeness, the booking photo from the jewelry-store affair. It revealed some things the video hadn't. Sacca had large brown eyes and rather delicate features. Despite the stain on his cheek, he was a type who would have attracted sexual attention from his fellow prisoners, particularly when he was a younger man. That fact, and a further perusal of Sacca's sins, strengthened Silva in his conviction that they hadn't yet found their killer. If Sacca had had a violent turn, he would have fought to protect himself from rape. There would have been a record of fights, maybe even stabbings, in the time he was behind bars. But there was nothing of that nature. On the contrary, the man had, again and again, been given time off for good behavior.

Of course, it was remotely possible that no one who'd shared prison with him had found Abilio attractive. More likely, Silva thought, he'd had one powerful lover or had been, in the parlance of prisoners, "everybody's punk." A man who'd put up with that and not fight back did not seem like a person capable of doling out the hideous damage done to any of the current victims.

Before they even spoke, Silva had a strong conviction that Abilio Sacca was not his man. That conviction was strengthened when he actually had Sacca seated in front of him.

Sacca's eyes were reminiscent of a fawn's, without a sign of even moderate intellect behind them. And he had a tic, an irregular spasm of the muscles around his right eye.

Silva found it disturbing, so disturbing that he was having trouble giving Sacca the fish-eyed stare he reserved for felons.

"Your eye always do that?" he asked, confronting the distraction head-on.

"Nah. I only get it sometimes," Sacca said.

"Like when?"

"Like when I'm nervous, that's when. What's this all about? Why are the Federal Police interested in me?"

"Come on, Sacca. You know the drill. You don't ask the questions, we do."

"Yeah, yeah, okay."

"I want to know if you were on TAB flight number 8101 from Miami to São Paulo, the one that arrived on the morning of the twenty-third of November."

Tic.

"No."

"I think you were."

"You can think what you want. Go ahead. Check the passenger list. You're not gonna find me."

"Not as Abilio Sacca, no."

Tic. Tic.

"What are you talking about?"

"Ever hear of a guy called Darcy Motta?"

"Never."

"Uh-huh. You should ask a doctor to check out that tic."

"I already did. He says it doesn't mean anything."

"You ever play poker, Sacca?"

"No."

"Let me give you a word of advice: don't."

"What's that supposed to mean?"

"Bluffing isn't one of your strengths."

"I'm not bluffing. You got the wrong guy. Somebody makes a couple of mistakes in his life and you never let him forget it. You know what this is? This is police harassment, that's what."

"We've got a DVD."

"You've got a what?"

"We have a video recording of you boarding the flight in Miami."

Sacca put a hand over his right eye in an attempt to still the tic and stared balefully at Silva out of his left.

"Not true," he said.

"The God's honest truth," Silva said.

Chapter Thirty-Four

ONE OF THE MOST traumatic events in Haraldo Gonçalves's life took place in the living room of his parents' home. Haraldo had been three weeks short of his eleventh birthday. It was the final game of the World Cup, the decisive game of the tournament.

Twenty-three minutes into the first half, with the score at nil all, Argentina's principal striker fired off a shot that narrowly cleared the top of the goal. Five centimeters lower, and Brazil's hated rivals would have scored. Young Haraldo, in his excitement, wet himself.

The last thing Haraldo wanted was to be saddled with a derisive nickname like Pisspants. Hurrying to his room, he slipped into clean underwear, changed his jeans, and, without giving it a second thought, grabbed a team shirt with the logo and colors of Corinthians. Then he raced back to the living room, clutching the fatal jersey in his hands.

He'd no sooner slipped it over his head when an Argentinean shot struck home. It was the only goal of the game.

There is an expression in Brazilian Portuguese, *vestir a camisa*, literally *to wear the shirt*, but also signifying support for any movement, group, company, or philosophy.

Corinthians was having a spectacularly bad year. To wear their shirt signified supporting a loser. By the final whistle, Haraldo's family, and their invited friends, had reached general agreement: young Haraldo had transferred Corinthians' bad joss to the Brazilian National Team. He was a *pé frio*, a

Jonah, a bringer of bad luck. He, personally, had brought on the disaster. That they believed this was bad enough. Worse was that Haraldo came to believe it himself. He took upon his young shoulders the heavy responsibility for Brazil's defeat.

Years later, Haraldo had tried to explain the sequence of events and consequences to a Chilean girlfriend. When he'd finished talking, she told him his family was crazy. And when he demurred, she told him *he* was crazy.

None of them were, but all of them were Brazilian. And Brazilians are superstitious. On New Year's Eve, they dress in white, light candles, and toss flowers, perfume, and even jewelry into the sea to propitiate Iemanjá, the *orixa* of the waters. Any other comportment on that night is, according to common belief, sure to bring ill luck in the year to come.

In Brazil, *Mães-de-Santo* read the future with cowries. Chickens are sacrificed on a regular basis. Offerings of cachaça and cigars can be found along rural roads and near waterfalls, mostly surrounded by the stubs of burned-out candles. There is no Brazilian who has not, at one time or another, wrapped a *fita do Senhor do Bonfim* around his wrist or ankle and tied three knots in it while making his three wishes.

Haraldo's family members were no more spiritually inclined than any of their neighbors, but certainly no less. By the time that year's Cup had rolled around, their *Candomblé* priests and priestesses had been busy for weeks. Blessings, hexes, sacrifices, prayers, all had been performed. And then Haraldo had undone the lot by slipping into that cursed jersey.

His mother didn't speak to him for two days, his father for a week, his sister for almost two months.

Now, almost a quarter century on, the superstitious child had become a superstitious man, the most superstitious man any of his colleagues had ever met. Gonçalves didn't walk under ladders. He would go around the block to avoid crossing the path of a black cat. His heart skipped a beat at the spilling of salt. He avoided unlucky numbers like the plague. It was, therefore, with great trepidation, and a drawn Glock, that Haraldo Gonçalves approached the door of room 666 in the Hotel Gloria. Something awful was behind that door, Gonçalves knew it. He'd taken his gun out of its holster even before he'd left the elevator.

"It's that superstition crap all over again, isn't it?" Arnaldo said. "You want to scare some innocent citizen half to death? Put that thing away."

"Innocent, hell. Clancy's in there with a woman."

"So what? No law against that."

"He's a priest, for God's sake! He's a priest and he's in there with a woman."

"Maybe he's just taking her confession."

"Oh, sure, right."

The elevator came to a stop, they got out, and the door closed behind them. There were signs on the wall. Room 666 was to the left. Arnaldo muttered something and started walking.

"What?" Gonçalves said, hurrying to catch up. "What did you say?"

Arnaldo stopped in front of 666, put a finger to his lips and knocked.

"Yes? Who's there?"

If Something Awful was behind the door, it had a sweet voice and an American accent.

"Federal Police," Arnaldo said.

"What do you want?" The woman sounded confused, not frightened.

"Open up," Arnaldo said, "and we'll tell you."

"Please show me some identification first," she said. "Hold it up where I can see it."

Polite. But firm.

Arnaldo fished for his wallet, held his ID in front of the tiny aperture in the door.

There was a short pause, then the rattle of a chain. The door opened, first a crack, then wider. The woman who came into view flinched at the sight of Gonçalves's Glock.

And what a woman she was. She had long blond hair, high cheekbones, and a perfect complexion. The areas around her blue eyes and full lips bore no makeup at all. She didn't need it.

"Senhora Clancy?"

"Yes."

"Your . . . husband. Dennis Clancy. Where is he?"

A voice behind her said, in English, "Someone looking for Dennis Clancy?"

"Yes, dear, they are," the blond responded in the same language. "They say they're federal policemen."

"I'm Dennis Clancy," the man said, stepping into the doorway. "You speak English?"

"Badly," Arnaldo said. It wasn't true. He spoke English quite well.

"Splendid," Clancy said, willing to accept badly as quite good enough. "So Petra won't have to translate. Come in, won't you?"

The room was small, the wallpaper faded, the carpet thin and stained. Chipped Formica tables flanked the double bed. A coffee machine stood on the chest of drawers, a television hung from a rack bolted to the ceiling, an armchair graced a corner. The only other piece of furniture, a writing desk, was butted up against a grimy window that overlooked an air shaft. Six sixty-six wasn't one of the Gloria's best rooms.

Dennis Clancy closed the door and directed the federal cops to the chairs. Gonçalves took the one at the writing desk. Clancy and the woman sat side by side on the bed. He took her hand in his.

"The coffee is quite dreadful," he said, "otherwise I'd offer you some. You already know our names. What are yours?"

"I'm Agent Nunes. This is Agent Gonçalves."

"Good. What can I do for you?"

"You can answer some questions. Did you arrive in this country on the morning of the twenty-third of November?"

"I did."

"On TAB 8101 from Miami?"

"Yes. But my visa is perfectly in order, and I haven't—"

"Just answer the questions, please. Why did you come to Brazil, Father Clancy?"

"Just Mister Clancy, or Dennis, if you prefer. We've elected to leave the church."

"*We?* Wait a minute. Are you telling me she's a nun?"

"He's telling you," she said, "that I *was* a nun. Sister Clare. Before and after that, I was Petra Walder. Now I'm Petra Clancy."

"You're married?"

"We're married," she said.

* * *

"*MERDA*," ABILIO Sacca said.

"Indeed," Silva said, "and you're in it up to your neck. Come on. Start talking."

"I got nothing to say."

"Yes, you do. Want me to tell you why?"

"Okay. I'll play along. Why?"

"Because we're investigating multiple murders, all performed by the same person."

"Not me. I never killed anybody in my whole life."

"With only two exceptions, the people who were travel-ling with you in that business-class cabin are either dead or they've been cleared."

"And one of those two exceptions did the killing? Is that what you're saying?"

"It's a distinct possibility."

"It was the other guy."

"With you people," Hector said, "it's always the other guy."

"And, in this case," Silva said, "the other guy is a Catholic priest."

"So what? Priests can kill people."

"They can. And maybe he did. But if I can't pin the mur-ders on him, I'll pin them on you."

Tic. Tic. Tic.

"Wait. Wait. Wait. You're saying you're gonna pin 'em on me even if I didn't do 'em?"

"Correct."

The Brazilian civil police framed people like Sacca all the time. Sacca knew this, and Silva knew he knew it.

"You got no call to do something like that," Sacca said. "I never done nothing to you!"

Silva shook his head, as if in regret.

"Sorry, Sacca," he said. "One of the murder victims was the son of the foreign minister of Venezuela. The president wants results. The minister of justice is on my boss's back. You see the bind I'm in. I've got to deliver."

"And you deliver by framing me?"

"Or the priest. Makes no difference to me, except I figure you'll be easier."

Tic. Tic. Tic.

Within Sacca's world, what Silva was saying made perfect sense. The little burglar rubbed a hand over his face.

"Maybe we can work something out," he said. "What is it you wanna know?"

"There was a boy in the compartment, traveling alone. Remember him?"

"Yeah, I remember him. I remember everybody. I got a good memory for faces."

"You were searched when you were going through Customs, right?"

"Right," Sacca said, cautiously, a wary look in his eyes.

"They didn't find anything on you," Silva said.

"Right again. So, what are you—"

"But they found something on the kid."

"I don't know anything about that."

"Ecstasy pills. *Your* Ecstasy pills. You were smuggling them in from the States."

"No, I—"

"You got up in the middle of the night, took those pills out of your hand luggage, and slipped them into his. The kid was busted with your pills. They took him away and put him in a cell with hardened criminals. An hour or two later, he was sent to a communal shower."

"Why are you—"

"Shut up and listen. Someone tried to rape him. He wouldn't have it. They killed him and raped him anyway. He was fifteen years old."

Sacca shrugged. "You know what the kid should have done? He should have just let them do it. I mean, he'd be alive today if he had, right? Sometimes you just gotta—"

"You framed him, didn't you?"

Abilio Sacca opened his mouth, closed it, and opened it again. At that moment, he reminded Silva of a ventriloquist's dummy.

"I didn't frame him," he finally said. "It wasn't like that at all."

"No? How was it, then?"

"I want to see a lawyer. I'm not saying another word until I see a lawyer."

"No deal," Silva said.

"What do you mean, no deal? I got a right to a lawyer. I don't have to talk to you guys."

"Thing is," Silva said, "I'm under a lot of pressure here."

"And what the fuck do you think you're putting *me* under?"

Silva couldn't count the tics any more, they were coming that fast. "Ah. But that's different," he said. "You're a convicted felon. I'm a cop."

"Jesus Christ."

"Talk. I need answers now, right now. I can't wait. And if you don't give me those answers, I'm gonna pin those murders on you."

Beads of perspiration broke out on Sacca's brow. "Look, how about we do this? How about you turn off that camera up there in the corner—"

"It's not on."

"You expect me to believe that?"

"Do you have a choice?"

"Give me your word."

"What?"

"Your word. Give me your word it's not on."

"You have my word. It's not. But, if it would make you more comfortable, how about we have this conversation somewhere else: out in the yard, for example?"

"Good idea. Now, I want your agreement on the rest. Then I talk."

"What rest?"

"I don't sign anything. I just tell you. You get me a lawyer, a good one, and you don't tell him shit about the conversation we're about to have. And you don't testify about it either. Not you, not this guy here." He pointed at Hector.

"All right."

"All right? Just like that? All right?"

"We've got bigger fish to fry, Sacca. You play ball with us, we'll play ball with you."

"I'm still not sure I can trust you."

"You're going to be happily surprised. Let's go outside."

* * *

CLANCY'S THREE brothers had opted for the secular life, but his parents, religious people to the core, had always dreamed of having a son who'd embrace the priesthood. They worked hard to steer him away from his sweetheart, Petra, and toward the Church.

"I wanted to please them," he said. "I managed to convince myself that there was something romantic about giving up the love of a woman to serve God. I began to see myself as a kind of hero, sacrificing his own happiness for a greater good."

Petra looked down at his hand and squeezed it. "When he first started talking about becoming a priest," she said, "I thought he'd get over it."

"What she *really* did," Clancy said, "was refuse to believe it."

She smiled at him and then at Arnaldo. "He's right," she said. "And I kept refusing until the day he entered the seminary. It wasn't far from my home. I hid behind a telephone pole and watched when his parents brought him to the front door. Then I hugged the wood, trying to make believe I was hugging him. I hugged it so hard that, when I got home, I found splinters in my cheek. I locked myself in my room, and I cried for hours and hours. I wasn't interested in other men.

The prospect of spending my life alone frightened me. I decided to join a religious order."

"A convent?" Gonçalves asked.

She raised her eyebrows. "Goodness, no," she said. "That wouldn't have suited me at all. I joined a small order. We help refugees in London, street kids in Nairobi, migrant workers in Florida. Here, in Brazil, I work—worked—with the rural poor."

"Meanwhile," Clancy said, "I was ordained. I'm not cut out to run a parish. I was doing social work. One day, I ran into Petra's sister, Heidi, on the street."

"She wrote me afterwards," Petra said, "told me what he was doing, gave me his address. By then, I was in this little town up north, São Bento. I doubt you've heard of it."

Arnaldo shook his head.

"No," Gonçalves said. "I never have."

"It's in Tocantins, near Miracema. Dennis and I began a regular correspondence. His work. My work. Nothing that you might call really *personal*."

"Not in the beginning," he said.

"In one letter," she said, "I referred to what we'd shared as 'puppy love.'"

"But I didn't think so," he said, "I thought it was much deeper, much more profound than that. And, in my next letter, I shared the thought with Petra. It was the hardest thing I ever wrote."

"And when I read it, I started crying again."

"The situation was driving me crazy," he said. "Most people go to psychiatrists when that happens, but I was a priest. I went to another priest."

"Damon O'Reilly," she said. "We'd known him all our lives."

"Damon died in Boston a month ago," he said. "Otherwise,

I wouldn't tell you this: there was a girl, in Ireland, when he was young. They exchanged a kiss. One kiss, and in more than sixty years, he told me, a month hadn't gone by when he hadn't thought of that girl at least once. He'd learned to live with it, he said, but if he had his life to live over again, he wasn't sure he'd do the same. He told me to come down here and talk to Petra, get it out of my system one way or another. One way or another, he said, but I think he knew what was going to happen. I wrote her straightaway."

"And I," she said, "told him not to come. I didn't think I could stand losing him twice."

"Damon," Clancy said, "was diagnosed with terminal cancer. He spent his last days in a hospital. I went to visit him, morning and night. Toward the end, he pushed himself up on his elbows and asked me what the hell I was doing there. He wanted to know why I wasn't in Brazil."

"Delirious?"

"Not at all. Sharp as a tack. Right up to the very end. I told him she wouldn't have me. He said he'd only kissed a girl once in his life, but he knew more about women than I did. He told me to go catch a plane."

"And you did?" Arnaldo said.

"Not until he died. He was the kindest man I ever knew. I wanted to be there for him at the end. I performed his last rites, and left for Brazil on the evening of his funeral."

"We traced you," Arnaldo said, "as far as Miracema. Then you dropped off the map."

"There are no hotels in São Bento," Clancy said. "It's a tiny place, a church, a few shops, no hotel. No airport, either, and no train, but there's a bus from Miracema. Petra fixed it so I could stay with a family."

"He showed up on my doorstep," Petra said.

They smiled at each other.

"There were classes to teach," she said, "and they had to find someone to replace me. I didn't want to scandalize my Sisters any more than I already had. We took care not to be alone together, not until we left."

"We got married in Palmas," Clancy said. "I called my mother to tell her. She hung up on me. Petra's family has been more understanding. They're supporting what we've done. Tomorrow we're going to leave for Boston and try to put things right with my folks."

"And then?"

"And then, Agente Gonçalves, we're going to have three kids."

"Four," Petra said. "And now, officers, you've heard our story. We'd like to hear yours. Why are you here?"

Chapter Thirty-Five

THERE WAS A WOODEN picnic table in the courtyard. Hector and Silva sat on one side, Sacca on the other. The federal cops asked to be left alone with the prisoner.

"It was like this," Sacca said when the guard was gone. "I'm in a bar in Freguesia. You know Freguesia?"

Freguesia do Ó, once a hilltop village, had long since been absorbed by its expanding neighbor. These days, it was simply one of São Paulo's many neighborhoods, with little to distinguish it except for the old central square with its church and cemetery.

"I know it," Silva said.

"So I'm up there," Sacca said, "in this bar, and a guy I know comes to me with a proposition."

"What guy?" Silva said.

"You don't have to know that, do you?"

"Maybe not. What was the proposition?"

"Carry a package to Miami."

"What was in the package?" Silva said.

"I got no idea. It was none of my business."

"None of your business?"

"Look, he doesn't tell, and I don't ask, okay? He's like, you want to do this? And I'm like, how much? And he's like, ten thousand dollars, American."

"Guy wants to give you ten thousand dollars to take a package to Miami, and you think it's on the up-and-up?"

"I never said that. I'm not stupid. I just said I didn't know what was in there."

"Uh-huh. So then?"

"So I tell him I've never been out of the country, and I don't have a passport, and, with my record, there isn't much chance of me getting one. And he says no problem. He's gonna get me a passport, and he's gonna furnish the ticket, and I'm even gonna travel business class. He'll pay me half of the ten grand before I leave. The person I deliver it to in Miami will pay the other half."

"All right. So you agreed, and. . . ."

"And he tells me to be ready to leave on Friday, meet him in the same place at seven o'clock, and bring a suitcase with what I need for a couple of nights in Miami."

"And you did."

Sacca nodded. "And I did. And he gives me the package, and a ticket, and a reservation for a hotel, and a passport."

"And the passport was in the name of Darcy Motta?"

"Yeah. And the photo in it was from one of my mug shots. But the background was different, and they took out the sign they make you hold on your chest."

"You think this guy is a cop?"

Sacca shrugged. "How else would he get one of my mug shots?" he said.

"And the passport? It got you into the States with no trouble?"

"Uh-huh. There was a visa in it and all, good for five years with multiple entries, if you can believe that. Multiple entries means—"

"I know what it means. If you don't overstay your welcome, you can keep going back and forth. Go on with the story."

"Yeah, okay. Well, it must have been a real visa because it had one of those holo . . . holo. . . ."

"Holograms?"

"Yeah, one of them on it."

"Where did you deliver the package?"

"He gave me an address. It was typed out on a piece of paper, and he told me I'd better not lose either the address or the package, because if I did, he'd cut my balls off. 'Just show it to a taxi driver,' he says. 'It's a bar,' he says. 'Get there at ten the day after tomorrow. Take the package with you. Leave it out on the bar where people can see it, and have a drink. Somebody will contact you.'"

"And somebody did?"

"A woman. An ugly skank, name of Maria."

"Maria what?"

"There you go again," Sacca said, showing peevishness for the first time. "Don't you get it? You do this kind of stuff, you don't ask people to tell you things like that. And even if you did, they'd lie. Maria, just Maria, okay?"

"Okay. Blond? Brunette? Redhead?"

"Blond. But not really. Her eyebrows were dark."

"What else can you remember about her?"

"She was old enough to be my mother. And she had rough hands, I mean really rough, with calluses and all, probably worked as a maid somewhere."

"Hang on. You're in a bar, right? It was ten at night. It was dark. And you notice her hands."

"Hell, yes, I noticed her hands. I didn't look at them; I *felt* them. She wanted to shake on the deal."

"What deal?"

"I'm getting to that," Sacca said.

Sacca asked for a cigarette and got one. Then he asked for a Guaraná, and Hector went inside to get one from the guards' canteen. By the time Sacca had finished drinking it, he was back into single tics.

"You're gonna get me a lawyer, right?"

"I'm going to get you a lawyer," Silva said. "I promised, didn't I?"

"Cops don't always keep their promises."

"This cop does," Silva said. "Keep talking."

"All right, all right, keep your shirt on. So this Maria coughed up the money, the other five grand. Then she asks me if I want to earn more. Sure, I say. How? So she spells it out. It's Ecstasy. You know Ecstasy? It's that pill kids take when they go to—"

"I know what Ecstasy is," Silva said. "Go on."

"This Ecstasy stuff, she tells me, used to come from Holland, mostly. But now, with a lot of kids there in the States into it, she knows a Dutchman who makes it right there in Miami. And there's another guy in São Paulo who will buy everything she can send him. That's where I come in."

"She wants you to carry Ecstasy from Miami to São Paulo?"

"Yeah. But there's a catch. She's not about to put the stuff in my hands and just let me walk away with it. What's to prevent me from stealing it, right?"

"Right. So what did she suggest?"

"This: I buy the stuff from her. She can get it really cheap, and she's already got the guy lined up to buy it. She marks it up fifty percent to me, I mark it up fifty percent to the guy in São Paulo, he marks it up a hundred percent to the kids who distribute it in the clubs, and *they* mark it up god knows how much. Everybody wins."

"Except the kids who consume it," Silva said.

"Hey, nobody's standing with a gun to their heads. It's a free country, right? They want to take the stuff, it's their decision."

"Finish the story."

"I'm getting there. So she makes the proposition, and there are two problems with it."

"She might be lying about the numbers, and she might give you sugar pills instead of the real stuff."

Sacca looked at Silva with something approaching admiration.

"Right. Exactly right. Although, to tell you the truth, I didn't come up with those problems on my own. While I'm sitting there, turning the deal over in my head, she does it herself. And then she gives me the solutions. She tells me to call somebody in São Paulo, anybody I want, and check on the street value of the stuff. That'll prove she's not lying about the numbers. She even offers to pay for the call."

"And to make sure she was selling you the real stuff? How were you going to convince yourself of that?"

"By trying it. She says she'll meet me at the airport, says I can put my hand in the cookie jar, pick out any pill I want, and pop it. If it works, odds are the other pills are gonna work too. And I don't hand over the money until I taste the goods."

"It didn't worry you that you were only going to try *one* pill, that she might have mixed some duds along with the real article?"

"I thought about it. But then I thought why should she? That's like killing the chicken with the gold eggs. She's talking about a long-term relationship here and, by this time, she knows I'm fixed up with a phony passport that will take me through customs like shit through a snake."

"And how does she know that?"

"Because I told her, okay? She's selling the deal to me, and I'm selling *me* to her. I'm interested, see? If it all checks out, I can make easy money."

"So you did what she suggested? Called São Paulo? Got a fix on the street price?"

"I did. And it was just like she said. And I got to the

airport early and met her. Early, so the pill I was gonna pop would have time to work before I paid her the money."

"And?"

"And she's got the pills."

"Which are in containers labeled as vitamins?"

"Yeah, that's right, labeled as vitamins. I choose one of those containers, break the seal, mix around with my finger, and choose a pill."

"And?"

"And I popped it."

"Right there in the airport?"

"Right there in the airport. Anybody who sees me, they think I'm popping a vitamin, right? It was cool. I never had Ecstasy before. I had my MP3 player with me, and I can see why the kids—"

"Get on with it."

"Okay. So I paid her."

"How much?"

"A thousand dollars. Not much, but then there weren't that many pills either. It was gonna be a trial run for both of us."

"And then?"

"And then she takes back the container I opened, pours the pills into a plastic bag and fills the empty container with some other pills from another bag. 'What are those?' I say. 'Vitamins,' she says, 'just an extra precaution. If the Customs guys want a closer look, they'll stop here instead of opening the two that are sealed.'"

"All right. What happened next?"

"I went through security, which gives me no trouble at all, and I took a seat in the departure lounge. That's when I saw the cop."

"Cop? What cop?"

"This detective, from Santo André, named Georgio Parente. I didn't notice him at first because I've got the buds from my MP3 player in my ears, listening to Chitãozinho and Xororó and grooving on the music. But then I look up and there's Parente with some lardass, who must be his wife, and a couple of kids almost as fat as she is. The kids are wearing hats with ears. I practically fell off my chair."

"Hats with ears?"

"Mickey Mouse ears. I figure Parente took the family to Disney. I put my hand over my face and sink down in my seat like I'm sleeping. Every now and then, I look through my fingers. Parente's kids are running around yelling and stepping on people's toes. The other passengers don't like it a bit. They're whispering to each other and shooting nasty looks at lardass, who's got her nose in a magazine and isn't doing a damn thing to stop it. But Parente is, and he's got his hands full, so he doesn't notice me."

"What makes you think he would have recognized you?"

"He's busted me three times. The last time wasn't six months ago."

"All right. What did you do then?"

"I sat right where I was until they called the flight. By this time, I'm thirsty as hell. That's another thing that Ecstasy stuff does to you: it makes you thirsty. I'm still buzzed, but I can't groove on the music because I'm worried about Parente. They call the first-class passengers. They board. Then they call business class. I get up, keep my back to him, and line up. On my way to my seat, I grab a newspaper off the rack. The paper's in English, and I can't read a word of it, but I buckle up and hold it in front of my face until we take off. He musta walked right by me on his way to economy."

Silva had an intimation of what was coming. "You were afraid of running into him during disembarkation?"

"Goddamned right I was. My tic was acting up like you wouldn't believe. He woulda taken one look at me and known something was up. If he'd asked to see my passport, I woulda been fried. Then they woulda gone through my baggage for sure."

"So," Silva said, "you decided to get rid of the evidence."

"Wouldn't you? It was the last thing I wanted to do. Those damned pills cost me a grand. But I figured it was either lose them or go down."

"So you waited until the middle of the night. You opened the compartment over your seat and took the pills out of your hand luggage. And then what?"

"I was gonna flush them down the toilet. But then, I got to thinking. What if I'd been wrong? What if it wasn't Parente? What if it was just a guy who looked like Parente? And even if it *was* Parente, what if I could get off the airplane and through Customs without him spotting me? Wouldn't it be stupid to throw all that money away for nothing?"

"So you took the Ecstasy and put it into Julio Arriaga's hand luggage."

"Was that the kid's name? Julio Arriaga?"

"That was his name. What did you plan to do if he got through Customs without a hitch?"

"I had this story all ready. About how I had my hand luggage in the same compartment as his, that I was looking for something there in the dark, that maybe my stuff got into his bag by mistake."

"Pretty thin. You think he was going to believe that?"

Sacca shrugged. "Maybe," he said. "And if he didn't, I was gonna take the stuff from him anyway. He was only a kid, not a very big kid either. He couldn't give me any trouble even if he'd wanted to."

"Didn't it occur to you that a kid that age was probably going to have someone waiting for him at the airport? Someone older, more experienced, liable to be suspicious of your story?"

"Yeah, it did. And it mighta been his father, and his father mighta been built like a gorilla, but I couldn't think of a better idea. Doing it that way, I had a *chance* of getting my stuff back. If I'd flushed it down the toilet, it would have been gone for good. What would *you* have done, huh?"

Sacca was looking at Silva as if he actually expected an answer to the question.

"One more thing," Silva said. "Tell me about the run-in with Mansur."

"Who?"

"Did you have any trouble with a man on the airplane?"

"Oh. That. Was that his name? Mansur."

"That was his name."

"Yeah. Well, he musta told you about it, right?"

"He didn't tell us a damned thing. He couldn't. He's dead."

"Good riddance, the prick."

"What happened?"

"He saw me stuffing the kid's bag. He was across the aisle, acting like he was asleep, but he wasn't. He saw the whole damned thing, and he heard me lie to the stewardess."

"And then?"

"He waits until the stewardess buggers off, and he comes and sits down beside me."

"And he blackmailed you?"

"He did."

"How much did you give him?"

"Everything I had, over three thousand dollars and almost a thousand reais. The prick."

Chapter Thirty-Six

ON THEIR WAY BACK to Hector's office, Silva posed a question.

"If you discovered," he said, "that it was Sacca who planted the stuff on your kid, and that Sacca was in a cell in Santo André, what would you do?"

"I don't know what *I'd* do," Hector said. "But I think I know what the kid's father would do."

"And that is?"

"Based on everything we know up to now. . . ."

"Yes?"

"And acting under the assumption that it's him, not Clancy, who's our man. . . ."

"Yes?"

"I think Julio Arriaga would try to get inside Sacca's cell and kill him."

"I agree. And we certainly don't want to have *that* happen, now, do we?"

"So *that's* why you agreed to get him a lawyer? So we can get him out of there, set him up someplace—and use him for bait?"

"Precisely."

"What if Arriaga doesn't come for him?"

"Then I'm barking up the wrong tree."

"How are we going to get the word out?"

"You're going to tell his ex-wife."

"You've thought this out, haven't you?"

"I have."

Hector stroked his chin. "I *did* promise Aline Arriaga I'd call her if I found out who framed her son."

"Yes," Silva said, "so you told me."

"When do I do it?"

"No time like the present."

"While he's still in Santo André?"

"Why not? But first, call that delegado, Carillo, and tell him that no one, *no one*, except Sacca's lawyer gets in to see him."

"Where do we get the lawyer?"

"I'll talk to Zanon."

"The public prosecutor?"

"Yes. He's as straight as they come, and he won't like it one bit, but he owes me, and he'll do it. When Sacca walks out the door we'll have people waiting."

"At which time I call Aline again and tell her he's on the street."

"Exactly. But this Arriaga character, if he is indeed our man, has already proven to be very resourceful. We mustn't underestimate him. Assign a man to cover the exterior of the jail, more than one if there are multiple exits. Provide photos of Arriaga and Sacca. As an additional precaution, put an undercover operative into Sacca's cell and tell him to stick to Sacca like glue, never more than a meter or so away. Make it a man adept at hand-to-hand fighting. Tell Carillo what we're up to and tell him, too, that our operative is to be the last person introduced into that cell, the *very last* person introduced into that cell until we get Sacca out of there. And tell him to keep the whole undercover business under his hat."

* * *

"I KNEW it!" Aline Arriaga said when Hector called her. "I knew my Junior was innocent! What did you say that bastard's name was?"

"Sacca. Abilio Sacca."

Her next words came right out of Silva's script.

"I want to see him," she said. "Where is he?"

"He's in a jail in Santo André." Hector gave her the address. "I have to warn you, though. They won't let you in unless he wants to see you, and he probably won't. It's his right to refuse."

"His right? A man like that has *rights*? How about my son's rights? He had a right to be locked up with other kids. He had a right to *live*. And who showed any concern for *him*?"

"I'm sorry, Senhora Arriaga. I know you—"

"Did this Sacca show any remorse? Any remorse at all? Did he even say he was sorry?"

"He's not that kind of man."

"When he gets out of that delegacia, where will he be going?"

"Perhaps to prison."

"*Perhaps?* Only perhaps?"

"These things are unpredictable, Senhora."

"You're certainly right about that, Delegado. If I've learned anything about our judicial system in the last three months, it's that it doesn't work. Will you do one more thing for me? Just one?"

"What's that, Senhora?"

"Keep me informed of this man's whereabouts. I'm not going to get a good night's sleep until I meet with him, face to face."

***

ALTHOUGH ZANON Parma was a friend of many years' standing, his pleasure in receiving a call from Silva quickly vanished when he heard what it was about.

"For Christ's sake, Mario, I can't just pull the guy out of there for no reason at all."

"I'm sure you'll find a way, Zanon. It's vitally important that you do."

Silence.

"Zanon?"

"Okay, okay, I'll find a way, but Jesus, Mario—"

"Just make sure of one thing: don't get him sprung without informing me first. I don't want Sacca walking out that door without half a dozen men waiting for him."

Silence again, this time more lengthy than the first.

Then Zanon said, "I've got an idea that will work, but it's gonna take time to set up. There's no way I'm going to be able to get him out of there before the weekend. Monday would be the absolute earliest."

* * *

"ZANON SAYS he needs another five days?" Arnaldo said the following morning. "Maybe six? What's with that?"

"Zanon is a straight arrow. He's not going to do anything illegal."

Arnaldo sighed. "And legal takes time."

"Always and in all circumstances. Unfortunately."

"And you can't push him any harder?"

"No. We'll just have to wait for his call."

"What do we do in the meantime?"

"Why don't we go have a chat with that delegado, Bittencourt?"

"Call him first?"

"Not on your life," Silva said. "Let's go in there with a show of force. Round up Hector and Babyface."

* * *

SERGIO BITTENCOURT was biting into a croissant when the four men barged into his office. One of them he already knew. It was that federal cop, Hector Costa.

Of the others, one was a kid who looked to be in his early

twenties, one was a tall man in his fifties who moved with the grace of a cat, and the last was a man of about the same age wearing a gray suit. The latter had black eyes that closely resembled Costa's.

"Chief Inspector Silva would like a word with you," Hector said.

Bittencourt stood up, brushed flakes of pastry from his white shirt, and stuck out his jaw.

"I've got a question for you, Delegado," the man in the gray suit said. "How much money did you take from Senhora Arriaga?"

"Did she say that? Did she say I took money from her? She's full of shit."

"Ah, so you fed her the information out of the goodness of your heart, did you?"

"Fed her *what* information? I didn't feed her anything. What the fuck are you talking about?"

"She wanted to know who was responsible for killing her son, correct?"

"Wouldn't you?"

"Just answer the question, Delegado. Did you, or did you not, tell Aline Arriaga that João Girotti raped and killed her son?"

"I did not."

"You're lying. She offered to pay for the information. You wanted the money. You gave her a name, you gave her Girotti."

"That's a load of crap."

"Why Girotti, specifically? Did his name just pop into your head? Or did you have something against him?"

"If she says that, it's no more than her word against mine. And who is she? A nobody, that's who! The word of a nobody against the word of a delegado? Don't make me laugh. Get the hell out of here. This conversation is over."

"Your response," Silva said, "told us everything we came here to find out. We'll be talking again before long."

"Is that some kind of threat?"

"Yes, Delegado, it is."

* * *

THEY WERE in the delegacia's parking lot when Hector got a call from Horácio La Selva, the undercover agent he'd put in the cell with Sacca. La Selva sounded agitated. Hector made a gesture for the other cops to gather around him.

"Some idiot," La Selva said, "forgot to tell the guards I was a cop."

"That idiot would be me," Hector said. "I told Carillo to keep it to himself, figured it would be safer that way. Safer for *you*, not Sacca. What's the problem?"

"The problem, Senhor," La Selva said, changing his tune, "is that Sacca got sprung yesterday afternoon at five. But me? I had to spend another night in jail."

"Damn! Is the delegado there now?"

"He just arrived, had some problem with his kid at school."

"Put him on."

There was the sound of the phone being handed over, then, "Carillo."

"What's this about Sacca being released?" Hector said.

"What we agreed," Carillo said. "Silva sent a lawyer."

"No," Hector said. "He didn't."

"Well, somebody did. And he had all the right paperwork, so we had to spring Sacca."

"Tell me about this lawyer. Did he give you a name?"

"He didn't have to. I already knew the bastard. It was Fonseca."

"Dudu? You're telling me Dudu Fonseca was the man who got Sacca out of there?"

"That's what I'm telling you. Hey, weren't you guys supposed to have a man stationed out in front?"

"We were, and we do."

"Then he's fucking blind, because Fonseca and Sacca must have walked right by him. There's only one way out of here."

* * *

"Well," Silva said when Hector related the details of the conversation, "that clinches that. Julio Arriaga is our man."

"Has to be. Aline Arriaga is the only person I told."

"And then there's Fonseca."

"Fonseca? What's with that?" Gonçalves wanted to know.

"Aline consulted him when her son was arrested," Hector said. "And then he got João Girotti out of jail."

"That shyster isn't cheap," Gonçalves said.

Silva looked at his watch and made a quick calculation. "Sacca has been out for almost eighteen hours. Three to one he's dead already."

"No bet," Arnaldo said.

Silva turned to Hector. "Do we have his home address?"

"We do," Hector said.

Silva turned to Gonçalves. "Call in the team we have standing by. Tell them to meet you there. If Sacca is still alive, put a protective cordon around him."

"How tight?"

"Loose enough not to discourage Arriaga. The last thing we want to do is scare him off."

"And if Sacca's already dead?"

"Call Hector at the office. He'll contact us. We'll meet at the murder scene."

Silva turned to Hector.

"Check Aline's bank accounts. See if she's made any

substantial withdrawals. Check the airline records to see if she might have been in Brasília around the time of Juan Rivas's murder."

"You think she's an accomplice?"

"Juan Rivas was a cautious man, concerned with his possessions, concerned with security. I'm still curious as to why he opened the door to his killer. If he looked through the peephole and saw a woman, that might have been all it took. He might not have regarded her as a threat."

"Whereas if he'd seen Julio out there. . . ."

"Exactly."

"Surveillance on Aline?"

"Immediately. Around the clock."

"Phone taps?"

"Home, office, and cell—and if she uses a pay phone, even once, initiate coverage on that as well. My guess is she'll be smart enough to use prepaid cell phones, but maybe not."

"I'll get right on it. Where are you and Arnaldo going to be?"

"First," Silva said, "we're going to find out what the hell happened in Santo André."

"And then?"

"We're going to have a talk with Dudu Fonseca."

***

THE MAN on duty in Santo André was right where he was supposed to be, directly across the street from the jail. He was Pedro Sanches, on the job since eight that morning and as reliable as they come.

"Morning, Sanches."

"Morning, Chief Inspector."

"You see La Selva on the way out?"

"Sure did. He practically bit my head off. He was *not* happy."

"So I heard. He tell you Sacca has been sprung?"

"He did. But I got no orders to leave, so here I am."

"Good man. Who was on duty last night at five?"

"New kid, name of Mendes."

"You have his home number?"

"I do."

"He live near here?"

"Matter of fact, he does."

Silva groaned inwardly. "Merda," he said. "Get him over here."

Mendes showed up ten minutes later.

He had a sunny smile on his face and a pristine band of gold on the third finger of his left hand. For Silva, the unblemished ring clinched it.

"All right, Mendes, save us both some time. How long were you away from your post?"

The smile faded; Mendes looked at his shoes. "Not long," he said. "Not long at all."

"How long?"

"From a little before five to almost six yesterday evening."

"Jesus Christ!"

"My wife and I are newlyweds, Chief Inspector. You're a married man, right? You know how it is."

"Give me your badge, Mendes."

"What?"

"Give me your badge, and your gun, and go home to your wife. You're suspended."

"Come on, Chief Inspector. It was just a little slip, could have happened to anybody. I'll be more careful the next time. You won't catch me slacking off again."

Catch me.

If he hadn't said that, Silva might have let it go with a reprimand. He hated to ruin a man's career.

* * *

MARA CARTA stuck her head into Hector's office and said, "Aline emptied her savings account."

"When?" Hector said.

"Yesterday afternoon, just before two o'clock. She had over twenty thousand reais saved up, and she took every centavo."

"And Brasília? Did she go there around the time Rivas was killed?"

Mara stepped into the room and leaned against the doorjamb.

"If she flew, she didn't do it under her own name. Her credit card receipts show no expenditures, not in Brasília, not anywhere along the route."

Hector was about to ask her who'd been assigned to the surveillance team when the phone rang. It was Gonçalves, calling about the murder of Abilio Sacca.

* * *

DUDU FONSECA'S offices were on Rua Major Sertório in Cerqueira César, just across the street from São Paulo's most elegant bar for meeting high-class prostitutes, a place called La Bamba.

The people in the lawyer's wood-paneled waiting room fell into two categories: felons, and the friends or families of felons. On observation alone, it was difficult to tell the difference.

The arrival of two federal cops caused them, as might have been predicted, not a little discomfort.

Fonseca didn't keep them waiting. Not, Silva thought, because he was particularly concerned about the delicate sensitivities of his clients, but rather because he didn't want those clients to panic, go running off, and give their money to a rival attorney.

With some effort, because he was very fat, Fonseca rose to greet them.

"Chief Inspector Silva. And Agent Nunes. What a pleasant surprise."

"Pleasant surprise, my ass," Arnaldo said.

Fonseca's smile faded. He dropped back into a chair that groaned in protest.

"I'm sorry to hurry you along, gentlemen, but you arrived without an appointment, and you've seen my waiting room. What do you want?"

"Abilio Sacca," Silva said.

"What about him?" Fonseca said.

"We want to know who paid you to get him off."

"I have no idea."

"Don't trifle with me, Dudu."

"I'm not, Chief Inspector. I can't imagine Senhor Sacca ever becoming a regular client, so I'd be perfectly willing to tell you. If I knew. Which I don't."

"Explain."

"The woman who came to see me paid cash. She gave the name Batista, but I somehow doubt she was telling the truth. She called herself Senhora, but she wasn't wearing a wedding ring. What she *was* wearing was a blond wig. It was a good wig, but it was a wig. She used dark glasses, glasses so large that they effectively concealed all features above her nose, including her eyebrows." He raised his hands in a gesture of helplessness. "I'd like to be of more use to you, I really would. But I can't. If I were to pass her tomorrow on the street, and if she wasn't wearing the same wig and the same glasses, I wouldn't recognize her."

"Maybe not, but tell me this: had you ever seen her before, blond hair, dark glasses, and all?"

"Once."

"When?"

"This wasn't Senhora Batista's first visit. She had come to me a while back about another man she wanted released."

"João Girotti?"

One of Fonseca's eyebrows rose in surprise. "Yes. Girotti. How did you know?"

"It doesn't matter. I just wanted to confirm it was Girotti."

"Well, indeed it was. The felon's friend, this woman. I don't understand it." Fonseca shrugged. "Maybe she has a passion for bad boys."

"Here's another name for you, Dudu. Do you remember a woman named Arriaga? Aline Arriaga? Came to you about her son?"

"Yes, of course. Her boy had a fatal . . . fall. He died in police custody. Doesn't say much for our law enforcement community, does it? The people who are supposed to be protecting us, I mean."

"Don't get snotty with me, Dudu. Just answer the questions. Did Senhora Arriaga look anything like this blond?"

"Senhora Arriaga is a brunette."

"And the blond, as you pointed out, was wearing a wig. We can, therefore, surmise that her natural hair color was *not* blond. I ask you again, could Senhora Arriaga have been that blond?"

Fonseca shrugged. "She could have been," he said, "but there is no way I'd swear to it. So that's a dead end for you there, Chief Inspector."

"How much did you charge her for springing Sacca? Something like that must have been expensive, huh? I mean, after all, they had the little punk dead to rights."

Fonseca frowned. "What I did was perfectly legal, Chief Inspector. Judge Miranda was kind enough to stipulate a bond, and my client paid it. As to my charges for the service, *that* information is strictly confidential. If you want the numbers, you'll have to subpoena me. Furthermore, I resent the implication—"

"That's enough, Dudu. Get down off your high horse and tell me exactly what the woman said."

"She said that an acquaintance of hers, that's what she called him, an acquaintance, was being held in Santo André. She wanted him out. I made a few phone calls. She sat where you're sitting while I did it. Once I'd analyzed the problem, I gave her a price, my fee plus . . . expenses. She opened her purse, took out a roll of banknotes, and started counting them out."

"What was going through your mind?"

"I beg your pardon?"

"Tell me the thoughts you had at the time. It doesn't matter if they were pure speculation. Just tell me."

Fonseca leaned back in his chair, put his elbows on the armrests, and touched the tips of his fingers together.

"This is a little embarrassing," he said, "but I'll be frank with you. When I saw that roll, I thought I should have set a higher fee. I think she would have paid it. I think she would have peeled off every note and given it to me. There was a kind of quiet intensity about the woman. She desperately wanted Sacca released, God knows why. And God knows what they have in common. *She* was a woman of some class. From my experience of *him*, he's an ignorant buffoon."

"What else?"

"That's it. That's the extent of it. I was kicking myself about that money. And now"—Fonseca, with the same difficulty as before, rose from his chair—"you'll have to excuse me. Please be careful not to let the door hit your asses on the way out."

Chapter Thirty-Seven

THE SCENE OF ABILIO Sacca's murder was already crawling with reporters. Gonçalves wisely kept his lip buttoned until all four of them were within the perimeter of crime-scene tape and away from attentive ears.

"The landlady is a widow," he said then. "Lives alone, works nights in a hospital. Over there"—he pointed toward the home of the closest neighbor—"we've got an old lady. She hasn't been out of her place in two days, but didn't see anything, and she didn't hear anything."

"Where's the body?" Silva asked.

"This way."

Gonçalves led them down an alley. Sacca's place was a tiny freestanding building in the rear of his landlady's home.

"Built for a maid," Gonçalves said. "There's just the one room and a bathroom."

"What's the landlady's story?"

"Around ten thirty this morning she went to collect the rent. The door was ajar. He was stretched out in a pool of blood. She didn't panic. Like I said, she works in a hospital. Says she's seen a lot of bodies in her time. She checked his vital signs before she called it in, told the attending officer the paramedics didn't need to hurry. He'd been dead for hours, she said. The ME confirms that the death was sometime between 1:00 A.M. and 4:00 A.M."

"He's already here?"

"The ME? It's a she. Gilda Caropreso. Inside."

Arnaldo glanced at Hector. "You and your girlfriend have to stop meeting like this," he said. "People will talk."

"How about Janus Prado?" Silva asked.

"He's off today, but they always keep him posted on stuff like this. He called me, asked me if you were coming. When I told him you were, he said to have fun and. . . ."

"And what?"

"And to tell Arnaldo Nunes he's so ugly that when he walks by toilets, they flush."

Gonçalves seemed pleased to be passing the message along.

***

GILDA CAROPRESO, very much at ease in a room crowded with men, was wearing yellow jeans and a pale blue blouse. The only concessions to her profession were latex gloves and a pair of plastic booties. She circulated among the newcomers, collecting kisses on her cheeks and giving Hector one on the mouth. Then they all went over and looked down at the body.

Abilio Sacca was a mess.

"I don't think he got anywhere near his attacker," Gilda said. "I'll have a closer look under a microscope, but there doesn't appear to be anything under his fingernails except dirt. There is, by the way, a lot of that. And the rest of his personal hygiene doesn't have much to say for it either."

Silva knelt. Gilda hadn't been exaggerating when she spoke of Sacca's hygiene. Close-up, and under the steely smell of blood, the corpse gave a whole new definition to the term "body odor." He squinted through the plastic bags to have a closer look at the victim's hands.

"Ouch," he said.

"Indeed," she said. "Whatever the killer was using, Sacca was trying to fend it off."

"So 'it' didn't get left behind?"

"No. Hector tells me you have a theory this killer might be the Arriaga boy's father."

"Not everyone ascribes to it, but I do."

"Poor man."

"Crazy man. If it's him, he's killed a lot of innocent people."

"A man like that belongs in a mental institution, not in a jail."

"That's for the courts to decide," Silva said.

"Yes," she said. "Unfortunately."

"Could the weapon used to beat him have been a baseball bat?" Hector asked with a flash of inspiration.

Silva stood and Gilda knelt for another look. After a while, she said, "Maybe. I'll check for wood fragments in the wounds. What kind of wood do they use for baseball bats?"

"Ash," Hector said. "The same wood the English use for cricket bats."

"How the hell do you know what the English use for cricket bats?" Arnaldo said.

"He comes up with that kind of stuff all the time," Gilda said. "He's a repository of totally useless information."

"And occasionally amazing instances of insight," Silva said.

"Once the killer got past the hands," Gilda said, "he concentrated on the head. There's considerable damage to the forehead, temples, cheekbones, nose, and jaw. There's also a second and very damaging blow to the crown. That one was probably postmortem, a final whack to make sure he was dead. And before you ask, yes, he was shot. Once. In the lower abdomen."

Chapter Thirty-Eight

JULIO ARRIAGA ENTERED THE stale-smelling apartment, put the bags of groceries on the kitchen counter and started opening windows.

Inez put one hand on her pregnant belly and another on his arm. "I'll air the place out," she said. "You go get the rest of the stuff."

He came back, lugging the heavy tent, to find she hadn't opened a single window. She was standing in front of the answering machine.

"You'd better listen to this," she said.

"What—"

Inez put a finger to her lips and pushed the play button. The woman who'd recorded the message was speaking in Portuguese, which was a good thing since Julio Arriaga's English, even after three years in the United States, was still nothing to write home about. When he couldn't get by in Portuguese, he used Spanish. And why not? Everybody knew you didn't have to learn English if you lived in South Florida.

Senhor Arriaga, the voice said, *my name is Solange Dirceu. I'm calling on behalf of Detective Sergeant Harvey Willis of the Miami-Dade Police Department. It's most urgent that Detective Willis speak to you. When you get this call, no matter what time of the day or night, please call me on my cell phone to set up an appointment.*

She gave him a number and hung up.

"Want to hear it again?" Inez asked, her finger poised above the machine.

Julio looked at his watch. It was almost midnight.

"Leave it for tomorrow," he said.

"No matter what time of the day or night," Inez said, quoting verbatim. She'd been a schoolteacher, and she still had a pedagogical bent.

"Oh, hell," he said, and went to get a pencil to make a note of the number.

The following morning, at the appointed hour of nine, Detective Sergeant Willis was on the Arriagas' doorstep. He was accompanied by some black cop, whose name Julio didn't catch, and an attractive brunette whose name he did: Solange Dirceu, the woman he'd spoken to the night before.

Julio settled them around the dining table, the only place in the apartment that had enough chairs. Inez, flustered to have three people she didn't know in her kitchen, served them coffee. After it had been established that his English really wasn't good, the rest of the interview went through Solange. What Willis told him next caused Julio to sit back in his chair.

"*Puta merda*," Julio said.

Solange translated this as "holy cow." She didn't approve of Julio's choice of words.

The entire interview, with Julio's approval, was recorded on a small device Willis had brought with them. They finished within half an hour and left Julio sitting at his kitchen table, staring at the wall.

***

"I GOTTA make this quick," Harvey Willis said, "so I can concentrate on my driving. I'm on I-95, surrounded by crazy Haitians. I even have one sitting next to me in the front seat."

In the background, over the noise of the traffic, Silva

heard Pete André tell Willis that racist honkies like himself
had no place among Miami Beach's Finest.

"It's about Julio Arriaga," Willis went on, ignoring his
partner.

"He struck again since last we talked," Silva said. "He
killed another passenger."

"No, he didn't."

"What?"

"Julio Arriaga didn't kill anybody. Julio Arriaga hasn't
been in Brazil. He never left the States."

"Harvey, are you sure?"

"Absolutely sure. He's been camping in Chekika."

"Chekika?"

"It's in the Everglades. He's been there for the last two
weeks."

"And he can prove it?"

"He can. You want to camp in there, you gotta get a
license. The park rangers come around to stamp it. I saw the
license, I saw the stamps, and I just got off the phone with
one of the rangers. He remembered Arriaga, said he's seen
him every day for the last two weeks. And I do mean every
day. He worked both weekends."

"Goddamn it. So that's another dead end."

"Far from it. Hold on to your seat. Julio says Aline took
his pistol when they split. Says he thought long and hard
about going down there for his son's funeral. He really
wanted to, but in the end he didn't. Why not? Because his
new wife is pregnant, and he was afraid of what his ex might
do to him with that gun. Turns out she blamed *everyone* for
the death of her son, *everyone* including him."

"But it's been months since it all happened—"

"Julio said he talks to Aline's mother every now and then,
said they always got along. The old lady told him Aline is

still as bitter as she ever was—and just as angry. According to her, Aline is keeping Junior's room like a shrine; pictures, votive candles, the whole nine yards. She even puts chocolates on the pillow of his bed. And she does it every single night."

"So Aline's insane?"

"'Crazy' was the word Julio used. And, oh yeah, Junior owned two baseball bats, wooden ones."

Chapter Thirty-Nine

THEY WENT FOR HER at eight o'clock in the evening.
She'd been home for more than an hour by then.

Durval Kallos, one of Hector's men, was stationed within
sight of Aline's front door. He'd found a convenient bench at
a bus stop, and stood up when he saw the brass approaching.

"Evening, Durval," Hector said. "Who's in the rear of the
building?"

"Serginho, Senhor."

"Your radios working?" Silva asked.

"Sim, Senhor."

"We're going to take her. You stay here, tell Serginho to
stay there. Neither one of you is to leave his post for any
reason. If she comes out of that door, and we're not with her,
bring her down."

Durval looked shocked. "Use my gun, Senhor?"

Silva nodded. "The only way she's going to get out of
there alone is to shoot her way out. And she'll be looking
to shoot *you*."

"You're certain, then? Certain she's the one we're looking for?"

"Not a hundred percent. More like ninety-nine."

"How many security guards covering the building?"
Arnaldo said.

Durval pointed with his chin. "Just those two over there,
the fat one and the thin one."

The other four cops turned to look.

"Like Laurel and Hardy," Gonçalves said.

Hector snapped his fingers. "I *knew* that fat guy reminded me of somebody."

The rent-a-cop who came to meet them was the fat one. Silva held up his warrant card for inspection. The guard studied it carefully before he opened the gate.

"You've seen my name," Silva said. "What's yours?"

"Virgilio, Chief Inspector. Virgilio Ycaza."

"Okay, Virgilio, listen up. We're going to arrest Senhora Aline Arriaga. You're going to help."

Virgilio looked mystified. "The four of you need help? With her? But she's just a little thing. No taller than that." Virgilio held a hand below his double chin.

"It's not muscle we need, Virgilio. Come along. I'll explain on the way."

Halfway to the front door, Virgilio waddling next to Silva, they were intercepted by the other guard.

"What's going on?"

"They're federal cops," Virgilio said. "They're going to arrest Senhora Arriaga."

"Why? What did she do?"

"Maybe nothing," Silva said. "Maybe she killed eight people."

The thin guard blinked, looked at his companion, back at Silva. "Why?" he said. "Why would she do a thing like that?"

"Revenge," Silva said.

"For her son?"

Silva nodded.

"He was nice kid," the thin guard said. "But *eight* people?"

"Six of whom didn't have a damned thing to do with it," Silva said. He pointed to the Taurus .38 lodged in a holster suspended from the guard's belt. "You know how to use that?"

"We're *Policia Militar*," the man said and stood up a little straighter. "Both of us are."

Silva had suspected as much. Most rent-a-cops were moonlighting policemen. If you were in the ranks, it was a stretch to live on your salary.

"Good," he said. "You stay here and cover the stairwell. If she comes down, tell her to lie down with her face to the floor. If she doesn't, or if she tries to get up, shoot her."

"You gotta be kidding."

"I'm not."

The guard's face paled. His hand went to the butt of his gun.

"And me?" Virgilio asked.

"You're coming with us."

In the elevator, Silva explained what he wanted Virgilio to do: "You ring her bell. You tell her you've got a delivery. When she opens the door, you step back. Not left. Not right. Back. Leave the rest to us."

Virgilio swallowed.

"We don't deliver packages," he said. "People pick them up downstairs."

"This time, you decided to do her a favor. She knows you, doesn't she?"

"Yes, Senhor. She knows me."

"So there's no reason for her to suspect anything. She'll probably think you're after a tip."

The elevator stopped on Aline's floor. All of them stepped out. Virgilio lowered his voice to a whisper. "What if she asks to see it through the peephole? The package, I mean."

"Then it will mean she's suspicious."

"What if she is? What if she starts shooting through the door?"

"I don't think she'll do that."

"You don't *think?*"

"Are the doors steel?"

The guard shook his head. "Wood."

"Good," Silva said. "Let's go."

Virgilio grasped his arm. "*Good?* A bullet goes through wood like a whore goes through condoms."

"I'm not thinking about bullets. I'm thinking about getting into that apartment. Let's go."

Virgilio didn't say anything else, followed along meekly, but Silva could see the tendons standing out on his fat neck.

The sound of a television program, one of the evening soaps, was coming from inside Aline Arriaga's apartment.

The federal cops drew their pistols and took up positions, two on each side of the frame. Silva nodded to Virgilio. Virgilio pressed the doorbell, a harsh, loud buzzer. Someone turned down the volume on the television set. They heard a woman's footsteps, approaching the door, coming to a stop on the other side.

"Who's there?"

"Virgilio, from downstairs, Senhora. I've got a package."

The chain came off. The door started to swing open. Virgilio stepped back. Hector stepped in front of him, holding his Glock in both hands.

Aline Arriaga was still in her work clothes. The laser sight from Hector's pistol painted a dot of red light on her white blouse.

She put a hand to her mouth. For a moment they all stood there, frozen. Then Aline's shoulders slumped.

"Put the gun away," she said. "I'm not going to give you any trouble."

But Hector didn't put the gun away.

"Take a step backward," he said. "Turn around. Put your hands behind your back."

She complied. Arnaldo stepped forward with his handcuffs, shackled her wrists.

"So soon," she said. "I didn't expect you so soon."

Her remark irritated Silva. He didn't think it was soon at all. Not soon enough for Bruna Nascimento, not soon enough for any of the innocent victims. He blamed himself for not having gotten to the bottom of it earlier. It seemed so obvious now.

"This is about Rivas, isn't it?" she asked.

"No, Senhora, it's about guilt and innocence. Someone is guilty of the murder of a number of perfectly innocent people. We think it was you."

"Don't you dare talk to me about guilt and innocence! My son was innocent. Someone is guilty of killing him. And how much effort did you put into finding that person? None at all, that's how much!"

She leaned forward, trying to get closer to Silva.

Arnaldo pulled her away, forced her into a chair and held her there. She tried, at first, to shake him off, but when she realized how strong he was, she stopped struggling.

"You say this isn't about Rivas," she said, "but you're lying through your goddamned teeth. You think I'm stupid? You think I don't know how things work in this country? How the rich and powerful get justice and the rest of us can go to hell? Rivas is an important man. Your superiors are on your necks. You need someone to blame. It's a simple as that."

"No, Senhora," Silva said, "it's not as simple as that."

But she wasn't listening.

"None of you gives a good goddamn about people like me," she said. "You'd sing a different tune if you'd ever lost a child."

At that, Hector, Arnaldo, and Gonçalves all looked at Silva. But Silva had eyes only for Aline.

"I had a son, Senhora," he said. "We lost him when he was eight years old."

Her mouth went slack, aggression replaced by pity in the space of a heartbeat.

"Did you have other children?"

"No, Senhora. We never did. He was our only child."

"Your wife. . . ."

"Never got over it. Neither one of us did."

"It's worse for the mothers," she said. And then: "I'm sorry. I didn't mean—"

"No. You're right. It is. It's worse for the mothers."

"What was his name?"

"Mario. Like mine."

"And he. . . ."

"Leukemia."

"Leu . . . kem . . . ia. I don't know what I'd have done if Julio had died of leukemia. I mean, it isn't even contagious. There's no one to blame."

"No. No one to blame."

"But there is when your child is murdered."

"Yes. Then."

"And what do you think the murderer of a child deserves?" she said. The manic glint was coming back into her eyes.

Silva looked at his colleagues, then at his hands. "There's no death penalty in this country," he said.

"I didn't ask you that. I asked you what a murderer of a child *deserves*."

Silva met her eyes. "Death," he said.

Chapter Forty

"So now she's got herself a lawyer," Sampaio said.

"Yes," Silva said.

It was the Monday after Aline's arrest. They were in the director's office in Brasília, just the two of them in the room.

"And the lawyer is that cheap shyster, Dudu Fonseca."

"He's a shyster, but he's anything but cheap," Silva said.

"Whatever. And her idea is he'll get her off so she can go out and kill that guy Salles, the one who really murdered her son."

"I'm sure that's her intention. But it isn't going to happen. The lab results are in. The gun, the baseball bats, the wigs, the sunglasses, we found them all in her apartment. Not even Fonseca is going to be able to get her off now."

"Fonseca would be making a big mistake if he did. Everybody from the president on down would have his balls."

"And he knows it. I don't think he'll try very hard."

"We've got her dead to rights? Guaranteed? No chance she's gonna be able to wriggle out of this?"

"No," Silva said. "No chance."

"Tell me this: how did Aline locate the people who'd been traveling in the business-class cabin?"

"She worked for the airline, remember? She had access to the passenger lists."

"Lists, okay, but how about the victims' addresses?"

"Rivas, Cruz, Porto, Mansur, Palhares, Neves, they were

all frequent fliers, all in the airline's mileage program. She must have gotten their addresses that way. Bruna, another airline employee, was no trouble at all. Sacca, we gave her."

"And Girotti?"

"Remember I told you about that delegado, Bittencourt?"

"Oh, yeah. Him. You bust him yet?"

"Not yet. Soon. We're still gathering evidence of his other indiscretions. The guy's as crooked as they come. We surmise he told Aline when Girotti would be getting out of jail. She waited for it to happen and followed him."

"But we don't know that for a fact."

"No, we don't."

"Why didn't she go after the old lady? And the guy with the weird name?"

"Senhora Porto and Marnix Kloppers? Perhaps because they were parents, too, the only ones on the flight who were. That's just a guess. I really don't know. I *do* know she consciously and purposefully excluded Lidia Porto. She visited her in her apartment, grilled her about the other passengers, and left without attacking her. Maybe because Senhora Porto told her she didn't rise from her seat during the entire flight."

"And what about the priest? Why didn't she go after him?"

"I believe she would have. If she'd been able to locate him."

"Crazy. How did she get to Brasília? And Rio?"

"Drove, probably. She owns a car, could have gone back and forth in a night. It would have been tiring, but it's doable. Ribeirão Prêto and Campinas are, of course, much closer."

"And now she's clammed up completely, has she?"

"Yes."

"So it isn't likely we're going to get any answers for the rest of our questions."

"No."

"You know what bugs me?"

"What's that, Director?"

"That pervert."

"Pervert?"

"That pervert, Big Castor Salles. He'll come out of this with nothing more than an add-on for rape and another add-on for killing the kid. The odds are, he'll be out before she will."

"The add-on for rape," Silva said, "is guaranteed. We have the forensic evidence to make our case. But he won't serve even a day for the murder of Julio Arriaga Junior."

"What? Why not? What about all the witnesses?"

"Everyone who was in that cell is frightened to death of him. He's a member of the PCC. He has friends. Zanon Parma, the public prosecutor, tried, but he couldn't find a single person willing to stand up in open court and testify."

"Are you telling me Salles is going to walk?"

"On the murder charge, yes, he'll walk."

"But . . . but if he hadn't killed the boy none of this would have happened. No one would have died. After all the trouble he's caused, a conviction for rape is nowhere near what Salles deserves."

"No," Silva said. "It isn't."

Epilogue

THE FOLLOWING ARTICLE APPEARED in *The Estado de São Paulo*, Brazil's leading newspaper, on the eleventh of March, 2008, three weeks and one day after the murder of Juan Rivas.

KILLER SHOT IN ESCAPE ATTEMPT

AT APPROXIMATELY 5:30 P.M. yesterday evening, Castor Salles, 28, was shot and killed while attempting to escape from police custody.

Salles, "Big Castor" to his cronies, was being transported to Federal Police headquarters when the incident occurred.

Already accused and incarcerated for assault, he was to be questioned about his involvement in the PCC, the country's largest and most dangerous criminal enterprise.

But upon arrival in the underground garage, he managed to slip his handcuffs. Using them as a weapon, he succeeded in stunning Haraldo Gonçalves, one of the agents accompanying him. He then made a grab for Gonçalves's pistol.

Salles was about to turn the weapon on his captors when he was shot to death by Agent Arnaldo Nunes, another federal policeman.

Hector Costa, the delegado in charge of the case, called the incident "a lamentable but clear-cut case of self-defense."

Mario Silva, the Federal Police's Chief Inspector for Criminal Matters, praised Nunes for his courage and quick thinking during the confrontation.